Whispering Memories
THAT HAUNT THE SOUL

KAY RICHE

Trafford rev. 06/06/2012

 www.trafford.com

North America & international
toll-free: 1 888 232 4444 (USA & Canada)
phone: 250 383 6864 ♦ fax: 812 355 4082

Whispering Memories
THAT HAUNT THE SOUL

The memories that whisper in the cool air night and the chills in our spines are the families' memoirs of the unknown.

Would you like to accompany me on an adventure that doesn't come with instructions or a map?

It's really a beautiful time in my life. You will see my energy, part of it, is magic; the rest is the love in my heart. You will also learn about my whispering memories that haunt my soul. On this adventure, you will meet the spirits of two amazing women. You will learn the hardship and dedication to success and yet the marvelous years of high school. The supernatural is different for everyone and cannot be blocked by anything while you use your creative talents that are deep-seated inside your soul. There are many questions about the unknown to be answered. Come along into my spinning world that I spent at St. Claire's Academy, in Philadelphia, PA. Surprisingly, the wind will lift the souls of the nonbelievers.

This is my journey; please join me on the roller coaster and have the blast of your life. My name is Annie Haverstein, and I was born in Harrisburg, Pennsylvania. I am considered to be a striking young lady. I have a thin frame, long, curly blond hair like my mom's, and the biggest blue eyes that anyone would wish to look into. I am extremely proud of my family and, most of all, my dad.

DEDICATION

To Alice Kathryn "Trout" Baldino, my mother, who was an avid
writer for *Reader's Digest* and *Look* magazine in the 1900s and
who also had a vivid imagination of soul-searching.

CHAPTER 1

_M_Y FATHER, RICHARD, IS A hard worker—with very broad shoulders—tall, and exceptionally good-looking. He's a member of the Pennsylvania Railroad and, over the years, has learned the railroad business with expertise. My dad is a senior engineer and is very well respected among his peers. He has a daily route starting at Harrisburg, to Altoona, then Lancaster, and the last stop is Philadelphia before returning home again. The train where Dad worked as an engineer was called the Dream Train. Many knew the reason for the selection of the train's name. My dad named it in dedication to my mother. Dad felt this was a perfect name even though it wasn't advertised or gossiped about. Dad had many dreams for himself and his family in his lifetime. Many thoughts and memories have been shattered since his wife had passed away several years ago.

Brenda, my mom, died when I was just four years old. She was a very powerful woman in politics and the performing arts. She was only forty-two years old, an outstanding, beautiful blonde, five feet and five inches tall, of slender build, with beautiful long legs and blue eyes. Mom was artistic, smart, and striking. I was her only daughter and looked so much like her. My mother was very involved in politics but had no time for utter hearsay in town. She loved making her home comfortable, her husband happy, and her children safe. This was her main objective in life. My mom died very tragically. Most of the townspeople couldn't believe the unexpected event and the hardship that it has put on my family and the town.

Mom, who was a renowned concert pianist, had performed the night before for a concert production in Philadelphia for a political campaign. This was a ritual for her to raise money for many idealistic causes. This usually made her extremely tired and overwhelmed with anxiety. It was a must that she performed with perfection.

At the end of the concert, the applause was gratifying and rewarding. The standing ovation, the cheers, and the applause were always worth the sacrifice. She always had to be her best no matter what her challenges were.

The next day, my mom went to the lake, as she has always done on a daily basis. Mom was an avid swimmer; some might say a remarkable one. While growing up, Mom entered many swimming meets and usually won all the blue ribbons. She was the celebrity of the town, headliner of the news bulletin. When she swam, most people wanted to be there in her company to cheer her on when she won. Brenda had an aura and charisma to her spirit; everyone loved and respected her.

The lake was near the town and up toward the flowing springs, where the townspeople loved to fetch freshwater from the rocks. On the winding slopes were also the wonderful bushes of the lilac flowers that were treasured by most. Mom would gather up flowers for her friends and enjoy the wonderful smell of the lilacs that she scattered around her house in her expensive glassware on her tables.

She loved to go to the lake when time permitted her to do so. After spending time swimming, bottling water, and cutting her beautiful flowers for her vases, she would return home. Many hours were spent on the lake since she enjoyed these moments that she could treasure with God and her spirit and say her private prayers. It was her time when she felt she could rejuvenate her soul and go back to her recollections as a young girl that had always whispered to her soul.

Most would identify with this phrase and realize the value of the words. Mom was very contented to have a moment with God and her soul up on the lake. This made her day exciting and superb. My mom was a believer and tried to give her family the same beliefs with God and love, to believe and trust in the Lord.

Before this day, many severe, harsh rains passed. Even though the sunshine was bright and warm to her body, she forgot that this kind of weather would bring out many other unheard species in the water.

The sign on the dock said No Fishing, but it didn't say anything about swimming. She approached the boat from the side of the bank. She pulled the boat into the water, grabbed the oars, untied the rope, and proceeded to go into the water. Mom ended up rowing the boat to the middle of the lake as she had done so many other times. Feeling so energized, she jumped overboard into the refreshing lake. Mom decided that it was way too hot not to go for one more dip. Oh, how she loved to swim.

Time had passed quickly that day, and before she knew it, exhaustion had set in. Even though Mom was so tired, she had to take that last desired swim. Jumping into the cool water and enjoying herself was a delightful way for her to end a day. Mom proceeded to swim around by the boat and enjoyed the coolness of the fresh water. She did a few laps and went back and forth from one side to another in the lake area. Mom always enjoyed the little ripples of cool water splashing on her body. This was a must for her to do; the planned course that she had chosen for herself each week was important. When her fingers officially turned into prunes, Mom knew it was time to get out of the water. She decided to head back down to the house. She ended this perfect day as a memorable one.

She was totally unaware that in a matter of seconds, her family and world would change. Out of the corner of her eye, she saw something approaching her rapidly. She whipped her head around briskly and saw that a family of poisonous snakes were wrapping themselves around her arms, neck, and then her legs in the water. A massive snake had already wrapped his body around her neck, making it almost impossible to breathe.

She tried aimlessly to fight them off, kicking and splashing, but to no avail. They were way too slippery and slimy and moved in an exceptional speed toward her body for their vicious attack. Even though she was a strong avid swimmer, this was too much for her to contend with. Sometimes you should listen to your body when it tells you to depart. However, instead you take time and gaze at the clouds and feel the warm breeze on your body and meditate into your emotions.

The snakes started to nibble on her fingers and then her ears; before she knew it, they spread themselves all over her body. There seemed to be millions of the little creatures, going after her eyes and biting at her face with tremendous force. Although she fought frantically to get them away from her, she was not strong enough for this fight. When the attack was finished, the snakes had what they wanted; they proceeded to leave her all bitten up. The school of snakes had won this battle.

It was exactly what we were all told to be aware of. Many stories were told of the poisonous snakes that come from the waters in the swamp area when it rains heavily on the slopes. The mud would come down the hills, and the brush was so thick that it was nearly impossible to see anything else. You just wouldn't think about the dangers of the slopes. If you looked up to the skies, you would see the most beautiful rainbows or hear the birds chirping in the trees and be able to feel the splashing of the cool lake water on your body. It never seemed that danger would ever be present at this spot.

CHAPTER 2

HE SKY GREW DARK, AND everyone was arriving home to enjoy dinner and an evening of some laughter. Dad was looking forward to spending time with his children. My dad loved coming home to the smells of the apple pie, the lilac aroma, and my mom's wonderful cooking. Mom's sister had all the children at her house for the day. Aunt Suzie was planning to go to the general store in town with us to get some baked goods for tonight's dinner. We loved going shopping with Aunt Suzie. Suzie was very good to my dad, my mother, and all the boys, but especially to me, Annie. Usually, Suzie allowed us to buy candy sticks or fresh baked apples. It was such a special treat for them.

Aunt Suzie was a gracious host and was often asked to prepare most of the special dinners for the officials in town. Everyone knew that Aunt Suzie was a wonderful cook and that she had the best variety of meals to offer in her home. She was a plump little thing, had a beautiful smile, and had a God-given talent to love everyone. All the townspeople adored her. She taught most of the children in town to knit and make throws. Her work was very creative. Much of her time was put into baking, teaching crafts, and helping others in the town.

So, when Aunt Suzie was going to take you to the store or watch you for a moment, you were ecstatic about this because it was special for you. My mom and dad were so thankful for the joy and laughter she gave us. She was a caring person and yet subtle about being funny and smart. I sure felt God gave us a treasure with our aunt and uncle.

The time waiting just seemed to become longer and longer, and yet no wife or Mom appeared. Dad was getting a little concerned for Mom's safety. Dad knew that she was going into the woods and up the hilly slopes to the lake to gather her thoughts. She did this so many times, especially in the pleasant weather. The day was hot, and he knew how she enjoyed rowing the boat and swimming in the cool waters. Time elapsed, and now he was worried about his precious wife. Dad asked Suzie to please keep the children while he went looking for Brenda. Dad replied, "Maybe she went to pick up material for a dress which she was expecting to make for Annie?" At this moment, Dad then decided to start walking down to the town to see if she was at the dress store or had just taken another road into town back to the house.

Clearly, no one had seen Brenda on this day. Many of the men told him they would go with him up the slopes since it was colder and darker than before. He needed help now and quickly. Time was starting to run out, and they had to get to the lake before the cold air would hit the hills and the temperature would drop extremely low. The dogs came, and so did many townspeople. Brenda was a critical resident and loved by all. She was one of a kind, most men told Richard. With her being a beauty so special, many wished that they walked in Richard's shoes.

The men in town decided to hit the slopes up toward the lake. Many rows of townspeople were scattered across the mountain slopes. The search parties hoped not to come face-to-face with wild animals that roamed around after dark. Fire lamps were in everyone's hands, so they were able to see their way through the bush. They carefully held on to them to avoid the woods catching fire. This was the best way to put fear into any unknown animals that might have been waiting on the slopes.

As everyone climbed the slopes, dogs barked and the evening air nipped at their toes and fingers. Everyone was eager to find Brenda quickly. Dan, Richard's brother-in-law, was really getting upset. He knew that the more hours they spent looking, the less hope there was of her being alive. The men had all reached the lake. After much time, they finally saw Brenda. In true horror, the sight that no one wanted to see was Brenda's body afloat on the water. It was nighttime, and it was cold and dreary to be at this place at this time of night. To see this sight was an outrage and an upsetting situation for anyone to be in. Richard stood like a stone brick wall when he saw her body. His body movement was impaired because of the loss of his wife. Uncle Dan became the strength to Dad at this time. Dad needed a strong shoulder to lean on. These two men were very close through the years since their wives were sisters. They had unspoken admiration toward each other and an undercover respect and love.

As Richard and the men looked on, Dan approached the water and very graciously grabbed Brenda's wrist to pull her out of the water to the body of land by the lake. The men gently took the weeds and brush off her body.

Neighbors Harry, Roger, and Edward helped Dan put their coats over the water-damaged, battered, bitten woman whom they all knew as their loving neighbor and friend.

Richard wept over his dear wife and just dropped to the ground on his knees. He looked at his dear brother-in-law and friend Dan and knew it was time for him to proceed with the others down to the town. The body was still intact, and they proceeded down the hills and into town, where everyone was waiting eagerly for the voice of hope for Brenda, but instead it was a knife-wrenching word that ripped their hearts out with tears of sorrow. As they approached the town, most of the townspeople were waiting. Pastor John was a man in the crowd with his parishioners. When the men were finally at the bottom of the hill, they saw the grief, crying, and weakness that presented itself all over the men.

The men carried her, their friend, carefully with respect and adoration. After all, she was their neighbor and loved one. As they all knew, they were lucky to have found her so early; if darkness had set in, the animals would have destroyed the body by the morning.

At this moment, the townswomen knew they had to comfort Richard. Since Brenda was such a believer in our Lord, they felt the best thing was to have a circle of hands and pray. As they saw the body pass by them, the sobs were loud and the screams increased with pain. Their wonderful friend, a tremendously good woman, a wife and mother, now was gone.

They would never see her smile again in their homes or parish or hear her laughter in their stores. Only the memories that Brenda left with them would be remembered. How could this happen to such a fine lady? One wonders!

Pastor John led the townspeople in prayer at this time. When Richard walked by, he nodded to reassure family and friends that this was comforting for him. This was a sad moment for the town of Harrisburg.

Dad could see the sorrow, grief, and horror on everyone's face. It was now time to tell his children the tragic news—the death of their mother. He thought about the sickening words that he had to tell them: that their mother was dead and would never return to them, ever.

CHAPTER 3

RENDA'S BODY NOW HAD TO be taken to the funeral parlor to be prepared for the funeral service. Richard, being so humble, thanked everyone for their thoughts and prayers and said very softly, "She died in her paradise." She died in the one place where she knew God was always with her in spirit and prayer, where she could enjoy her beautiful lilac bushes and pick a few to always bring home.

It's hardly a surprise that as Dad's final day with Mom ended, he was stressed. You could practically see the sweat forming on his brow, which was not the image that everyone had of him—the strong and all-together man. What was surprising was the source of tension showing on his face. The heavy breathing from Dad and Uncle Dan projected so loudly that most could almost hear their hearts beating rapidly and strong. You heard the scared and tense voices, their worried and defeated look that was on both their faces.

It was so intense—the pain, anguish, disappointment, and sorrow. We all knew there were things we could control and things we could not, and this was one thing that no one could control.

Dad now had to do his worst job ever—to approach his children and Aunt Suzie and tell them about the heartbreaking disaster that Brenda had encountered. As the doors opened into the dining area and the family saw the anguish on Richard's face, no one had to speak any words. An old saying is that your face tells all. Since I was only four years old, it was difficult enough, but for my older brothers that had a few years on me, they seemed to understand it better. Of course, their approach was different from mine. I just ran to Daddy and asked where Mommy was; where was my Mommy? My brothers, of course, asked the why and how questions. Dad knew how to handle these circumstances; he told us all to sit down on the couch as he held me in his arms. I do remember the sobs from everyone. Aunt Suzie and Uncle Dan repeating, "She's so young. It's not fair such a wonderful woman." With the best explanation that a father could do at this time, he explained about the attack of the snakes and in terms that we were able to grasp, how the snakes took Mom's life.

As he went into the brief details very meekly, he told us to grab hands and bow our heads and pray for Mom. Respectfully, he repeated that she would be missed and God would take care of her. Dad told us to remember her continually in our hearts and that sometimes the days would be longer and sometimes shorter, but when we need her, we just raise our heads to look above and Mom would be present. "Now let's do our best to get ready to sit down to enjoy our dinner and rejoice, for Mom is in God's kingdom, where we will all meet in time. Amen."

Dad had planned to sit with Aunt Suzie that night to go over the funeral. Most likely she would not agree with his decisions. Sisters can be demanding and controlling. Aunt Suzie usually wasn't this way, but you had to recognize her sorrow of losing her close sister and loved one. Richard knew he had to sit down with Suzie and Dan to discuss the issues at hand. It was very difficult, but it had to be done. Suzie had an agenda written up for discussion with Richard and the children.

Anxiously, her voice squeaked and she said, "We have to discuss the flowers, burial, organist, singer, church, minister, and invites to our home. We have to try not to hurt anyone in the end." Richard knew that she had bitten off more then she could chew by trying to do this by herself.

Dad was so devastated that he had to plan his wife's funeral. It really didn't seem to be a reality until now. He knew that having a life insurance policy would have solved the calm after the storm. However, like most, he thought this was so distant in their lifetime; why worry?

No one wants to believe that he or she will ever walk down this road. His wife was young, brilliant, energetic, and realistic in life. Why should they worry about death? He knew now that if he had some insurance for this difficult time, it would have eased the burden.

Nerves were at an all-time high; everyone was counting on everyone else to know what to do and when. After all, Mom and Dad were a young couple, and things were all right in their world. What could possibly go wrong? Death of a loved one is something you wake up to and are not prepared for. Nevertheless, who among us really are? Not many.

Suzie and Dan knew what burial issues were on hand. Suzie had just buried her great-aunt Nellie about a year ago, and she knew the bills that would arise. Burials could be expensive, and she knew that her brother-in-law was not one to set money aside for emergencies. He was just making ends meet now. Dan, however, was a senator and was able to put money aside for the unknown. They all had to sit down at the table to discuss the concerns that came with death. Uncle Dan told Dad not to worry about the bills. He would take care of everything.

We're all family, and we were there for one another. We would conquer whatever was presented in front of us on a daily basis. All of us would climb the mountain together, hand in hand, and when one fell, the other one would pick the other one up. Whoever felt this was going to happen at this time and age? Who really knew when God would make a calling and see fit for one of us to be rewarded at the golden gate? We go! As Mom had felt, this was rejoicing in her life, to see our faith be challenged and see her God.

Dad turned to all and declared, "Everything is now crushing me, and I feel that I can hardly breathe. Nevertheless, I know I have to bounce off the bottom of the pile, and come back strong and really fulfill the promise of what Brenda and I started, to keep our family safe." Now it was, time for everyone to see who Dad really was, the dependable, responsible, independent father and husband. None of us would stand alone; we would all walk the road together, picking up the pieces of each other on our own.

Dad was considered to be strong as an ox, but now he was just a man of despair, missing his loved one. He turned to all with a soft, meek voice and said a soft-spoken thank-you. That was enough for everyone to understand. When asked if he believed in God, he shrugged good-naturedly and said, "Some days." He had to get ready to take this task in hand and be ready to take it by storm.

We knew that we would never remove Mom from our hearts and souls. We also knew these tough times would continue. In time, the hurt would diminish, and we would always hold on to the love of our mother forever. My brothers turned to Dad at this moment and replied, "Dad, our back and our shoulders will be your strength until you feel free to climb off. Until then, hold on tight and we will carry you."

The pastor came down to console our family as well as the townspeople in talk and worship. He wanted to discuss death in general. Pastor John told us that Brenda's death would be felt by all. Our emotions come out of the subconscious, of a nonreasoning mind. They all held hands, made a circle of love, and prayed loudly to get past some of their pain.

It ripped my heart in half to see Dad sobbing so much. It was at this moment of time that we all took notice of the love we shared with one another and our relatives. Pastor John wanted us to repeat to ourselves over and over again that our mother and friend was gone and was in paradise with God. He thought that this would help to heal our pain and it would heal our hearts to repeat it out loud. Did it help? Maybe a little.

He proclaimed to tell us that a chapter has ended in our book of life. "The second chapter is now opening. It's that Brenda loved you. She wouldn't want you mourning over her death for a prolonged period, if any at all. She would want you to go on with your life, be happy and a healthy person, wouldn't she? Now often people lay guilt on themselves by saying 'I should have gone to see her more,' 'I wish I had or hadn't done this or that,' 'But all of that is water under the bridge,' 'It makes no difference now.' What has happened is over, and your feeling guilty isn't going to help Brenda a bit. Most likely, it has a bad effect on those you love who are still around you. For the benefit of yourself and those you love, you must disconnect the guilt. These exercises will help you do that because it says, 'It will disconnect you from all the emotional upsets you will experience involving your loved one.'

"You must understand that this makes sense. You can't change the past. However, you can change your reaction to the present. 'Do you want your kids and friends moping over your wife's death when it's time to let her go?' I asked Richard. 'Give your wife the same consideration. The good memories and feelings will remain after this exercise, but the upset feelings will be gone. When you think of Brenda, their mother, your wife, in the future, only good feelings will come. How fortunate you are to have had a good woman, and them, a wonderful mom. Some people will not have either in their lifetime."

Pastor John continued to discuss his claims that these exercises would work. What makes this exercise better than others is that another person has to say it to you in the right way and repeat the words that your beloved mom has departed from this life. You can believe what I speak about, but it still needs the connected service. Pastor John continued to say that this was effective in time of death.

He stated, "Try to get into your feelings of your loved one when you lose them." If you are longing for your mother who has passed, get into your feelings the best way you can when you hear the exercise. This exercise shows control of the nervous system during the voice message, which is where you want to be. After a day or two, you can always repeat the exercises. Soon after a death, I have found this necessary for me to do. To calm us, we all took his knowledge and wisdom to heart. Pastor John has been in our church for a long time. I can remember Pastor John doing services when I was really young and attending them with Mom.

We knew that this would get us past some of the bad times, but for now, the funeral was tomorrow, which we had to think about. The pastor left our home, and then Dad told us all to go to bed since tomorrow was going to be a long day to endure. Aunt Suzie made some coffee for Uncle Dan and some of their close friends. It seemed as if the night would never end for us and I'm sure for the rest of our family and friends as well.

Pastor John was angelic, as he should be, and had wisdom about him that would soothe people in despair. This was just what Mom would have ordered; we knew this, and so did Dad. It was time for the worst day of our lives and everyone that knew my mother. She was having her funeral service and burial, and I had no conception of what anyone was talking about. My brothers and I did exactly what was asked of us. My mom's body was prepared for her to go on to eternity and her soul to be lifted to God and his world. My Aunt Suzie and I had decided on what my mother should wear.

The dress was my mother's wedding dress; what choice could have been better? She would have part of her love with her, the piece of material that wrapped her body in the coffin. This attire represented her love on the day she was married to my dad.

I knew her angels were beside her everywhere since the spirit force moves. I felt them in the air; it was so intense, the feeling of our angels. It should scare most, but my mom talked about them often. Angels are messengers who must be heard in their own language. Angels may be visible or invisible, but all angels bear a message of love and contentment. The most important thing for those who wish to talk with the angels is the ability to hear and understand their messages. They do carry a strong impact on you and the one that has died.

The day of the service was very dismal, and the rain was falling slightly. I was sensing that it was heaven's tears since my mother believed so much in God. As the rain fell, I wanted the tears to touch my face so I may feel a piece of love on my skin. I was just so little and young to appreciate the meaning of the pastor's talk in church. The choir was singing, and the voices in church sounded as if we had a choir of angels. There were so many sobs and crying, some intensely and some quietly. But looking on everyone's face, you knew of the pain. As my mother's body passed by me and my brothers, I wondered why they closed the door on my mom. I felt she was sleeping and she would wake up soon. Little did I know until I was of age to realize that that door never would open again. She was carried out by Dad, Uncle Dan, and some close friends of ours. Dad told everyone that this was his love, his wife, and no way was he not going to carry her to her resting place. We had a resting place on the top of the hill, but the walk was long. It was a place where Mom's and Dad's parents were buried.

On the way to the burial site, we had to go through a wooden bridge with the lake running under it. On the sides of the hills were bushes of lilacs, which were blooming in full force. It was the perfect walk that Mom would have made if she had to choose. The townspeople lined up inside the bridge and prayed loudly as we passed. Women and men were so shaken up by the way poor Mom had died. As I passed through there holding on to Aunt Suzie's hand, I did feel that the angels were over the ceiling in abundance. When we came out of the bridge we saw a glorious rainbow which went from one side of the lake to the other. It was like an arch with radiant colors bearing my mom's name on it, or so I believed. What do you expect? After all, I was only four years old, a very innocent child, and so were my brothers.

We finally reached her resting place, and the pastor asked us all to pray. We sang beautiful songs together, and the clouds behind her were moving so fierce, I wanted to grab one of them so they would stop. When it was all over, we passed by her open grave and threw a lilac on her ground, but strangely, now the door was open. Then I saw my mom being lowered into the dirt and the door closed again. It was an awful time for all, but for me and my brothers, it was quite an experience to accept and understand. Of course, no protection was there for us, the young children. It was her time now to be with her maker, our dear God, and that had to be accepted.

It was a long time passing that these vivid imaginations were out of my head. I cried for many nights and years for the loss of my mom. As time passed on, we did what everyone does when losing a love one. We tried to remember the good times and realized that someday we would all meet her in God's kingdom. I knew the angels would take care of Mom, and I knew that someday, when needed, Mom would return in her spirit to take care of me, Dad, or my brothers.

CHAPTER 4

*S*EVERAL YEARS HAVE NOW PASSED. Where did the time go? Dad kept us all on our life's path. He made sure that we would continue what he and Mom started out to do. Mom would have wanted us all to be strong, determined, responsible, educated, and successful, but most of all, happy and loved. We all did a wonderful job of keeping her ideas true to heart.

Dad, after all, was a father of seven children and kept very busy trying to feed and provide for us in many ways. I was the youngest child of the family. The family consisted of six boys and one girl—me! The boys were all good-looking, broad, strong, tall, bright, and very protective of little ole me, Annie. Time has passed by since that night of horror with the coming of Mom's death. My passion of love was to play the piano just as my mother did. Everyone was amazed that little Annie was just as talented as her mom. I really did not know my mom well but heard so many stories about her. It seemed like every day she was present in my surroundings. I just wish that I had more time with Mom before she left this earth.

My joy was coming home from school in hope that one of my brothers would be there to play. Usually, I did not see them until they came home from work at 5:00 p.m. Some of my brothers worked on the railroad with Dad. Waiting for Dad and my brothers to return home at the end of the day was my biggest joy. Once I saw them coming up the path to the porch, I ran as hard as I could to jump into someone's arms.

It was the highlight of my day, and I was hoping theirs too. When the gate swung open, you could be sure one of them would pick me up and swing me around. Enjoying this moment was grand for all of us.

Since I was the only girl in my family with six brothers, it was easy to get really spoiled. Which I certainly was! Aunt Suzie and Uncle Dan also went out of their way to spoil me. I expected my life always to be this way. My brothers were typical boys, playing ball with me when they had the time, and if they didn't, they made the time. They sure loved to rough it up with me. I played baseball, skated, hiked, and fished as well as any boy in the town. I enjoyed competition on any level. Ribbons galore hung in my room for anyone to glance at if they had the time. I was very proud and just loved to display my accomplishments.

Aunt Suzie's job was trying to keep me grounded; after all, I was her sister's daughter. Being a lady had to come to the surface sooner or later, I hoped then in my teen years. Aunt Suzie knew that I was a looker, smart and tough, but she was not so convinced if she would be able to make me into a fine woman. Her niece was a wonderful catch for any young man to pursue.

Dad had a hard time dealing with me. With so many brothers, he was concerned that maybe instead of being this sweet, wonderful lady, I would turn out to be a tomboy since most of my day was involved with men. Dad absolutely had no idea how to handle me and turn me into a fine woman.

This was my mom's wish that she always had for me. Her dreams for me were to be one of the finest, respectable women in town. Working on the railroad took many hours for Dad, with no care for me. Aunt Suzie usually took care of me when needed. Dad wanted to keep me grounded in every aspect.

Aunt Suzie tried daily when the boys were not around. She taught me cooking, knitting, and sewing, how to select the right material—whether it was checks, stripes, or plaids for a new dress or for curtains. This was a hard chore to endure, as I liked playing with my hat on backward.

If my aunt was busy and unable to watch me, my dad had to hire someone to stay with me during the day. Aunt Suzie now had her own baby to take care of. However, since she was Dad's sister-in-law, she always found time for me. She was the best bet to watch over me while Dad was working. This was sometimes hard to endure for Aunt Suzie. In today's world, hiring someone to take care of a young one is expensive and difficult.

Since the baby was born, coming home from school was so joyous. Little Claire always greeted me cheerfully. Walking baby Claire in the carriage and through the town was delightful for me. Aunt Suzie was somewhat pleased to see that I did this. She knew those motherly instincts were buried in my soul. Women sometimes do not realize that they do have them. Aunt Suzie was definitely going to find my good womanly qualities and make them rise to the top. That was for sure!

Suzie was so delighted that the two girls were always together. She knew age was now an important thing, but in time, when both of us would be married and have children, those twelve years would not make a difference. Claire just loved her cousin and always laughed and smiled when I entered the house or yard. Learning and feeling guided by motherhood with my cousin was a good time for me. My Uncle Dan thought that I was a natural teacher. He loved me being with baby Claire. My aunt was right; I did have the caring that you needed to be a good mother and to raise children. Suzie was relieved, knowing I had those motherly instincts. Aunt Suzie felt somehow that this had to be projected more in me for others to see. She knew her sister would want more for her daughter than just horsing around with the boys, playing ball, or fishing on the dock. There was always a time and place for everything.

Dad thought long and hard about this situation. He had many nannies and many challenges in his life, thinking about my education, friends, and suitors. He knew that the young men would call on me later in life. His plan was to get me into a prestigious school where I could use all my attributes. Dad wanted more than anything for me to achieve good education and to be able to grow up to be a fine woman.

Dad had his trials and tribulations with the boys, but they grew up responsible, strong, wise, and bright. They were hardworking young men and knew their place in their family with Dad and their little sister, Annie.

The Haverstein family was a strong respected family in the town of Harrisburg, Pennsylvania, and he meant to keep it that way. Wherever we went, friends waved and smiled. Just to know this respectable family was an honor. After all, Uncle Dan was a senator working at the capitol, and Dad was an engineer for the largest railroad.

Let us not forget Mom, one of the greatest concert pianists in the Northeast. Who would not want to know us? Before Mom died, she was always a headliner in the papers, playing for charities, doing fundraisers, or playing for political parties at the capitol building. Don't forget Aunt Suzie; she also did her part—always helping to solve problems with either family or friends and showing young women what they needed to know to make their talents a success.

Uncle Dan's political party was always trying to get him to run for higher office. This was not for Uncle Dan; he wanted his feet grounded on the land of Harrisburg, not in Washington, DC. He did not want to travel and leave his wife and baby for long periods of time. Unacceptable! Uncle Dan was truly a family man and had a few extra worries on his plate—us. I am so proud to be part of *this family*.

CHAPTER 5

Harrisburg was a thriving, well-known railroad town. This was the capital of the state and was very popular in performing arts, education, and sports. For example, our baseball team, the Harrisburg Clippers, was well-known. They played in a prestigious baseball league known as the Tri-State League. This team played in the states of Pennsylvania, Delaware, and New Jersey.

Dad put his energy and mind into finding a private girls' academy for me. He needed to put all my talents out in front and find the best schooling that was available and what he could afford. He found a girl's private school in Philadelphia, Pennsylvania—St. Claire's Academy. Dad felt this was a good fit for me based on my talent, my grades, and my personality.

Since Dad worked for the railroad, there was a special fund available for daughters of employees that wanted to advance their talents in the arts. Dad knew that I was smart enough to get some extra money toward my tuition, but I had to pass the test and get accepted first at St. Claire's. St. Claire's was a parochial school run by the Bernadine nuns in forbidding black robes. Some fear? I would say so.

The John Harrison Kennedy Foundation provided financial assistance to the daughters of railroad employees. The goal of the foundation was to help the family enable the daughter to mature into a responsible individual. The foundation encourages each grantee to pursue her education, capabilities, and interests and permits a student to cultivate her good health habits in the belief that such encouragement will aid her in achieving a richer and more fulfilling life.

To qualify for a grant of financial assistance from the foundation, the daughter must attend a school that has met standards with the foundation. The student also would have to maintain a good health program and receive high academic grades while attending. Each grantee is also encouraged to participate in religious services of her faith. Applications for grants must be approved by the board, and such approval, as well as continuation of the financial assistance under such grants, lies within the sole discretion of the board of trustees.

This was definitely something I would apply for to help with my education. I was so excited to take the test and try to help Dad with funding. Dad was going to set up an appointment for me at the foundation and with St. Claire's. It finally hit me on my head that I could be leaving town and my friends and could be going away to school in my near future. Exciting, scary, and maybe a little intimidating—yes, all three to be exact.

I thought that I should not jump the gun yet. I still had to pass all the tests to get accepted. St. Claire's testing first and then the foundation. One step at a time, I told myself. Baby steps if you must.

His little girl was not so thrilled when Dad talked about it with the boys. It seemed now that it was a little bit more of reality, hearing it. Leaving my brothers, family, and friends behind would be difficult. However, Dad would be the most depressing, hardest, and saddest to depart from. This was so overwhelming and nerve-racking after all, I was just a kid. Thinking about all the changes in a new school in an unknown territory was scary. I knew this was my upcoming future.

I was confident of my talents and knew that with what Dad saved, getting state aid, and a scholarship from the John Harrison Kennedy Foundation; things would be easier for Dad. I certainly was not going to let him or my mom down.

After all, I was always the princess and taken care of by all my men in my family. They were always my protectors, loved ones, people that I could count on whenever the need arose. I thought, how I was going to be able to leave my dearest cousin Claire, my childhood friend Samantha, and my best friend Jessica? This was a question only my heart knew for sure.

The family sat down at the dining room table, and Dad explained to all, "If Annie can get into St. Claire's; it would be a big accomplishment because most that do apply are not accepted. Only a small percentage of girls are accepted at this school." The school grades ran from ninth to twelfth grade. This was a prestigious all-girls' boarding school with very high standards in academics, charm, and concert piano playing. I thought to myself, *Good thing I'm not boy crazy!*

He contacted the master of the school and spoke too many of his railroad attendees that traveled back and forth on the rails for their comments. The feedback from everyone was very positive. Mr. Grumbling, the headmaster, spoke to Dad about all the issues that had to be reviewed before my acceptance at the school.

The first call of duty was the entrance exam and a tour of the school. Dad and I decided after eighth grade graduation to make an appointment for the last day of June. The weather would not be too uncomfortable for the testing, and it was a good time for Dad to take vacation time. I was now in eighth grade and would graduate this coming June. Spring came and went before you knew it; I was at St. Claire's taking the exams that were needed. I also had to make an appointment for the exam at John Harrison Kennedy Foundation.

Dad and I entered the school for a tour, to meet the teachers, to see the rooms. I immensely enjoyed walking briskly across the grounds. It was so peaceful and breathtaking. We both had a good feeling about the school. Little did anyone know why.

We managed to take in some sights off campus and enjoy the surroundings. During the day, we had a picnic lunch for both of us by the school's lake. It was delightful at this part of the school. The ducks were swimming fiercely, and the birds were singing so beautifully.

While waiting by the lake, a teacher came out to get me, it was now time for me to take the entrance exam, which I was nervous about. I had to meet the head nun called Dame Mother Teresa Harris. (*Dame* because she had been honored for her achievements; I never knew of what.) She had this stern look on her face and was not really so pleasant. It seemed that she was angry all of the time.

She certainly was frightening to a fourteen-year-old girl. The one thing I will remember will be her advice to me to watch out for fear itself. At this time, I could not really understand her advice, but I am sure that as age approached me and I got little smarter, the word became more of a reality. I was confident with the academics that I did pass the exam with flying colors. Dad asked me how I made out on the test, and I told him that I did very well. Stage two that day was to take a test to play a musical piece of your own choice on the piano. This was a big decision; what do I really play that seems great for the listeners? What would they enjoy? What would Mom tell me to play? For this teenager, there were too many questions to answer.

Dad was going to wait in the lobby until the process was completed. He ended being so impatient with the long process that he came into the room where I was going to play. His nerves were on edge. I entered the room, and there were a display of teachers and good old Dad waiting to hear my performance on the piano. I glanced at Dad and smiled; he gave me his special wink of the eye, and I totally understood his message. He just loved me so much. He could not let me be there all alone. At this point, I knew Mom would have never left my side either. I started to play *Clair de Lune*, a masterpiece of a work, and it went brilliantly. I felt the chills up and down my spine, even if knew no one else did. This was a wonderful experience, and I knew I did my best. I hope that they all felt the same.

Mom, for sure, would have been bursting her buttons off her chest. The writing tablets came out on the teachers' laps, and I noticed that many of them were taking notes. Dad and some students were in attendance in the classroom also to hear the performance. After performing my piece, the applause and cheering was exhilarating and breathtaking. Dad, of course, stood up so proudly, and his clapping of hands spread over the classroom with loudness and much love. He simply showed his admiration toward the piece I was playing; it was

Mom's special selection at concerts. Simply overwhelmed, I was very gracious to the hosts. At the end of the piece, I stood up and bowed humbly.

Waiting for the mail and results of the tests was going to be exciting but anxious. *It is going to be a long summer,* I thought. Until I received my final comments and grades from the schools on how I did, it would be a worrisome summer.

School was now over, and now another summer was there to enjoy. Every day during the summer, I would run to the mailbox at the end of the walkway, open it up very carefully, and hope. I was always waiting for the big brown envelope to appear. I had not decided yet if I wanted the results and the letter to be an acceptance or a rejection. In my eyes, I was not very sure of leaving all my comfort zones and trying on a new life.

Summer was going by quickly, and my family and I waited everyday for that special time when the results would be in. Then we would know my faith. I ran to the mailbox as usual one day wondering, *What if it finally has arrived?* I went to get the mail as usual, not knowing the outcome. To my surprise, the envelope was there. I rushed into the house, hanging on to the big brown envelope by the corner. Telling myself, *Do I want this or not?* Anxiously I decided to slowly rip the corner and proceeded to read the letter.

Lo and behold, I was accepted with a scholarship and full honors in academics plus on my talent of piano playing. At the end of this day, I was bouncing off the walls with joy. I just couldn't wait for someone or anyone to come home. My voice was quiet and meek, and I just wanted to scream to the top of the roof about my accomplishments. Best of everything was that I even received a monetary payment. Now I had to tell Dad and my brothers that the day was finally here. I would now have to leave home and my family this coming August. I now knew, at the end of that summer, that everything would be completed and all would be put into order. For sure, I was now accepted at the school and would start this upcoming fall as an incoming freshman at St. Claire's Academy. Who knew! The entire make-believe process was finally a reality that this was going to happen to me. I was truly going to St. Claire's Academy. How great was this? What an accomplishment for me, and what a way to end my summer. Boy, it sure was a cool day.

I never envisioned that my high school years would be attending St. Claire's Academy. I was simply going with friends to Camp Curtain High School where all my brothers went. I did enjoy having a mass audience when I played, and I knew you would get this kind of reception at St. Claire's. *I could be the leader, stand up in the middle of the audience, and take my bows so deserving of myself,* I thought.

When the application selection for St. Claire's was decided for me, I wasn't sure if I really wanted to depart. I had been truly blessed for this moment in my life. I was able to help Dad with some of the money. I received financial awards from the state of Pennsylvania, John Harrison Kennedy Foundation, and St. Claire's since I was an A student and a superior musician. A top student, in return, would get help from donors who helped the school financially. This was a monetary blessing for Dad and quite a relief.

This school had a very select group of young women being accepted. I never did foresee seriously considering going to a different school. It certainly wasn't something I ever thought about—leaving home, a better school, a new community, and new friends.

My first question to the teaching staff would be, am I able to be featured in one of your holiday shows? I knew that I would love the luxury, style, and artistic playground of this world, but would I shine? Who wouldn't want to come here and wear the world's most beautiful clothes for their concerts?

Was there an endless parade of gorgeous, eligible, wealthy men to meet? I knew all the students had to be supportive of one another rather than participate in the so-called girls' cat fights. This is what some girls will do during a competition—scratch each other's eyes out for the prize. This would not sit right at this school; everyone here was equal. If you performed for special occasions, you truly earned them. "Good girl, great job," you will be told. So now, the waiting time took place.

CHAPTER 6

THERE WERE NO SURPRISES WHEN the townspeople heard that I was accepted at St. Claire's Academy. Since talent and brains were embedded in my family, all the townspeople knew there wouldn't be any challenges for me to endure. By the end of the day, the story was told among my friends. They knew that I would attend the academy. Everyone was truly excited but tearful. I didn't realize that my piano playing would have the highest value of self-expression to most. Maybe the fault lay with schoolteachers who, with the best intentions, tried every day to make an art of acting or have music playing be less intimidating, telling the kids that it was all about letting whatever's inside you come out to play and exposing it. This was great advice, but when you found yourself under a spotlight as everyone was enjoying the school holiday concert in the audience, you could have less courage. Then the line between self-expression and self-absorption became very thin. The road to pathological narcissism wasn't long and winding but perilously short. I guess I listened well and followed their advice.

Who knew that enjoying what you love to do could make you succeed? I would have to say, my teachers obviously understood my future outcome. It wasn't just piano playing that succumbed to this inward gaze. It was evident in everything from bad to good about people just like them. "Express yourself"—it was that dreary anthem of practice that launched these million piano lessons. The main artistic value you should bring to the stage is not "self-expression" or a compelling backstory but empathetic imagination. You would have the ability to throw your entire vocal prowess into singing about people who were nothing resembling you. You would have confronting emotions and crises you've never encountered. Instead of trying to make every piece about you, you should make yourself about every piece that you play.

Think big; imagine deep. Try to be one person on whom nothing is lost. Or, if that's too over the edge for you, just draw from the more accessible artistic piano playing that you hold. Open your heart, and free your mind.

There's always something to be anxious about. The question now is whether it lives up to your hopes. How do you fulfill their expectations in an unexpected way? What should we demand of ourselves? I welcome that. I was feeling stressed by the whole thing to start with, just not knowing anything about my origin and where I would fit in with the school. I guess, if I was lucky, I would join all the open discussions and figure it out for myself.

CHAPTER 7

THE JOURNEY WAS HARD FOR me since I had to leave my heart behind with so many loved ones. My home, family, and friends were the only surroundings that I had ever known. This would be hard to depart from while still being able to demonstrate that I was a big girl now. As my brother Adam said, "It's now time for Annie to reach for the stars and look into the heavens of life to achieve the best. To do this, you have to go knock at the front door and walk in proudly. Climb over the mountains, holding on to only a few hands or doing most of it on your own. Whatever challenges are put in your path, express joy on this road and overcome them successfully."

I bowed my head proudly and nodded to Adam, the oldest of the bunch. I knew it was now time for me to fly and clip the wings from my family. My brothers, cousins, and Dad helped me pack my belongings. They made sure I had my best clothes and the uniforms that I would be wearing. My special boxes of ribbons, hair clips, and jewelry were packed first. The most important item for me was my mirror that was left to me from Mom.

My mirror was beautifully trimmed with hand-painted flowers and had a slender handle made of gold. The mirror had a few chips, but it was Mom's; it didn't make a difference if it was old or worn out and maybe even chipped a little. I imagined when I looked long and hard that I could see Mom and me together. I was able to feel Mom's soul, which gave me much strength. It was comforting for me to know that this was mine to hold. It was wrapped in tissue paper and packed very carefully on top of my baggage to take to school. This was one item that made me feel at ease and reassured me of my soul. If I looked long and hard into my magical mirror, I thought that I was able to see my families' love and support.

My friends came down to the house to say their good-byes, which was so heartbreaking. My best friends Jessica and Samantha were the first ones to show up at the house. I was also expecting some neighbors, relatives, and believe it or not, some teachers before I left. Good-byes were always so awkward and uneasy. We had our hugs and tears, and then we realized that time would pass, and before you knew it, I would be home for the summer. We felt if we closed our eyes for a little bit, when we opened them, we would be with one another again by the fishing pond. It just wasn't easy for fourteen-year-old girls to depart without a scene. This was the first time since we all grew up that one of us had to leave the nest. We were above and beyond ourselves, making a circle of friendship and hanging on to each other for dear life. This gave us the sparkle to our existence. It was as if life's direction had passed us by, but then we got the energy and excitement to wake up to see our friend in front of us again.

Jessica lived right next door to me ever since I could remember. We played hide-and-seek together and ran down to town for our candy sticks with Aunt Suzie. It would be hard leaving Jessica. She was so sweet and a gentle, kind person. A friend like no other that no one else could imagine. To leave Jessica was as if my heart would crush in half. Samantha, on the other hand, was my conscience of not getting into trouble by the fishing pond or anywhere. I never really wanted half the time to just go into the water as I was supposed to—walking in. I would rather hold on to the rope and throw myself into the cool lake. Samantha made me keep my feet grounded; otherwise, I think I could have been in plenty of trouble most of the time. Samantha was so incredible and so smart. She was the one who, when I didn't understand my homework, would help me figure it out. I sometimes felt she was an older sister to me even though we were all the same age. It was going to be hard to leave the best friends a girl could have. I knew in my heart that when I would return home, the summers would be thrilling with one another. I couldn't wait to come home to go to the barn fires and hear the stories of my old school and about my friends from town.

It was tricky and unpleasant and maybe quite a bumpy ride leaving one another. Knowing that the holidays come up fast made all the apprehensions become no concern. Our uneasiness of me departing became a jumping-up-and-down command for the three of us. Our spirits dominated us and gave us the authority of power to scream, cry, and get a little bit out of control. Just what teenage girls are expected to do, I guess.

When I looked on the porch, there was Aunt Suzie with her hanky, wiping her tears from her eyes and blowing her nose. Uncle Dan was holding in his arms little Claire, who was trying so hard to say my name, Annie. Claire had just learned recently to say my name and was trying so hard to repeat it again. Uncle Dan looked at me with a comforting look as if to say, "It's going to be OK, Annie. See you soon. Love you!"

Of course, behind the crowd of well wishers were my brothers and good old Dad. My brothers were all so proud and excited. They yelled at me to be good, enjoy, and love every moment of this stage of my life. Dad of course had said his personal good-byes to me when I was packing. He knew that he had to let me go to do his job. He also told me that if, for any reason at all, I wanted to come home, the door will always be ready to accept me back with open arms. No shut deals here! He hugged me so tightly and said a prayer over me, as he had always done since I was a little girl.

He then gave me a hundred kisses all over my body, as if I was four years old again. I kept yelling to him, "Come on, Dad, enough is enough. I'm a big girl now." Nevertheless, I loved every moment of his caring. We finally looked into each other's eyes, both full with tears, knowing it was time for me to go.

Dad just couldn't stand there to watch me board the train, to watch his little girl go to the big city and big school and go away. It was way too hard for anyone to watch. He would have too many tears and not be able to tear his heart from me. I was a special girl to him; after all, I was Daddy's little girl.

I turned to them all one more time as I walked down the path and through the gate. I waved and sent a big kiss to all. I jumped into the carriage, and Al put my bag on the other side of me, and we then proceeded to go to the train station. My brothers Samuel and Al waited patiently until the train came to make sure I was seated and boarded properly. The conductors all knew me and that I was Richard's daughter. You just knew that I would be safe until my arrival in Philadelphia, Pennsylvania. Dad told Mr. Nicolson, the conductor, to take special care of me until I reached my destination.

We arrived shortly it seemed; this time the ride seemed shorter than before. Maybe the anxiousness of arriving at my new destination was now embarking on me. The trip was enduring and tiring by the time I arrived at school. I was surely exhausted and somewhat a bit edgy. When I arrived at the train station, Ms. Hornet was there picking up a few girls that were coming in at this time.

She gathered up the group and informed us all to board the carriages. "We can't be tardy for Mr. Grumbling," Ms. Hornet replied. "He was expecting us to be on time. Being late is totally unacceptable."

When we arrived, Ms. Alice was there to meet us; all the girls other than me were upper classmen. I was the only freshman for this pickup. Ms. Alice advised us to visit the ladies' room and wash up a bit since most of us have had long trips before arriving. Ms. Alice called out my name first and told me that the headmaster, Mr. Grumbling, and I will meet me in the library. "Snappy please," she added.

Mr. Grumbling was pleased to see me again. He informed me that he was sure after my musical piece that I would be one girl for acceptance. He was so proud of his selection of incoming freshmen this year. My welcome from Mr. Grumbling was a pleasure. It was gratifying that he would take his time out to welcome us individually. After this meeting with Mr. Grumbling and listening to some details of information, my brain was in overload at the moment. Mr. Grumbling discussed lessons, expectations, grades, support, friendship, summertime, and holidays that we would have off during the calendar year. It seemed that he went on and on until Ms. Alice walked in and clapped her hands for me to rise as Mr. Grumbling was done with his speech. At least Ms. Alice said so. Thank God. I was so glad to see Ms. Alice; I was able to escape from Mr. Grumbling's long deliberation speech.

The headmistress, Ms. Alice, came down to the library to take me to my room, where I would now live until I leave the school on graduation day in four years. I was startled by Ms. Alice's clapping, but somehow I knew to rise up and stand. She had a slight smile on her face. I knew I would be an obedient student. Huh, little did she really know me. Who was I kidding? I was an obedient child (girl, lady, woman, etc.). My nervousness and fear had now gone out the window you would say. I knew now there was nothing to lose sleep and fret about.

CHAPTER 8

As I gathered up my belongings—my book bag and suitcase—I proceeded to follow Ms. Alice to where my room was situated. It seemed that we walked for a while, so many steps to climb and so many rooms I passed. I peeked in on some; other girls were trying to organize themselves, speaking to old and new friends. Everyone seemed happy, friendly, and enthusiastic to be here. I just couldn't wait for the joy of being here to strike me over my head. I had to understand that this was all true and real. I knew I would achieve my dreams in the long run. I couldn't wait for me to become conscious and grasp the thought that I wasn't hypothesized. It had better come soon and quick as I was starting to get the creeps that maybe I shouldn't be there. I went down some of the hallways to check them out and to see who was on my floor. I couldn't, like other girls, be so patient to meet my next-door neighbor to my bedroom. Will she be pretty, will she be nice, and what can I expect? Time would tell.

We finally approached my room. Surprisingly enough, my room was bright and cheerful and was situated on the corner of the building on the third floor facing the lake. It was bright, very clean, and organized. I was actually nosy and proceeded to walk over to the windows. I wanted to know, for the next four years, what I would see looking out my window. What would I see daily? I noticed a family of ducks, looking so content. I felt it was cool to be able to see this every day. It was so soothing to see the mom and dad ducks with their baby ducks just hanging out on the green manicured lawn. How cute was this? It was quite amusing to watch the ducks and birds on the lake; it was quite peaceful, if I say so myself. I knew in my heart that this was going to be it for a while, and I had to make the best of my new world.

Ms. Alice informed me to get acquainted with my room and my neighbors and make new friends. I thought to myself, now, how was I supposed to do this? Have a siren and call everyone out to meet little Annie? I poised myself and realized she was talking about the other girls in my hallway and wing. I then contained myself thinking how dopey I was not to know the obvious. I settled myself in, put some items on the shelves, and hung my uniforms in the closet. The rest of my things I put neatly away in the drawers.

My best moment was when I took out Mom's mirror and I laid it gently down on the dresser with extra love and care. This was how I always handled my mirror, oh so gently; after all, much love was in this mirror that I was looking into. When I held the mirror and looked in to it, for a second, nothing but heaven and love was rolled into this package. I knew that I was having plenty of hysterical awkwardness during this time of remembering. Oh, so hard and yet, so lovely.

I looked up gently to see the cross hanging over my bed and then knew to look up into the skies and seek Mom out. She was there all right, her sun shining brightly, the clouds so perfect, and a warm, gentle breeze coming through the trees. I just bowed my head and replied to Mom, "Thanks. I'll see you soon. Stay around please." I knew there was no way Mom was going to abandon me, all alone away from family and friends in an unknown territory. It was a moment of mine that brought me back to those whispering memories that haunt my heart.

I did everything I was told to do quickly and efficiently. I watched all day as the entire incoming freshmen received their schedules and room assignments, just as I had when I arrived. Ms. Alice, by the afternoon, had escorted so many girls to their rooms, some upperclassman returnees and new recruits. So many of them seemed quite interesting, and some seemed to me the likelihood of maybe having a new friend. This was a difficult time for most, to just tap someone on the shoulder and ask her to be your friend. You had no idea if she would like you or not or if you would like her. I knew some situations for the first months would be difficult, but the learning experience would be worth more than the moment of silence. I couldn't wait for the next morning to meet my teachers and meet new girls who soon would be good, fond friends. So many stories to share with all—excited, yes, very!

The next day, the bell rang very early in the morning. This was the call for all the girls to get up, take baths, and get in line to go to breakfast and start their day. The day started at wake-up at 5:00 a.m. and the line up in the hallway at 7:00 a.m. to go to breakfast, classes, do chores, piano lessons, charm school, and learning, learning, and more learning. Before you knew it, Ms. Hornet was in the hallway, tapping away as usual. Everyone was very punctual.

Sure, if one thing was told to us during Mr. Grumbling's meeting; it was that if you were late, extra chores would be handed to you. Who the heck wants that! After all, this was a group of smart girls; no one could be that clueless.

We all marched down to where breakfast was being served. This was my first day, so important and yet nerve-racking. I walked into the room that was pointed out to us to have breakfast. I actually was sitting in a school cafeteria for the first time in my life. I realized, I didn't know a single soul. Like, where do I sit? Where do I go? Go around the line on the left side of the older girls or to the right? Many questions and advice for incoming freshmen to adhere. It seemed in a flash that two girls named Marybeth and Kaitlin appeared in front of me and grabbed me off my feet. They took hold of my hands and told me to follow them swiftly. I felt very relieved that someone fetched me. I didn't know how I was going to sit there alone and not know anyone.

Marybeth, Kaitlin, and I hit it off from the first moment they captured me. I knew that they would be some of my best friends in this wonderful learning experience. We picked up our trays and proceeded to go on line and seek out what we thought was the best spot in the cafeteria.

What did we know? We were only freshmen, but thinking that we were at least the smart ones and the cool girls. After four years of schooling, I hoped all my friends and myself would have it all—the charm, talent, and wits. I told them, I saw them both in our hallway when I was unpacking my things in my room. "You looked like an ideal twosome to be with. My thinking was, can I just pop in on both of you and announce myself? I just had to decide how to meet both of you without looking childish. Now, I didn't have to, as you both found me. What luck, finding friends who would be gracious and charming."

The environment in general was pretty good. All the girls were laughing, smiling, and getting along well. During this time, the teachers just stood by and let us unwind and have conversation with one another. They all knew this was the time to let us be noisy, curious, and maybe a little bossy, until we all settled in. Most of the girls were now in school, and maybe a handful just hadn't arrived yet due to time changes of trains and other things. School was now in session, and there would be no time for fooling around. This we surely knew.

CHAPTER 9

*F*OR ONCE, I THOUGHT THAT women had really an incredible legacy. Women and this institution celebrated, and will celebrate for years to come, their successes. They could feel fabulous no matter who or where they came from. I saw at the end of the hall that a dispute was going on among some of the girls. They certainly weren't agreeing on an issue. I watched curiously and called over Marybeth and Kaitlin to see what was happening. We watched intensely as a group of five girls got together and finally ended handling things appropriately, conspiracy-like but as a team. It was a dispute that we didn't want to question or get involved in. Marybeth, Kaitlin, and I had to go downstairs anyway to pick up some of our books for classes beginning tomorrow. After we finished our assignment, we went to the field outside to relax a little. Our newfound friends seemed to follow us to the same place. They wanted our opinion on this squabble, but we knew enough to stay out of this type of mess. We told them that our objective here was to get a good education and possibility end up being a star. Certainly we were not taking sides in who was right or wrong. Who wants to get in the middle of this type of argument? Certainly not us.

It all comes down to one thing: hold on to your friends and your families and keep love tightly secured next to your heart. Life would always walk you down the right path. Change is always good, I guess. We would have to see what happened next. I was there for a while and didn't plan to leave soon. It was pretty cool, this place, or maybe I was just blessed. It was a pinch of lightness, an adventure or wait. I think there is another word I'm searching for—*fun*. Yes, that's it, pure fun.

We all sat down with our food, and Marybeth decided to introduce herself first. Then it was easy for the rest of us once she opened the first page of our new beginnings. It seemed that we all bonded pretty quickly. I started telling the girls about my family and my school that I left behind. I would miss those special girlfriends of mine from home. I suggested to some and others, "Let's try hanging out tonight and getting to know each other a little better."

It seemed that after my story telling, I also told the girls that we should take a little tour of each other's rooms. Imagine me, the not-so-prominent person on the school grounds, taking the lead at this prestigious school—how unexpected! Stepping up to the plate is hard, but after all, someone has to make something happen. Does this make you a leader? Sometimes.

Marybeth invited me to meet her by the music hall after English class. Marybeth was earlier and arrived way before I did. While she was sitting there waiting for me, she had time to think clearly about her new friend Annie as a person. She felt that Annie was a new girl that she had just met in school this year with Kaitlin. She knew truly that I was going to be one of her best friends forever. My philosophy was to chat your way to happiness and that everything was not so serious. Think light, think big, and life will give you what you set out to achieve. *This was the way to go according to Annie. Boy, did she enjoy talking to people and making conversation. So charming was she that once Annie got a hold of your ear, it was a delightful experience. Everyone loved her smile, her charm, and her caring qualities that she showed to all. Whether you were a personal friend or not, she popped that little individuality out of her chest for everyone to enjoy. Her thoughts on people were that those who spend a lot of time during the day talking to new and old friends and loved ones are much happier than the silent types. The happiest people engage in both idle chitchat and several deep conversations per day, most say.*

This is my new friend Annie, I am so lucky to have found her. I just know that the next four years together will just be a blast. Imagine the best of friends—little ole Annie, Kaitlin, and me. I now have to see Annie to discuss how our schedules mesh with each other on practices. I do hope she shows up soon. I'm really getting tired using my brain with all my recollections of Annie. Whew, I finally see her coming. I do hope we are in class and practice together. To be in practice with Annie is a miracle in itself. Her imagination and her talent are so magnificent for anyone to be in her presence. I will keep my fingers crossed until I talk to her. I keep telling myself that God is good.

Annie was so excited when she saw me waiting for her. Annie yelled to me, "What's up Marybeth? Did you decide to change your music, or are you just having a bad day? Well, my friend, I am here now, so together, we will accomplish your fears or hopefully your happiness that this school brings to you. No fears now, I will help you get on the tracks and yield to the right or maybe even stop if you have to. What do you say? Sounds good, huh? Believe me, Marybeth, you couldn't ask for a better friend." We both laughed and continued to go to our math class. I did know in my heart that what Annie was saying was the truth. I knew it, and so did she. On to a new day!

St. Claire's Academy was a boarding and refinishing school for girls, located in Philadelphia, Pennsylvania. The school had about three hundred girls from grades ninth to twelfth. It's in the middle of town, surrounded by many buildings, lakes, businesses, and local shops. In the distance you could hear the whistles of the engines blowing, which was a familiar sound to me. It was a joy for my spirit to hear these sounds. It made my day peaceful and was something for me to rejoice about. It brought me back to my memories of Dad and my brothers; after all, most of them worked on the railroad. Those memories will always be part of me, no matter how far away I am from home.

During the day, I would hear the train whistles blowing loud and strong across the city. I would sit quietly and fold my hands gently and pray, as Mom did to keep us all safe. I knew that Dad didn't send me to this school to hurt me or to get rid of me but to turn me into a fine young lady. This school would enable me to have all the advantages that only one person can have in a lifetime.

Oh, I was proud of Dad and loved him so much that, if I thought about him hard and long, my heart seemed to beat fiercely. I sure missed Dad, but I knew that when I would hear the old whistles coming from the railroad tracks, it gave me peace and tranquility. It gave me that extra inner faith and support so I could do this. Do what? You might say. What am I expected to do? What handful of miracles was granted to me not to spoil? Would I be a star, or would I just have a magnificent time at this school? Maybe find my true love? I was so excited to see how the scorecard would add up for me. Time would tell what was in my future.

St. Claire's was a very strict school. Scattering among the property campus were dorms for girls and academic and administrative buildings to mention a few. The school had high gates around the campus and winding roads beyond your sights. The decor had dreary cold hallways but peacefulness to its surroundings. I felt, what was my possibility of me learning in these halls? In time, I would leave these dreary hallways someday and know that I would have many memories from my classmates and friends during the next four years. When I'm done here, my life would follow me on the outside of these walls and into the uncensored adult world. I would then have to expose myself and give a signal to show that I am ready for this adult world.

All new friends, teachers, and a continuously busy scheduled day was overwhelming, to say the least, yet ecstatic. As the days finished and the weeks added up to months, I realized that this was more than a chance for a wonderful life. After leaving the school on graduation, I would have four cherished years to remember and know that my hard work would pay off for me in the future. There were endless opportunities that I could achieve here more than anywhere else I knew.

CHAPTER 10

ON THE FIRST DAY OF class, we were told that we had to enforce strict rules. One was never ever to enter the room in the attic. It was the forbidden room to all. Of course, this meant never to mention the room in conversation to anyone. During this time, from September 1 to November 1, I always heard musical notes being played in the forbidden room in the attic. My close friends and I did whisper about the notes to one another. Many thoughts were on our mind of what this could possibly be. We did hear the notes being played every night since our first day of school. This was a topic that no one would ever speak about and really couldn't.

Marybeth was absolutely not curious at all and would have dreadful dreams at night if we spoke about the attic. Kaitlin was a little bit more curious but a little bit wimpy, not a risk taker at all. We made a pact though—hands crossed, fingers gathered, and crossing our hearts twice—not to repeat this to anyone else. I, on the other hand, was quite bold, curious, and had a little bit of craziness. After all, I grew up with six brothers; nothing was sane in our house. It was clear-cut that my brothers and I were definitely inquisitive children growing up.

I knew in time that I would reach out and go into that forbidden room. No matter what gossip was said about the room, I would take the chance. My bizarre prying was greater than my patience of the unknown.

I made up my mind, after several weeks of listening to the magical musical notes from the classrooms and the whining charms through the hallways, that this was the best place for me. I loved playing the piano; I was gifted with this talent, just like Mom. Mom was a wonderful composer and piano player, which I had been told often. I sometimes wished that I would have been able to recollect the times since many of their family friends talked about the parties that they participated in with Mom. I liked being the focus at most of the gatherings as I grew older. I would love playing my music, entertaining, and leaving much harmony, laughter, and joy when people were with me. Only at this time did I truly appreciate my mom and her not being here to be part of my life.

Brenda, my mom, was all I could think about when I played my music; my music came across as mom's did—full of jubilance! When I had my way, I would go into my dreams and remember the stories told and hear her music in the air being played. The good times that was had by all. After all, the memories were hard for me since my lifetime with my mom was a short-lived one. Clearly, I did remember so many good times with my mom. I remember her smile, love, and affection, but most of all, Mom playing the piano. My finest memory was when mom tried to teach me to play while I was sitting on her lap. It was sometimes hilarious to witness us in action. Oh, how cute both of us were when trying to do duets together.

Mom was so talented in composing music, and she played in many concert halls where most important people attended. Dad, my brothers, and I were very proud of her. She was the best part of our lives and had the impact of always having people attracted to her presence. My family was considered to be influential and the cream of the crop. After Mom would perform at one of her concert affairs, the outcome was that everyone would wait at the stage doors to just see Mom or get her signature. After taking the cheers and applause outside the show, anyone and everyone of importance would retire to one of the town pubs. The other performers would also proceed to go to the pub where you would hear the most laughing and cheering. It was surely not a hit-or-miss to find the right pub; just follow the crowd and listen to the music being played and the clapping and stamping of feet. When you walked in and saw half the town celebrating the triumph of the concert, you knew that the show had a home run. Most of the crowd was the audience or the players. This was a huge high spot for the town when the concerts were finished and the town celebrated for a job well-done. Since we were all so young, Mom and Dad made sure we left with a caring relative to tuck us back in bed.

Their life in the beginning was hectic, with the traveling and the crowds always shouting at them. The money issues seemed less pressuring when Mom worked for an evening. Dad was a proud man and wasn't about to let his wife be the only breadwinner. He drove himself hard to succeed in life as his wife had. He would not be a beggar or look for help from anyone. This was his family to take care of, to feed and shelter on his own. He was so proud of her music; the love in her heart always came across in her talent of playing and singing. She was a headliner to remember in this time. I so wished I would have seen the tremendous respect and admiration that everyone had for her. Dad took many engineering classes in order to succeed in his lifetime to become an engineer for the railroad. He was a very successful engineer for the Pennsylvania Railroad and a highly respected person.

Mom was so proud of good old Dad. Dad was a humble man, but his buttons would burst when you spoke of his children and his wife. This couple in town had so much to be thankful for. God had been good to my parents and us. Even though our life was so short with Mom, the time we had with her was so precious and loved.

Thanks to all the stories I have been told. I know that I possess her talent and charm; of course, let's not forget the good looks, ha! I've always had the talent and loved the musical notes in the air. Dad made much sacrifice for me to attend St. Claire's school. I also realized that my family loved me and was doing this to keep me safe and secure. Eventually, I would have a good life. I knew this for sure.

During the time I stayed at school, I always heard the sounds of music and the tapping noise coming from the terrible winding staircase that led my thoughts to the dreaded attic. No one was permitted to set foot in this horrible place, the forbidden zone. It was never spoken about even though all of us understood the musical notes being played. It was very frustrating to most that we could not quell our curiosity. No one just ever would speak about the music or the room. The only words that might be mentioned in the morning were "How did you sleep?" We all knew what the other one thought.

None of us wanted to talk about the musical notes being played in the evening. The attic notes and shrill sounds would sometimes get the advantage of you while sleeping. The phrase was not to gossip about this; you surely didn't want any extra chores. Heaven forbid, not us.

If Ms. Hornet and Ms. Alice ever found out what we thought about, which was the attic, for sure, trouble would be brewing for those that did believe or talk. Most of us did hear the music coming down from the attic. If they found out that we did believe, there would be severe consequences for us. All we needed to have happened was for the head nun or any nun to hear of our foolish wonders. After all, somehow, they would want us to clean our thoughts and get these notions out of our heads. Sister Harris or Sister Beettlemen then would walk us right to the confessional booth for prayer. The nuns were part of our school, but their presence was not always known. An action like this could cause you ten Hail Marys and God knows how many Our Fathers. Let's not even mention the extra chores added to your list.

Mum was the word from all of us. After all, how did we really know that this was true? Was this just our imaginary hearing that went on in our heads? Since most of us were away from home for the first time, maybe we felt it was what some would call homesickness. We decided that if this was what people would call homesick, it sure was scary.

Ms. Hornet, the music teacher, was a great intellect, but looking at her would put anyone into shock. She wasn't so pleasing to the eyes—not to be mean or anything, but that was what it was. Her personality matched her name perfectly. She was uptight, rigid, pale, and unhealthy looking—to be frank, exceptionally frightening. She had a mole the size of a giant ant on her chin, making her appear to be one of those witches that you read about in books. Nothing on a good note to speak about when you saw her. When spending time with her, you just had to think about your notes and try really hard not to look at her. There would be no way possible to think about what you were playing if you concentrated on her face. I know this isn't really nice to repeat, but somehow it just took the sweet notes being played to be heard in the air and made them into sounds of a tom-tom drum.

When I entered the classroom, I wanted to go in reverse and go backward into the hall, but to where else? My choices were limited, but I accepted them with grace, knowing I would be better off for this continued academics at St. Claire's. Ms. Hornet was not one to worry about her looks; she was a talented teacher and was able to pass her learning down to us here at St. Claire's. At least I kept telling myself this. She made you shiver and speechless. You played and tried not to look up much; just looking up made you play the wrong keys. Some laughed at her, made fun of her, but God forbid if you were caught. I tried not to get caught up in this with some of the girls. If Dad thought I was rude and disrespectful, what was I learning with all his money? To do this was shameful, quite childlike.

Ms. Alice, on the other hand, was the headmistress and taught charm school for the girls. She always presented that charm and possessed the ladylike mannerism that she was going to teach. She knew we all had it buried somewhere inside us, and it just had to be pulled out. It was going to be Ms. Alice's job to search for it before we finished our four years at St. Claire's. Ms. Alice was petite and slender and had long, flowing brown hair that hung over her shoulders, with curls and clothes always so perfect and fitting. Her hands and face were so smooth, and she always spoke calmly to all of us. This was a class we couldn't wait to participate in. *This is what heaven is*, we thought.

In Ms. Alice's charm class, you learned about makeup, hairdos, and selecting the right clothes for the right occasions. Let's not forget how to walk and sit with proper posture. The charm class was an exciting one, and who knew, after four years, if the ugly duckling would turn into a beautiful swan on graduation day? Could someone turn from a black swan into a beautiful white one? Only time could tell.

I knew my heart would never let go of the music sounds from the attic. I heard these notes over and over again each night. I just couldn't bear not knowing who was there, who was playing them. Maybe someone was hiding out in the attic? Maybe a nasty old person chained to something and couldn't get out. Was it my place to release him or her? Or was it the pleasant memories I wanted to believe in that it could be my mom? I had to find out the mystery of the notes sooner or later. My heart was full of joy and yet sorrow that I did not know the unknown. Yet I knew in time that I would be able to untangle the beats of my heart to challenge the forbidden staircase.

Ms. Hornet gave strict rules every day to stay in the classroom until we were told otherwise to depart. During class, she would examine all our fingers before approaching the pianos to see if they were long enough to play. Long enough to play—what was she thinking? She didn't want anyone to embarrass her or the school. We would laugh silently at this long enough; did she really think our fingers would grow overnight? She had to get a reality check on her brain if she thought this was really going to happen. I understood her looking for blisters or cuts on our fingers, but growing? If she found any unexpected mark on your fingers, there was no playing for you. Now, missing a day of practice was crucial. This was an essential part of the day of our musical playing of the piano.

No one ever wanted not to be able to practice. This was why, when retiring for nighttime, everyone was told that they should soak their fingers in warm water with a little bit of oil; this soothed and helped your fingers relax and stay soft. The nuns told us many times not to forget this procedure. It surely did work. I reminded Marybeth and Kaitlin to make sure they didn't forget. What are friends for?

When we all retired to bed for the evening, you could hear the nuns praying in the church downstairs. Sometimes their singing echoed through the hallways, like beautiful white doves.

If you really listened hard, you could hear their meek voices praying to God; this was so significant. It sometimes made you wonder; maybe this is the life I should lead. Then I would think again and say no way.

Morning came so swiftly, and before you knew it, you were getting dressed, brushing your teeth, and grabbing your books to get on line in the hallway before Ms. Hornet came with her tapping cane. We didn't look forward to Ms. Hornet, but the old crabby nun, Sister Meredith Beettlemen, was way worse. She sometimes would replace Ms. Hornet if other duties occupied her.

Ms. Hornet was strict in her own way but had flair to her. She always had a concern about where we were and what we were doing. After all, she also had part of the planning process of who would attend St. Claire's and who would be able to participate in the holiday concert. She had many talented young ladies to select from. Her duties were endless and quite important. Mr. Grumbling looked up to her with the utmost respect. She was extremely dedicated and had been in the school for at least 20 years. Her opinion did matter to him and her coworkers. She was not to be reckoned with. Ms. Hornet was smarter beyond her years. Yet, so clever to knock you down a peg without you even knowing it was being done.

I had to work long and hard to do my lessons. I remembered always to hold on to the learning process and keep straight A's. After all, I was able to attend the school on a partial scholarship. I didn't think Dad could have done this otherwise, no matter how hard he would work. This was my part of keeping up with the standards at school. After all, in my mind, Dad and my brothers were working very hard and long hours to keep me at the best school. I learned from the best teachers with the most creative and talented minds. Mr. Grumbling, the headmaster, and Ms. Hornet were a few who taught us well.

Ms. Hornet stressed to us that this was the only life that we would all know for now. Playing the piano and being the best was not easy but, in the end, well worth it. Ms. Hornet told us to be aware that we would be contented and pleased with ourselves with the result. After four years of high school, we would thank her later in life for this eternal gift of letting us be on cloud nine. In the next four years, we would all possess this talent and realize how fortunate we were to be at St. Claire's. When this happened, you would be joyful, ecstatic, and blessed. She informed us that whatever talent we had, and if it was not released, she would pull it out of us. Be reassured that this would happen, to some sooner than to others.

We left the classroom when Ms. Hornet departed. She was planning to go around to the other classes to check the rest of the girls. She knew the endurance each one of us needed to perfect our talent in the next four years at school.

When entering the room, she demanded respect, which everyone always gave to her. We all wanted to impress her immensely. I watched as she went to each piano student and checked us all the same. If the music did not match the keys, Ms. Hornet proceeded to hit your fingers with the ruler and quite hard. Others were more pleased when she walked by them and gave a sly smile from the corner of her mouth, which meant that Ms. Hornet was somewhat pleased with their progress. As she approached me, I prayed that she would not hit my fingers. After all, I was so delicate and my fingers so slender. When she came by me and put my hands in hers to check them out, I was dying and waited so patiently to see her reaction. She looked at me and said, "Good girl, Annie, keep up the good work." I sighed for a moment and gave myself a pat on the back. The missed keys were unacceptable to the dedicated sheets of music for Ms. Hornet. I knew she must have heard my notes not being played correctly. I also knew I was one of Ms. Hornet's favorites; this did help.

CHAPTER 11

The bells rang loud and strong; it was time to proceed to a new class. The teachers in class knew who the new kids in school were; it was so obvious. As I entered class, Ms. Braxton asked everyone to stop to meet me; after all, I was the new kid on the block. I was very anxious and very intimidated with the circumstances of a one-on-one. This was an advanced math class, and I knew this would be an easy A for me to achieve. I had scored really well on my entrance exam in math; as a result, I was put into a class with sophomores. I ended up being the only girl to be introduced in this class today. No problem, it was another way for me to meet other girls in different grades.

This was all so new to me—all the new faces, a very rigid schedule, and no time for anything else other than a learning process of some kind. After all, I knew nothing except being with my brothers and dad. When things were grim, I tried to remember the whispers of my mom's voice in my heart and the love she had for me in my soul. After the long hours of lessons—ten hours daily to be exact—my fingers sometimes felt weak and limber and really ached so bad at the end of the day.

School was finally over for the day, thank goodness. I had time to go back to my room and get some homework done before dinner. I was glad that I wasn't on chore detail for this evening in cleaning the crumby old fireplace for the woodburning stove.

It would have caused some issues with me since I had to go back to my piano class after dinner for extra practice. As I proceeded back to my bedroom on the third floor, all I had on my mind was to soak my fingers in oil to make them feel refreshed and soft. With practice tonight and regular playing tomorrow, I knew that my fingers had to get stronger and stronger to be the best. The holiday concert was gaining on me fast.

St. Claire's was an old castle with many floors, so many buildings, gray concrete walls, and no curtains and was very cold and dreary. Not the best image to imagine. All the girls had a narrow bed, lamp, end stand, sheet, pillow, blanket, and dresser. Let's not forget the cross that hung over our beds and the Bible in our dresser drawer. After all, we weren't here for comfort but for learning. It wasn't the best decor but suitable for young ladies like ourselves. You could say it sure wasn't home.

In the evening, someone would have the chore of keeping the firewood burning all night on each floor. This was known as the chore from hell. I was looking for Marybeth and Kaitlin, wondering if they were the chosen ones for tonight. When doing the fireplace, your clothes really get full of ashes and smoke. You were lucky if you were able to take cat naps during this chore; after all, the fires had to keep burning all evening to keep everyone warm. In the morning, you quickly brushed yourself off and picked up your books, got into line, and proceeded to go to breakfast to the beat of the tapping stick of Ms. Hornet. Dirty or tired, it made no difference to the staff; you still had your classes and chores to do. A chore was a chore in the eyes of the nuns and the school, no excuses accepted. No matter how many hours of sleep you got or how dirty you may have been, you still had to do your chores. What a nuisance!

The classrooms were bright, and each room had two pianos, which the girls rotated at different times during the days for practice. We all had a schedule to follow that was rigorous. All schedules were posted on Mondays on the bulletin board for everyone to check. They tried to be fair and rotate the times between grades and girls. Some of the girls were not first-rated and needed to get worthy to the standards of St. Claire's. Those girls had to do more preparation and training time on the piano. More practice meant that they were eliminated from doing the chores. Lucky for them!

Part of the day also included manners, walking, sitting, and handling yourself properly as a lady. Going to charm class was needed for every young lady to succeed in today and tomorrow's world. We all knew that this was an important part in a young girl's life to succeed. Knowing the correct way to flirt properly, we thought, could be another asset. Many times, we would laugh at how the teachers would approach this class and try to teach it. It was truly how to attract a man but still be a lady. Classic, not bold, meek, and not aggressive was the way of a St. Claire's girl.

My dad was attracted to my Mom because she had possessed this ladylike charm. Dad wanted me to learn this behavioral training. Advantages in our time were so little and far in between; like all, you had to make it work and overcome the hard challenges.

CHAPTER 12

AFTER MUCH TIME PASSING AND still listening to the notes in the hallways, I just couldn't resist anymore to explore the unknown. I was going to wait for the still of the night when everyone would be in bed and bed check was completed. I was determined to go to the attic. I made sure no one was awake in my wing. I didn't want anyone to know what I was planning to do. I proceeded to walk up the narrow stairs to the attic, where the lovely music was playing, and put some peace in my mind about the enduring nights of music when I slept. I had to see the room. It was a curious ambition that I had, to find out. As Dad always said, "Annie has to always snoop to find the results, whether good or bad."

I slowly walked up the stairs, which were dark and creepy. The staircase was very cold and smelled really bad, with a terrible odor to the room, maybe mildew. I approached the forbidden room, very scared and frightened. I proceeded to enter, anyway. As I entered the room and slowly opened the door, I peeked in quickly. I was way too curious to turn back now. I saw a ray of moonlight coming through the cracks of the roof. I felt that there was a mist of clouds over the chest of drawers in the back corner with an image of a figure standing there. I questioned if this was a man or a woman.

I turned around quickly to the beautiful sounds of the music that were being played, but from where—the chest, the corner of the room, behind the wall—and by who? I couldn't recall why I ever thought about going upstairs when I was told not to do so! Did the devil make me do it?

No, I knew that an alarm went off in my head to be inquisitive. I heard the bizarre and weird noises coming from the room, and they were intriguing. I had to find out, simple answer!

The sound of the beautiful notes of music being played in the back of the attic was definitely unusual. The piano music was way too perfect not for me to pay attention to the sounds. It was magnificent and not ordinary, but remarkable. My heart was racing as I listened. Now, I began to go into a cold sweat but enjoyed it immensely.

In the middle of the whole thing, I was starting to get a little startled about the whole aura, the mist, the music, and the dreariness of the room. When in the room, it gave me moments of relaxation. While I was present in mind, the mist turned into beautiful clouds, and I started to question this unusual sight. It was as if you could just reach out and touch the white clouds of softness. Then I breathed in the romance of the season's most fragrant flower, the lilacs, and told myself to exhale. "Sit still, Annie. Just watch the spin of a colorful pinwheel and enjoy it." This setting was a place that took me back to my memories with Mom to those lazy days at the lake. Moments like these should last forever, and no one should ever take these treasures from your heart and soul. These are my whispering moments, which will always haunt my heart and follow me into my lifetime. I will never forget the visit and my meeting place with whom I felt was truly my mom. I certainly will revisit her again in the future.

I decided, before I got a little wild with my imagination and it got the better of me, that I should run as fast as I could down the stairs and go back to my room. Once my spirit decided within me to leave, I took off as fast as I could. When I departed, it was really dark to go down the winding staircase. I jumped over some of the stairs and stumbled on one or two of them, proceeding to get to the bottom of the staircase. At first, the door seemed impossible to open. It was as if it was stuck or maybe the sprits on the other side were holding me in.

I knew no one could hear me. I had faith and comfort in God and knew I would get out. I panicked and was almost to the point of screaming. I wanted out and now. I pushed on the door hard, and it popped open. Thank goodness, to be trapped in the attic would be intense and a horrible experience for anyone. Mom or no Mom made no difference!

The shutters were clacking in the wind; the moonlight now turned to nothing but darkness. Only the smell of the lilacs in the air gave me some reassurance. As I was running down the staircase, even that old mildew smell turned sweet. Once I smelled the lilac smell, I then had the guarantee and assurance that I was going to be OK. After all, these were Mom's favorite flowers. So I told myself that no harm could come to me.

I ran quickly back to my room without any hesitation, not ever looking back. I couldn't wait to get back to my room and under the sheets and wait for the bells to ring to get up. If I heard the bells, then I knew that I was safe and could continue a new day without being rattled. Once I was in my bed and tucked tightly in, I just couldn't explain in my mind the experiences that went on that night in the attic. I never had an occurrence or an incident that put a spell on me for a short period. I sure wished my friends or someone could have shared with me this chapter of my life or at least the evening of shock.

Now, I reflect on my conversation on my interview with Sister Teresa Harris about the word *fear*. I had forgotten what she actually said to me until I was in the attic. She proceeded to tell me on my school interview that we should all be aware of fear. It had much power and importance to everything in life. It could stop you from doing stupid things or rewarding things.

However, it could also stop you from doing exciting or devilish things. Your judgment of others and yourself could be clouded if fear got in the way. This could lead you to all types of evil. When we understand, only then can we control ourselves from temptation and curiosity of our personal fears. One of the most important battles in life is fear. At this moment, I knew Sister Teresa Harris was a wise and kind person without letting us know her real personality.

I think now is a good time to conquer my anticipation of my fear. Now I'm a bit edgy and I am completely out of my comfort zone. Meeting someone who is unknown and in a dreary attic sure makes a difference on how you think. I knew it was a soul of a good person but did not know who. Why was this person allowing me to hear the beautiful sounds of music being played? Why did this person or these persons feel maybe threatened?

Was I the one to reassure them that all is OK? Many questions for me to find answers to, but as Sister Harris said, "Fear can't come into play."

Somehow today, God's angels were given a command to protect and guard me under any circumstance. The attic was one of their requests of protection for me. I knew the angels would hold me up in their hands and find a way for me to dash as quickly as possible and as fast as my feet would carry me out of the forbidden room. I knew in my heart absolutely nothing was going to happen to me. Maybe the shadow in the attic had some rumbling and confusion with the angels, but certainly not me.

My parents always told us to listen and we would learn. It was an important lesson in life to accomplish. Me listening on that special day to Sister Harris, I absorbed everything and was so glad that I did. Life could become so much easier when you listened and learned. When I applied to school and had my interview with Sister Harris, and when she started to discuss the word *fear* with me, I felt she was crazy. Now I know she was telling me discreetly about the unknown room. Some girls found out about the room, but they couldn't cope with the unknown events. Talking about the word *fear* makes it simple to apply that rule if you get trapped in the forbidden room.

Once I was in my bed and snuggled up, I felt my ankle throbbing. I thought maybe I had sprained it running back to my room. My ankle was starting to hurt me now. I knew that, before I woke up, I had to take the time and wrap my ankle before classes started. How was I going to walk around the school and do my lessons without explaining myself? The limp would tell it all. How would I cover this up? I wondered.

I didn't realize until later that I had hurt my ankle so badly. I went down to the kitchen before Ms. Hornet caught me in the hall; I needed some ice and bandages. All I had to do now was to run into a classmate or a teacher who had bed check in the halls. How would I explain myself? I especially couldn't let Ms. Hornet or anyone know that I got hurt going upstairs to the forbidden room, where I didn't belong. Climbing down the back stairs, I managed to get what I needed and then crawled back into my bed. I closed the door and put the blanket up over my head. I was a little bit shaken, thinking about the mist that was moving over the entire attic. It was going to be enough for me not to tell anyone about this mystery and hard enough for me to try to sleep peacefully before the sounds of our wake-up call. This would be soon. What a night to remember!

I wanted to close my eyes and try to get a good night's sleep or what was left of it. Soon the tapping of Ms. Hornet would be heard in the hallways in the early morning dew. I knew that I would return to the room of mystery and the unknown questions to be answered on another day; morning would surely not come soon enough for me.

CHAPTER 13

THE NEXT DAY SEEMED WAY too early for me to open my eyes. Since my mischievousness during the night, I just couldn't move! Today was very exciting since we were having a group of invited guests to tea. Some guests were coming in from different states and many other countries to tour the school with their daughters.

I remembered what the girls would be going through or would go through once they were led into the library for tea. This was a very important day at St. Claire's. We were told to wear our best attire and present ourselves as fine young ladies and, most of all, to be very polite. We had mastered the charm, the standing and sitting properly, even the way to hold a cup of tea. Ms. Alice loved to show off her girls; after all, we were a reflection of her learning. We were known as the best performers and academic achievers. Our schedules had to be adhered to by all of us. It was beyond any belief that anything today would go wrong; it just couldn't. No mistakes ever on presentation day for new recruits and their parents. It was unacceptable.

It was now time to put on my best dress, my shoes, and let's not forget, our white gloves. At this split-second, I looked into my mirror and fixed my hair with one of my ribbons, so wide and colorful. My mirror was on my end table, so beautiful as always. It was at this instant when I looked into Mom's mirror and reflected back into time and missed her. It was so pleasing. I had to check myself out in the mirror. I needed to know if I looked OK or the way I should. I asked Mom if she thought

I was presentable enough for our guests. I liked talking to Mom—that comfort zone, my heart beating so fast as to really think that she was listening. I loved doing this especially since I attended school away and Mom had passed when I was a small child. It was reassuring to think she was always with me. Sometimes your imagination stretches a little far, but it's OK if you get comfort.

My strength was given to me by looking through my magical mirror; at least, I thought it was. It enabled me to see beyond my years of growing up. It gave me the opportunity to go back in time with Mom. Do we need an excuse to remember our loved ones? Not really, but sometimes we do need to go somewhere where we are safe with just them and us. My mirror did just that for me. It was my safe haven.

Another day was upon us, and we received high praise from Ms. Claire and Sister Adele Bernadette for our ladylike charms that we perfected. I must say, we were very fast learners and alert girls in listening to what had to be done. Ms. Hornet was tapping her stick in the hallway for all of us to get lined up to continue to the library to greet our guests. To our surprise, we didn't realize that we would be having royalty at our tea. We felt this was only idle gossip to get us to be on our toes. We never really felt that the families from other countries would show.

Nevertheless, lo and behold, there were a few girls with their moms and dads from foreign countries, checking out the old place. Our school was renowned all over the world and in the States. It was highly respected for our musical talent, education, and elegant school of charm for girls. Only the best were selected for acceptance, which everyone was very much aware of.

Applications were many, but Mr. Grumbling, Ms. Alice, and Sister Teresa Harris, our head nun, were the professionals that made all the decisions. We had talent beyond our expectations that many people respected us for. Not knowing why my father had decided to school me here was not a reality to me when I left. But now it stood to reason why. Now I did realize on this day that Dad was trying to turn me into that lady of culture and prestige. What I should be and what Mom already had been. This was very captivating. It was well worth the sophistication, the chitchat, the politeness of most. I finally believed that I was to have something special in my life, as this would tell in time, with age, and after my graduation.

All very ladylike, we walked as fast as our feet could carry us to the main ballroom. This room had high ceilings, massive velvet chairs, chandeliers, and imported marble tile on the floors. It was a magnificent, elegant room. If I was a new possible recruit, this certainly would impress me as a student or parent. They knew what they were doing by making this room the first impression. I too remember that day with Dad and entering this grand old room. It was breathtaking, all the details and money that were spent on this one room. It certainly did the job for me and Dad. After seeing the welcoming room lobby, Dad and I couldn't wait to see the rest of the tour and the school grounds. I knew that this was a wonderful place for anyone to be during their high school years.

The hardest part of going away to school was leaving my family and friends from home. You had to look at it in another positive way though, look at all the new loved ones you would find between these walls the next four years. It's like looking for new love—very simple, enchanting, and life lasting.

It was a drooling day, very tiring and intimidating. To hold those smiles all day was an effort. We reminded ourselves in the hallway before coming down the stairs to make sure we didn't get any tea on our gloves and to smile, smile, and smile. Ms. Alice made the selection of girls that would make the school's best presentation for new students. How good we looked, more than that just great. We mixed with the crowd, parents, girls, and people of wealth. I now realized on that day that Dad wanted me to be one of these respectable ladies. Our guests left after tea and toured the classes, grounds, and met with students and teachers. Most important was the piano teaching; this was the talent that set our reputation higher than most private schools.

We had several princesses of different countries entering our world. They were here for the tour and a day of festivities. So marvelous were these young ladies, smiling graciously, holding the teacup properly, and knowing when to sit and when to stand. Very impressive for those that was watching.

The older girls were able to present their pieces, which were accelerating in themselves. I truly had an adventurous day and a moment to remember. I captured the guests, our music, and the presence of everyone in my heart and knew never to forget this second. I pranced into the library and down the halls, trying to act like a big shot. Little old me a big shot, imagine! Of course, I did it all with elegance and flare.

We had fine delicacies served, and many fine young men from St. Pete's school came over to help with the servings. Some of them stayed at the entrance, helping the guests in and out of their carriages. The upperclassmen boys from St. Pete's flipped the napkins properly on their laps, pulled the chairs out for our guests, and sat them at the correct tables. The boys had a big day, making sure they did all the right things. After all, it wouldn't be appropriate if our choice was the freshmen boys and they end up making a fool out of themselves on this special day. They were just not mature enough and as responsible as an upperclassman would be. However, they were cute as a button!

At the end of the day, all the horses and carriages pulled away to the direction of where home was for them. Many had to catch trains or maybe even boats to get back to their loved ones. I waved eagerly to them with my clean white gloves to say good-bye to my newfound friends, maybe. I hoped that in the fall, some would be able to return. Finally peace of quietness came over me, and I was settling my thoughts. Good old Ms. Hornet tapped her cane in the hallway—which echoed in the cold, dreary walls of the castle—to move on. The day was over, and so was all the excitement. We knew that she wanted us up front, which was usually in the ballroom. Our presence was required immediately for attendance. We all knew the tapping of the cane meant business.

When the last family left, the boys were picked up by their headmaster: Mr. Airy from St. Pete's. Mr. Harry Grumbling and Ms. Alice Snap were very pleased with the attendance at hand. Mr. Grumbling went in front of the library and asked for our attention. He stated that "the board was quite pleased with the way all the girls and boys presented our school at our open house." Then smiling, he started to clap, and with no hesitation, so did everyone else.

Mr. Grumbling and Ms. Alice were pleased with our performance and the boys'; we represented the school very well that day. After all, most of us were beginners really outside our element. It seemed to us that we outdid ourselves. "Magnificent," one parent expressed.

In five seconds flat, we were all checked in for attendance, and the boys departed. At this moment, it was already 6:00 p.m., ready for us to sit down to dinner in our dining room, which was by the ballroom. The dining room was elegant; some called it a big kitchen, but the chairs were nicer, the marble floors colorful, the chandeliers sparkling, and the cheery, bright windows making it very charming. Some of my friends had to go help the chefs prepare and set up since this was their chore for the day. Tonight, we all walked down to the dining room for dinner instead of the usual cafeteria. The dining hall was serving duck, which was a delicacy for me and most. I was used to having chicken and eggs in my hometown. It was a very extraordinary day, very impressive. I'm sure, along with me and the rest, we would never ever forget this marvelous day.

CHAPTER 14

*I*T WAS NOW TIME TO end the day and sleep well for the days ahead. As the sun was breaking through the morning clouds, I heard the musical notes in the hallway, which I heard most of my days at St. Claire's. It seemed, when questioning others, that this was not music to their ears, only mine. I sometimes thought the soothing notes I heard was a way for me to feel safe in my own world away from home. The comfort of the notes made my soul and heart feel powerful and comforting. It was somewhat creepy that no one else could hear the notes being played in the unknown forbidden room other than myself.

I spoke to Marybeth in confidence about the notes. She never wanted to talk about them at all; I thought sometimes she worried about me being crazy. As my friend, I asked her to share some of my concerns with me as I had no one else to talk to about them. Marybeth explained that the noise in the room was quite scary and wasn't a comfort zone to her. It made others very nervous and uncomfortable to think that they may have heard the notes.

Most of them felt it was weird to hear something from someone you didn't see. Kaitlin felt that maybe they were present and surrounded us but they had to prove themselves musically and give evidence to us that this was true. The musical notes, for her and Marybeth, were not relaxing but alarming. It made them frantic at night of the possibility of the spirits flying around the hallways and peeping in on them as they sleep. She indicated that when she put her head on her pillow, she took the noise out of her head so she could rest peacefully at night. Marybeth thought that it had to be haunted souls. Maybe someone was buried alive or was killed somewhere in the castle and his soul had to be released by playing music.

Sometimes her prayers would give her the courage she needed to close her eyes. It was unpleasant even talking about the spirits; it made her nervous. She needed a lot of bravery to think about their souls and to make conversation about them. Marybeth and Kaitlin asked me to stop, no more stories about the forbidden room. They couldn't sleep when I talked about it. Marybeth indicated she would have vivid dreams, and then when the torches burned out in the hallways, forget it. I felt whoever or whatever was upstairs in the attic would come down and play notes and walk the hallways at night. These spirits had to release their inner souls, and somehow, I did believe they were possessed with some terrible evil.

After all, our halls were dark even though the lamps were lit along some of the hallways. It wasn't a place that you roamed around after check in for sleep. Marybeth was concerned for me and told me to please listen to Ms. Hornet and Ms. Alice and leave the topic well enough alone.

"How do you know that no one is locked up in that attic? A crazy person who may kill you!"

"Oh, come off it, Marybeth."

"The musical notes weren't that frightening, unless I am too stupid to think that this could be anything else other than my mom playing. I am convinced about this."

I told Marybeth and Kaitlin that they were making more of a big deal out of this fable.

Marybeth replied, "Oh yeah, I heard a man hanged himself in the attic over a loved one. It seems that the girl was a student here and he worked at the school. That's most likely why no one is allowed to speak of anything. Imagine a student and a worker falling in love? What would this news do for the school and new students? How could the school let something like this happen? It would send out bad reviews and kill the reputation of St. Claires. I know if my dad heard something like this, he may have questioned himself about sending me here."

"OK, you can have this conversation at this time, but try to keep an open mind that maybe the souls of others are here to protect us. I understand your fears, Marybeth, but I know the good spirits will overcome the bad ones. This man wasn't labeled as a maniac. He was just in love. I know someday I will show you and Kaitlin that your fears can be lifted. We are protected and will be taken care of every day while we attend this school. Trust me, please."

"Trust you, Annie? You're asking us to feel comfortable about the unknown and the strange noises and the piano notes. It keeps us up at night scared to death, and I wonder when one will decide to stop in my room for a second. I am certainly spooked."

"I won't visualize a ghost, spirit, or something hurdling over me at night, and now you tell me it's your mom? Come on, Annie, I know you miss her and I don't blame you, but this is not within reason, your lifelike visions of your mom. Maybe school, grades, and just being away from home is getting to you? All right, maybe some of what you say is realization, but overall, it's not the spirit of the man who hanged himself but a pleasant person who needs to feel needed and loved. I am sure of this."

"Why can't this just be my mom's spirit? OK, believe in what you want, and in time you may get a grip of your notions and get back on track. Sleep well for tonight, my dear friend, I will see you in the morning."

I thought long and hard about what they were saying. I did so believe in my heart that it had to be Mom. Mom definitely was here to protect me and help me succeed and accomplish what she and Dad had set out to do. I put the chatter of Marybeth to rest because I didn't want to accept her fears. They weren't mine, and it wasn't going to be mine. I was assured that the magical notes were a sign of Mom telling me it's OK to have a mystery about a loved one. Face your challenges full speed ahead, and tackle them headfirst; at least that's what my brothers used to tell me. No fear in my heart, at least not today.

So, in my days of curiosity, when I wanted to challenge the forbidden room, I would tackle my feelings headfirst, as the Haverstein family has always done and then deal with it later.

The days and nights turned into one another; as timed passed, my curiosity got the better of me again on the mystery of the attic. It was a few months since I had returned to the attic. It was still frightening and scary not to know. I had endured the rigorous discipline and, of course, hours of piano playing. Who was I kidding? All of us had to. No one wanted to admit to the sounds after dark because, if you did hear them, what would Ms. Alice say or do? I would listen for hours to the harmony of the music in the attic until I closed my eyes and fell asleep. I felt an intense magnet was forcing me to enter the attic again. What a fool I was.

The sounds put me in a slumber and had a magnet so forceful that I was completely drawn to the music and the strength of the character. While I lay sleeping, he or she had the guts and determination to try and enter my inner self with a life force bigger than me and them. The atmosphere in my room became tense, and the mood would change my essence. As I lay there under my covers, I could see a flowing mist fly by in my room and hallway. This sometimes left a feeling and mood that my surroundings had a ghost present. Who or what this was, did one really know? Not when the spirits are trying to release themselves to you and leave you with an impression of who they are. I knew time would give me a handle on what this was all about and why me.

It looked as if someone was reaching out to hold my hand and letting my heart know that this was a safe place. I knew that this would satisfy me and reward my soul in my lifetime. I told myself that I would have inner peace within these walls of the unknown. I did challenge myself every day to listen to the school rules of not going to the forbidden room or thinking about it. On a personal note, I attempted to confront and explore the profound mysteries of human existence and asked my friends to be bold and do the same.

They confronted me head-on, reminding me that other things were on the table right now. We had to be caught up in the holiday concert without any delay, not a make-believe ghost story and a room that we should never enter or speak about. No one had time to think about idle chitchat of the forbidden room. There were too many things that we really had to concentrate on, like getting flying colors for our tryouts when we performed. The girls advised me to let it go for now and to concentrate on my musical pieces that I was going to play for the concert tryout. Marybeth and Kaitlin told me that we had priorities and I needed to put them in order. The spirits were for sure not the number one item for here, today or tomorrow.

CHAPTER 15

*T*IME PASSED QUICKLY; THE HOLIDAY concert was upon us again, which was beautifully displayed. The invitations, as usual, went out vigorously. Invites to special, important people were on the top of the list. The journalists, cameramen, colleges, and of course families and friends, not to mention a few, were always asked.

This year's competition would have a total of twenty-five girls being accepted to play piano masterpieces of their choice for a lead spot. Forty girls were selected for the choir. I was one of them. Ms. Melissa, our singing teacher, suggested her choice of vocals for this year's performance. She was going to pick one girl to do a solo. I knew that an upperclassman was going to try out shortly, so I waited backstage to listen. Christine, who I knew only slightly, was a junior and had vocal cords that were outstanding. I heard her backstage as she performed. She was dynamic and gave an amazing performance that was ready anytime to be sung. The lead vocal was now eliminated. For those who thought about trying, forget it. Christine had it in the bag with no problem.

Alessandra, a friend in my grade, decided she was going to try out for the lead solo in the choir this year along with several other girls. Christine, a junior, was also trying out on the same day as Alessandra for lead solo. I decided to wait backstage and listen to them both. Christine's tryout was magnificent. After listening to her, I wasn't quite sure if Alessandra had any shot for the solo lead. As good as she was, I didn't believe she was good enough to beat Christine.

We listened intensely to Alessandra's tryout. She also was brilliant and was certainly gifted with her voice. Well, I knew Alessandra accomplished what she wanted to do this evening. I just couldn't wait for her to finish and applaud her. After all, what are friends for?

Alessandra had finished her song, and she knew I was backstage, listening to her brilliant voice. I wanted to give her the encouragement that was needed.

"Alessandra, how did you feel about your performance?"

"It was hard," said Alessandra. "The best thing was that I could use everything that I was feeling in my singing performance—my anxiety, nervousness, messing up, and desire of perfection. I hope it works for me. Maybe I sounded amazing?"

"What you shouldn't do is second-guess yourself because everyone wants to be so perfect. Your conclusion was powerful and unexpected," I told Alessandra. "The notes were clear, and I am confident that you handled it the right way. I have obtained a degree of respect toward you for the way you ended your song. It made me feel happy and delighted to listen. I hope the teachers feel the same way."

I wanted to play the piano in the concert, but if nothing else was available, we had to be thankful that at least we had the opportunity to sing. Oh well, there was always next year. My friends and I were very talented, but so were many other girls. I hoped that my best friends and I would all be part of the show somehow.

The freshman girls in our class seemed funny to watch as they ran around helping the nuns with the lights and stage scenery. It was hysterical behavior. Some of the girls were on committees of decorating, food, and beverages. Special groups handed the selling of the tickets. Advertising also played an important part in the holiday show. This was a spectacular moment for St. Claire's Academy in Philadelphia; after all, this was the New York City for us.

The tryouts took place for days, and shortly, at the end of the week, names were posted and the pianists had their pieces and the choir their songs. Christine, as we expected, made the lead for the singing solo. With some disappointment, the three of us made no list this year, but we were satisfied that we were all singing in the choir. We all felt that this was the calm after the storm since none of us were going to be on stage or be headliners. Not this year anyway. Watch out, girls, next year will be another story. We shall prevail! No time for playing around now. Everyone had extra jobs to perform plus many hours of practice, and we all had to be on a serious note.

Before you knew it, evening was here and the excitement unfolded like a fever in your head. Guests were seated, and our audience was here. Finally, the curtains were going up. Authentic performances were rare, but some were going to be their own star and shine that evening. We trained for months before production, and it was pretty exhausting. We were up for the hype; it was there. Excitement was in the air, a few of the girls' hands were shaking, but overall we knew to perform and to perform well. You would have much satisfaction when you finally performed your piece with perfection.

I think, once you attend a performance as fabulous as this one and see your children; how far they have come is surreal. Our parents, teachers, and friends were taken back by the fact that we were children; where did this talent come from? It was one of our challenges at this school and one of the most rewarding things that would happen in our lifetime by far. The visual splendor was on display. There was an eye-popping audience who was thrilled at the idea of seeing a huge success. The evening came with no glitches. The teachers, parents, and all of us were so proud of our outcome. The show was dazzling and sparkled with a shining, bright star looking down on us. Maybe Mom?

I was somewhat tearful that I was not selected this year to play a musical piece. I was good but only a freshman, and this was a special event. Thank God, Marybeth and Kaitlin also were not picked.

This year Marybeth was helping out with the selection of music and practice with the choir. Kaitlin was picked for helping out with the selection of food. Her mom was a famous cook in her own restaurant in Pittsburgh, Pennsylvania.

Why wouldn't she want to be on the food committee? Ms. Melissa asked me if I would please help set up the organization of the music and who would stand or sit where. I thought to myself, *Wow, this is a big job. If someone doesn't play first or maybe I have them play last, what are going to be my consequences? Will they all be mad at me? No more friends?* I was proud to be selected but nervous about the conclusion of it all.

I sat long and hard and thought about this dilemma. I could be in or out with my friends within a matter of a performance. How would I select and make the right choices? I knew that I was strong, outgoing, and very persuasive—and yes, don't forget smart—to make it all work out. I accepted this job with a smile. Ms. Melissa was quite pleased.

Our seniors were first picked, and rightfully so. It would be a tall order next year to top the game plan and be able to get picked on your achievements all for one night. You really have to blow people's minds with a magnificent program and dedicate your time. Meanwhile, the teachers and all the deserving credits were in the backstage, waiting to perform and take their bows. Finally, names were called out one by one or by groups. The tremendous applause and standing ovation were for those that deserved the credits. Bravo, till next year.

We had our Christmas break, and before you knew it, we were back into school. Springtime passed and school was ending. The end of school was finally here, and my first year at St. Claire's was finished. I said my good-byes to my friends and really hugged Marybeth and Kaitlin, whom I was going to miss the most. We did finger crossing and promised one another that we would write at least once a week to keep one another posted on our summer crushes.

It was truly the end of my first year of growing up and becoming a young woman. I had vacation time now and went home to visit with Dad and my brothers, whom I missed terribly. I couldn't wait for the reunion with my family and friends. I boarded the train to Harrisburg, and I was on my way home. My first steps on the train; I knew Dad would be there to hold my hand up the stairs. He was the engineer today for this trip. Sure enough, I looked up and saw Dad with his smile and charming personality. He reached his hand out to help me board.

It was a moment of sincere love. Oh, how I loved my dad. I gave Dad my big bear hug, as I had done since I was a little girl. Dad picked me up, not too high anymore; after all, I was now going to be fifteen years old. Not the little four-year-old girl that he once played with, bouncing around. Once I boarded, Dad led me to a seat by the window. It was a charming ride through the other cities. What a beautiful day. This was an unforgettable moment that I would always remember into adulthood. As I sat there gazing out of the window, getting really excited about seeing my family and my friends, I started to dream about how summer would be this year. I was sure like others—a blast. As my Dad said, there was no substitute for fun. If you were not having fun, what's the point in all this then?

Before I knew it, I was home. I was now at the railroad station where I loved to wave to Dad when he was departing for work. My brothers Tom and Randy were there to pick me up since Dad had two more stops to make before he could depart off the train and go home. Tom and Randy were really my buds; it wasn't surprising that they were the two to pick me up today.

Tom and Randy had a million questions. How was I? Did I get straight A's? Did I want to go back? Overall they were good questions to be answered by me. I told them there would be plenty of time to go over my school year, and most anxiously, I did want to tell some of my brothers about Mom. It was important to choose the right brothers for this discussion, not one that would think I was completely crazy or nuts. Timing would be very important for this conversation, I thought.

It was like old times when I arrived—so much action, excitement, and confusion. Aunt Suzie, Uncle Dan, and my sweet cousin Claire were at the gate. Little Claire now was walking so great, solid on her little feet. She looked at me with her little hands in the air, like somebody attempting to communicate. It was powerful and moving. My brothers, those who were home, also couldn't wait to take me in their arms and toss me around a little. I went from one of them to another with a twirl and got dizzy when they were all finished. Aunt Suzie had a special meal on the stove cooking and of course made her apple pie for my arrival.

Oh, how I missed these good old times. However, I knew that at school, I was creating new memories with new friends. It was all summer fun for now.

Tom, Randy, and I horsed around a lot when we got home and decided to plan a game attack for Dad. It seemed that this was the reunion that good old Dad deserved. In growing up, the three of us just had to be the devilish ones. We were the three that would cause the ruckus in the house, all the confusion, and the added trouble. One big issue that Dad had with us usually was when we didn't do our schoolwork or decided that it wasn't necessary to do what was asked of us. This was logical for us to think that way; after all, we were children. We only wanted to play ball, fish, and swim.

With us being little guys, Dad would tell us to go pick the apples so Aunt Suzie could make an apple pie. Of course, we went apple picking, all right, but decided to have a snowball fight with the apples. What a disaster—the smell, our clothes full of the apple-juice stain, and wondering how we would explain ourselves this time around.

Boy, those were good old days, and yes, we did get into mighty big trouble with our pranks. So it was only right that we could think of doing something to good old Dad. I goofed around with my brothers today and remembered our moments together as we had in the past. This was part of my growing-up years with my brothers and moments that would never be shattered.

Now I was looking forward to being able to be with my neighborhood friends, see old teachers in town, and be with my family. The beautiful surroundings of my hometown seemed so perfect. I waited so patiently that evening for Dad's arrival. It was nearly 6:00 p.m., and as I was helping Aunt Suzie in the kitchen. I heard Dad open the gate and walk up the path to the porch. I just couldn't wait for him to come into the kitchen.

I called to Tom and Randy that Dad was coming up the walkway and to get set for the mad dash up the stairs once we fooled him. We had decided to let Dad think that supper wasn't ready and Aunt Suzie never showed up. Boy, I didn't know if he was going to like this joke so much. I ran and jumped into Dad's arms when he opened the gate. I now felt I was truly home. Dad laughed and said to me, "Annie, are you now back to being four years old?" I replied, "Dad, in your arms I'm always a little girl."

With this, Tom and Randy came out yelling to Dad that he would never believe what happened today—a no-show from Aunt Suzie and no dinner to eat. Dad looked like he was going to explode; he was exhausted from today's work and mad. I looked at the boys and told them they had better tell Dad about our childish prank to relieve him of any anxiety that I saw was building up. After all, I didn't want Dad to have a heart attack or something. The boys came yelling into the room and told Dad that they wanted to fool around like the good old days.

"We just wanted to see your reaction, Dad, but we knew today wasn't the day for any jokes. You looked so tired. Everything is done. Aunt Suzie is upstairs, and we just finished washing up also. Now is a good time to sit down to enjoy our dinner." We apologized to Dad; he understood and laughed it off, remembering our childish ways. Dad said he needed a good joke played on him. It made him realize that he was not indestructible either. "Good one, kids, let's eat. I'm starved."

Vacations at home felt well like a compromise. However, we soon discovered that there was a lot to like about a summer break that's low stress, inventive, and allows you sleep with your own pillow under your head. It was great to have my own bed, sheets, curtains and my little joys of treasures around my room. Each one of them had a story to tell me. Here, for sure, I didn't question or hear any playing of notes, and for sure, no mystery of any forbidden room was at my house. I wanted to open my bags now and put everything back into place. Especially Mom's mirror. I laid it down on my dresser; it was so dainty and so magnificent. I knew that my mirror and I had had some whirlwind of a year. I knew there was more to come and she would be by my side. The day was dark now until I saw the fall again. I told myself, "Annie, it's time to get a good night's sleep."

Summer was knocking at my door. Before the heat really got cranked up, I had a few ideas to make the scorching days ahead be at ease. I would make plenty of time for Dad to cook outside, do outdoor activities, do a little fishing, maybe swim, and rocking on our big old porch swing with little old me seemed just fine. I sometimes skip the most important part and that's the promise to, for a significant block of time, disconnect from my everyday school life and soak up the pure joys of summer. When I do that, even a single day can be a refreshing break and who couldn't use a little more of that?

I waited each day for my brothers and Dad to come home from work, and of course, even though I was becoming a young lady, I was still the little sister and precious little girl for them. I loved playing ball and being roughed up. It brought back those special days when we all would be waiting for Mom to cook one of her fabulous dinners. Now it was Dad's time to do so. He made a wonderful roasted chicken with so many fresh vegetables, homegrown of course. Aunt Suzie and Uncle Dan came over several times a week with baby Claire, who was so darn cute. I would have to say, she looked a little bit like me. I couldn't wait to rough it up with her and give her advice on being a young lady.

My oldest brother, Adam, took me swimming during the summer months, something that he and I loved doing together. Going fishing and putting the ugly worms on the sticks were a special moment with my younger brothers Randy, Elliott, and Samuel. Sometimes we would climb on the tire on the old oak tree and flip ourselves into the water; it was so refreshing.

I never took the fish home, as I felt, like me, they would never see their mother anymore in this lifetime if they left on a hook.

Before you knew it, summer was starting to end. It was already August. Dad had suggested that I come with him one day and take a train ride through some of his cities. I really got so excited on this summer day when Dad suggested this great idea. Dad and I left early for work, and when we reached the train station, Dad boarded me on the train and gave me a perfect seat to look out the window close to him as he ran the train.

The first stop on the train ride was Altoona, Pennsylvania, which was a town close by. I sat there very quietly and didn't whisper a word.

My schooling came in handy, and Dad was so proud of his now young lady. No one ever would question the engineer in charge if a family member was on board. Dad was so proud of me and my brothers, especially the fact that I was going to St. Claire's girls' academy in Philadelphia, Pennsylvania.

St. Claire had a reputation of being a prominent school for the most talented young piano players. Most of the graduates went off to play in concerts or for world-known figures abroad. My thoughts had always been that travel was a continuing education and a never-ending adventure. I'm naturally a very curious person, and so much of what I've learned in life is from the people I've met. My commitment to the earth is crucial. I want to see as much of it as possible.

As the summer came to an end, I truly reflected back on my summer day's home with family and friends. It was truly a joy as my heart grew solemn for departure. This was one of my most rewarding days and yet one of my most troubled ones. My understanding and my development as a great piano player was well worth the element of change. I knew the school was everything my dad and brothers hoped for besides the learning experience of concert piano playing. I was also working on how to be fine woman for years to follow.

Summer was almost over, and I was grasping the concept of who I was. I did discover in the very beginning, who I was, and I was proud of it; I will never apologize for what I do. This year was insane and out of sight. At the end of the day, I was just another girl; I just had more brothers than others and my best friends, Jessica and Samantha. Jessica didn't want me to go away to St. Claire's school, which was so far away. She just felt that this school was on another planet and she wouldn't get to see me as she has done in the past. Our plans were that we would go to school together and share those special high school moments that teenage girls shared. She and I were best friends since the beginning of grade school.

Samantha, on the other hand, moved in when she and I were about two years old. Our mothers were friends who shared their ideals together as women on raising kids, farming, and making great apple pies. Samantha's mom was heartbroken when she lost her dear friend Brenda, my mom. To my understanding, it took many prayers and visits to mom's grave and soul-searching for Mrs. Knipe to accept her death.

Her dad worked with my father on the railroad as a conductor. My brothers told me she had a hard time when I left; she seemed so glum and most of the time so serious. Time seemed like an eternity for her that would never pass. She waited patiently with Jessica for my return home. They would walk through the town together, stop at the ice cream parlor, and then sit on my porch during the day. Don't forget Jessica and Samantha now had to share me with other girls and new school memories that they didn't have with me during their school year. There was also my piano playing and a new life style that I would have with others to experience that they would not be part of. My best friends were hurting dearly. Thank God, our friendship was very strong and loving. This was also the reason why it would survive.

Well before I knew it, I was packing and going off to St. Claire's for my second year of school. I received my train ticket from Dad, and as usual, he gave me the talk—to be careful and learn everything that would be taught to me. I was saying good-bye again to my brothers, my aunt, my uncle, and baby Claire.

My neighborhood school friends came down to the house before I departed. It seemed that I had little time to spend with Jessica and Samantha during this summer. Now I was giving them hugs and remembering some of the crazy things we did over the summer. It was always tough to say good-bye. Knowing I would not see them for a while was hard. When I left, believe it or not, I was already planning my return back to school and the excitement that would follow.

As I boarded the train and waved good-bye to my two brothers, I sat back and relaxed for the trip back to school. I couldn't believe that I felt jubilated about my returning. The train was on time for me to depart. There were tears, excitement, and joy, and yet our hearts were wrenching with precisely what the years of dedication will bring to my table this year, for rewards? Now this was my new outside world for me to explore through my growing years. I knew this would all be worthwhile. The impeccable training I will receive will let my talents rise to the best of my achievements of who I will be, in my future.

CHAPTER 16

*I*T WAS A LONG JOURNEY but I was so pleased. I couldn't believe I was anxious to see old, mean Ms. Hornet. She will pick up the girls that arrive at the station from the trains and bring them up to the school grounds, as she has always done. We finally arrived at the school and as I entered I remembered the cold walls, and dreary atmosphere. I was excited to be back! I now knew that this new world had circled my heart, emotions and my desires for me to be the best that I can be. It was all I cared about now and what I wished for.

As we entered the main hall, good old Sister Teresa Harris was waiting. No surprise to anyone for her to be there. Sister Adele Bernadette the pleasant sole greeted us with her charming personality. We couldn't imagine where Ms. Alice was though; missing in action was not her style. Not seeing her was disappointing for most of us. Ms. Hornet saw the frowns on our faces from not knowing where Ms. Alice had disappeared. With a nod to her head, she said, "Do not fret, girls, as Ms. Alice was having trouble getting some of the bedrooms in order before your arrival."

My room was cold like everyone else's, and I had one sheet and one blanket to keep warm. September wasn't really a month that you needed much fire, but in this old school, it sure was damp. You almost couldn't wait for the fall leaves to fall; most likely, you were guaranteed a little heat. The smoke would go up the hallways and into your bedroom just like it did last year.

Smelling the dry wood in the fireplaces in early October would make it seem like yesterday never left me. As the weeks passed by, my heart was led to my room in the attic. All my suspicion and concerns were all in my head again. I tried immensely to wipe them out, but I knew there was a special love and a special protection for me up there. No matter what anyone felt or said, I knew this place was not all bad.

It was exciting and exhausting my first days back in school. I had to leave the questions of the unknown to my thoughts. I got up as usual during the evenings at school. Tonight wasn't any different. I could not bear the sounds of the beautiful music in the halls during the evenings, echoing through the halls. These magical notes were always able to calm me down to sleep. It was while I lay still during the night that I was able to hear these musical notes of mystery in the halls.

I knew some of the other girls heard them too but were so afraid of speaking up. They surely didn't want Ms. Hornet or Ms. Alice to be aware of their secret that they kept about the notes. I sometimes thought that all of the girls in my wing heard the soft gentle music being played. As life gets sometimes too complicated, most of us can't handle the unknown.

During the first week of school, when everyone was tucked into bed, I heard the wind howling loudly and the shutters on my windows clacking back and forth. I raised my head in a little fear to peak from beneath my blankets as to see who showed up. Shadows of mist were over my bed, and the wonderful smell of lilac was present. I realized that good old Mom wanted to welcome me back to school.

Raising my head to acknowledge Mom since I knew she could see me but me not her, I threw a kiss into my hand, hopefully one that she caught. Time would come again when I will be able to visit my second home of peacefulness.

Before I knew it, daylight had entered my room, the sun was bright, and the birds were chirping fiercely and loud. When I took a breath, I knew the day was going to be wonderful. I sometimes believed that the birds were always talking to one another. The unknown mysteries that haunt our souls are the questions that you may have no answers for but will torment you in life.

I had to go about my day without my dreams and desires in my head. I needed to concentrate on my lessons in my classes. Our schedules were so busy. Practice, practice, and more practice. Learning the languages of Latin and French was so difficult for me. In class, I had the answers for my questions. Was the word correct, the adjective used correctly? Did I make sense of the sentence? Those questions could be directed or answered by myself or others. The attic was not so cut and dry. Truly, mysteries of the unknown will remain lingering in my heart until solved.

Shortly, more rehearsals would come. The holidays were almost upon us, which meant peace, fellowship, and a marathon of practice. You learned to be technically flawless as a piano player and didn't lack inner fire. I was the ultimate overachieving student, executing each finger playing with supreme "perfection" by the book. This meant that I was the best to play in the saintly concert as a top pianist. I pushed myself to extremes from the inside out not to be detached from my inner soul. I also observed the activities as part of a series of hard work.

We now had been in school already a period of a few months. Everyone had new schedules and new teachers, and most of us had met new friends and had seen our old ones. Ms. Hornet, on the next day, ordered everyone to come to the ballroom for us to receive criticism and be praised on our individual talents. The teachers came and brought some tea; we were now young ladies learning the proper way to take advice and criticism. We sat up straight, legs not crossed, laughing; for once, calmness was felt in the air. After the deliberation of good and bad news from Ms. Hornet, we would return to class and rehearse. The headmaster came into the ballroom and welcomed us to the return of his great school. You could think that this was conviction of days to come.

The freshmen girls were so in aura about what was going on. Now they had new classes, teachers, and rooms that most likely they hated, like we did. Missing their loved ones and not knowing so much about the expectation of being here. *Can I do this? Will I make friends? Will I be happy? And most of all, will I succeed in the new lifestyle handed to me? Will I make my family proud?* Looking at them, I could see their little heads turning in wonder. I just wanted to go over to all of them, hug, and give big kisses to make them feel comfortable.

I couldn't sometimes endure thinking about the intensity for the holiday concert that was coming soon. I was on dinner detail tonight with Marybeth and Kaitlin; not so bad doing something with your friends. We made it fun and enjoyed it somewhat. Extra times were had by all of us spending it together, no matter how. Chores were done, and certainly it was a long day. I was exhausted; my head was twirling with so many answers, questions, and scheduling. I needed to make sure everything would work smoothly. At the end of the day, I proceeded in the direction of my room as I did every night. Whew, what a delight to see my bed. I took my bath and soaked my little fingers, which were killing me so much, and then started to relax in bed. I had some homework to do and a history test to study for. I wasn't so worried about this one; it was going to be a piece of cake since history was my favorite subject.

As I lay in bed, starting to get cozy with my pillow, saying some special prayers, I started to doze off a little. I then heard the notes rapidly spreading everywhere in the halls, but only to my ears. Or at least, the only one who wanted to admit it. I listened intensely, and one note was more wonderful than the others.

What happened? Maybe I was too tired to explain the beautiful sounds. I was dazed and anxiously awaiting the outcome of choice for the concert, which would be announced in the school in days to come. I couldn't believe that I concentrated on the concert more than the mystery of the forbidden room. I was sure that this was most likely a good thing not to take the space in my brain. I had to be good, better than good, to perform. I wanted this so badly, like the rest of the girls, so intensely.

That evening, I heard my beautiful notes being played, but this time, I knew everything was going to be OK with the tryouts. I knew by the soothing notes that life was wonderful in my world. It was going to be supreme. Somehow peacefulness came over my body when I listened to the magical notes. I knew the time was coming soon for my entrance to be seen again in my private, forbidden room.

The objectives required skill; missions were frustratingly fuzzy. Puzzles demanded little more than tapping the notes a few times on the piano. The fighting didn't require much thought either between us and them. You sometimes could punch your way out of most challenges blindly. This challenge would be a little tougher than most. Yet, I knew I was going to win the battle. My sword was laid down, and the triumph of victory was in my heart. Win I will for sure. My accomplishment was to be selected for the concert, and this was the destiny of my focus.

Tomorrow, everything would be told once the girls were announced. The holiday concert had to be viewed as a night of mucus, choking, gagging, and then some beautiful singing, maybe some comedy, hugging, and an occasional awkward silence in the air. The debut of a show! You knew you could lose the attention of your audience but still win the hearts and minds of your family friend viewers.

I realized that after the selection of the mentoring for each girl was done, no one could miss a rehearsal anymore until decisions had been made on the concert. It was endless days and nights for everyone; it seemed that the days turned into months. Again, it was a whirlwind. It was hard to imagine that I had survived so far the endurance of it all. I was now in my second year of school and thrilled to be there.

CHAPTER 17

HEN THE CLASSES WERE DONE, we proceeded to walk with our friends to our rooms. It was always cold in the hallways since the fireplaces really didn't get fired up until supper. I couldn't wait for the fireplace to be blazed and hear the burning wood crackling and the wood smell in the air. Marybeth and I were so excited since we were right next to each other's room as we were last year. Marybeth was kind and sweet, an only child. Her father was a famous artist and made a tremendous amount of money on his paintings. The only time we had to share our ideals of graduation and families were at bedtime. We were so tired by the time we were able to share news, we hardly would be able to stay awake. I knew that someday, I would tell Marybeth about my special thoughts of the attic. It wasn't the time now, but maybe in the future. After all, she was always one of my best friends since the beginning of my school years at St. Claire's. Who else would I trust and tell my deep thoughts to and be honest to?

As the night grew closer to sleep, I decided to lather my hands with my oil and rub them down for the hard work that would proceed on the following day. Work, work, and more work. I wasn't at the school that long to know everyone, but I did notice a girl that was a striking beauty yet delicate in her ways, almost too perfect. She was perfect for the school though—a class act, you would say. You knew by looking at her that she was an established lady from a charm school prior to this one. I certainly didn't remember her from last year. Having so much schoolwork and chores and practicing on the piano, I didn't even realize she existed until now. She was delicate, beautiful, and an educated woman, some would say breathtaking.

Another student informed me that her name was Rebecca, a princess from the country of England. She was one of the girls that came for the pre-exam testing for enrollment this past spring. It was a good choice to notice her and see how she handled herself.

I knew that she passed the exams with top grades and was happy to be there. I prayed that somehow she would be my mentor since seniors took that role with underclassmen at St. Claire's. Rebecca was just on the other side of my bedroom, so close to me. Somehow, I had to talk to her, maybe walk into her, or meet her in the bathroom or dining room hall for a meal. I could be lucky to have chore details with her. Making up my mind to meet her was now another challenge that I had to endure. I knew that she was going to be my friend and somehow more than that to me but, at this point, didn't know how or why?

I inquired about my curiosity to others. One of the girls told me that her name was Rebecca and she was from a family of eight, which included six brothers, herself, and her dad. Rebecca's mother passed on when she was about four or five years old. Weird, I thought, same scenario too much, fit for two girls. I was amazed that she had the same circumstances as I had. In disbelief, I was so excited to hear this, yet my heart was troubled for her. I knew the pain she must have had growing up without a mom and all those brothers. Sometimes you just wanted to have girl talk with someone. I knew I had Aunt Suzie; I sure hoped she had someone too. The result for her and me would be a great outcome for both of us. I just felt it in my bones.

Rebecca was a senior and I a sophomore now, but what if we never got a chance to meet? Our classes were different; our chores, teachers, and mealtimes also conflicted. The only good thing was that she was on the third floor, right next to me. I knew our closeness to each other's room was ideal. If nothing else happened, I would have to make our meeting unforgettable. I was going to have to be aggressive and just go to her room. The time had to be right; otherwise, I may lose a dear friend that I never even had. I knew in my heart this had to done. It was a desired strength inside me that kept pulling me toward her.

The headmaster now was deliberating on his choices to select seniors to mentor underclassmen. I sure was hoping that we would be a team. The headmaster came in and said that he had decided some of the girls for matching mentors. As I waited breathlessly, the headmaster, Mr. Grumbling, said, "Rebecca, Alessandra, Marybeth, Kaitlin, and Annie will be our first team." I jumped with joy and was so ecstatic. I was extremely delighted, you couldn't imagine the great day and the new journey I knew I would have with Rebecca and my friends. Rebecca held her composure, as she always did, just nodding to us with a little bit of a half smile on her face. She made us feel wonderful and good to know that we would share this year with her.

I wanted to write Dad and my brothers quickly to let them know my great day today. Rebecca came slowly over to me, hugged me, and said, "I can't wait to guide you and be a soul mate, just you and me. I know the others are part of our team also, but I feel something is special between you and me, as if we had a bond. It will be great learning from each other. I know some have told me our families are so much alike." This was a great day to have a big sister who I knew would take care of me and guide me properly. I had already adopted her into my family, a girl that I could really tell my feelings to. Rebecca was older and so much wiser than me, Marybeth, Alessandra, or Kaitlin.

How grand was this? She was so worldly and had this extreme, gorgeous look to her presence, smart and yet so charming. I was so excited about her being my mentor for the rest of the school year. Meeting this way, Rebecca explained, made us soul mates. This was weird; most girls would never say soul mates in explaining a friendship. Gee, what a great day I was having, so special.

I went back to my room and sat down to begin my letter writing to my family. I just didn't know where to begin with my start of the incoming year with Rebecca. I expressed to Dad my sincere thanks for the treasure he gave to me with this selection of the school. I now knew what this would do for me later in life. I told Dad about Rebecca, that she was bright, educated, a great pianist, and surely an attribute to womanhood. I couldn't wait to get my letter picked up and sent. Dad would be thrilled since I knew his heart was weighing heavily on him for sending me here. It was hard for him not to see me on vacations and some holidays. It was way too expensive for our style of living for me to travel back and forth from school. Even though my brothers were helping with the expenses to take care of me, it was draining.

After the announcement, Rebecca approached me in my bedroom with her confident way, smiled at me, and made the notion that tomorrow would be a great day. Rebecca picked me up in front of my bedroom for breakfast. This was the start of a new whirlwind for me with Rebecca. She would prepare me with her expectations and mine for me to be the best I could be. Challenges were beyond belief. We both had no idea how far the circle would close between the two of us. Kaitlin and Marybeth were at the end of our hallway and went to the cafeteria and classes by another staircase. They were going to meet us downstairs for breakfast. Usually, a senior was unable to sit with you, but since Rebecca was our mentor, there was no problem.

Rebecca told us that she came from a family of seven children, with six brothers; she was a princess from a long family line in England and the only girl. Rebecca explained that she lost her mom at a very young age and could also play the piano extremely well. I was always amazed that Rebecca never looked at the keys while playing. Rebecca and I started our new adventure together in school, not knowing our lifetime would be a lasting one forever.

For months to follow, Rebecca and I enjoyed each other's company. We had grown to respect each other's privacy and enjoyed the bookwork that also had to be learned. Rebecca had done many pieces of music and expressed to me not to keep myself locked up in one style of playing. "Broaden your horizons," she would say.

I listened intensely, followed her lead, and played, hard, really hard as she advised. I learned my lessons, did chores, and played the piano each day with notes that could melt your heart. I really enjoyed Rebecca's company as Rebecca did mine. I felt it was now time for me to tell someone about the forbidden room. I knew that I could trust Rebecca and she would understand my feelings and thoughts. I explained to Rebecca about the notes in the attic hallway in the forbidden room; my curiosity was beside myself as to the beautiful music. Rebecca laughed a little when I told her of this haunting story of the attic. I had to tell someone that would keep my secret safe. Rebecca then told me not to be alarmed. "I also hear the beautiful musical notes from the forbidden room."

It had been challenging for me not to embrace the room of the spirited souls. Rebecca was in amazement that my mom and hers both played in concerts and both women were well-known to all. It was such a weird thing yet an excitement; we felt maybe our moms set this all up in their world that they now lived in. To believe or not to believe, your choice.

It seemed like everyone on the third floor heard the notes during the wee hours of the morning. Maybe it was our wake-up call to rise and get going to class and practice. We all knew not to go near the room and never, never ever to go in it! Most of the girls were scared but tried not to think about it. They never wanted to confront Ms. Hornet and bring it up. On our first day of school, when we were freshmen, we were told never to talk about this room. As obedient ladies, we struggled to obey the rule. I had a real hard time not discussing this or dreaming about the unusual noises and notes that embraced the hallways and the forbidden room.

I thought to myself, *If anyone ever found out that I entered this room, life would be over. I would have to leave school, my friends, and my new life. I just couldn't or wouldn't let anyone know my secret.* Things were going so well, I didn't want to get into trouble with the headmaster or Sister Meredith Beettlemen. She was in charge of the noncompliant students. If anyone knew or gave details about me entering this room, it would mean a big dilemma. A disobedient student could have ten days of washing dishes or doing all the bathrooms twice a week and other unmentionable stuff to even talk about. *I truly don't and won't even think about this. It will spoil the rest of my day. I will have a complete breakdown and worry about my mess. How much misfortune could I be in? What if they did find out?*

Rebecca sat many hours by my side in my classrooms on the hard wooden chairs when I practiced. I learned to endure the pounding of the piano keys and always tried to make beautiful sounds of music. I told Rebecca how much I missed my mom. It had been such a long time since her death. I tried not to erase her memories. I wanted to keep the image of her smile in my mind, her delicate touch, sweet smile, and her loving arms. I was so little that it seemed that as I got older and older, she was fading away from me, which was frightening. Rebecca replied, "When I feel the same loss, the whispers and taunting memories of my mom, I close my eyes and try to remember the good times with her." She too replied that it got scary to look as if you could forget your mom's smile and her touch. We both knew their love could never be taken away from our hearts. We had these memories that would remain with us forever. Knowing what we felt in our hearts for our moms was something that we would cherish in our duration.

It was a nice moment that we could both share with each other. Rebecca told me that when I felt like this, I should go to her room. There I could enjoy the peacefulness of closing my eyes and remembering the good times and the love that my mother and I had for each other. "In time, this will be easier to handle. Annie, I will comfort you and reassure you of your sad memories or fears and turn them into wonderful dancing pixies and beautiful blue skies. Try only to remember the good stuff, the memories of today and only the memories of yesterdays that have gone by."

That evening, I remembered having my discussion with Rebecca over my fears and her advice to go to her room if I got scared. While walking in the hallway that evening, I really got startled. I heard moaning and felt a terrible vibration on the floors, and there was a chill in the air.

I almost thought someone had died since it was so terrifying. Weird I thought. I decided to go to Rebecca's room as she suggested me to do so if I got scared. Rebecca was at her desk, writing to her family.

I told her that I didn't want to interrupt, but I did think I needed her lap. She brushed my hair away from my face with a few strokes of her fingers and smiled. I started to calm down and went to sleep quickly. It seemed as if I was sleeping for a decade when I woke up. Rebecca told me it was only a few minutes but peaceful sleep.

I was surely contented knowing that I had Rebecca there to comfort me. She gave me the security and relaxation that I did need. All I needed now was too tiptoe back to bed and not be heard before bed checks were officially done.

The following day at dinner, I turned to Rebecca and mentioned I had to return to my room early for the rotation of my chores. She understood the torment and weight on my shoulders until I finished. It was so hard to do all your chores and still be able to get extra piano practice in the evening to play. I wanted to make my family and everyone at school proud of me. Most of all, to excel in life would be a rich flavor to enjoy.

As the days turned into weeks and months, the holiday concert tryouts were coming upon me soon. I had never envisioned something so grand at a school. I did love the mass audience, the select group that would attend; it would be a source of pleasure. Never considering seriously that I would go to another school other than my hometown school was amazement in itself. My first thoughts were, *Would they be able to put on such a grand show?* I thought that maybe I could do a magnificent piece, feature me as a great individual, which was somewhat ironic. I really talked and embraced ideas to myself from a female point of view. I loved the luxury, style, and artistic playground of this world, and then I asked who wouldn't want to come here and wear the world's most beautiful clothes?

An endless parade of gorgeous, eligible, wealthy young men would also be present at the concert. I knew that I had to be chosen. Most of the girls were trying to scratch one another's eyes out rather than be supportive to one another. Everyone wanted the lead spot in the concert. It seemed to me that if you had any spot, you should be grateful. Displaying that character would not get you far at St. Claire's or the outside world.

CHAPTER 18

*I*WENT TO MY ROOM EARLY that evening and was dreaming of the good times, as Rebecca stated. In the chill of the cold evening, I heard the mystery of the notes again. I proceeded again for the second time to enter the room; it was such a long time that I didn't approach the attic. I opened the door, which creaked; climbing the staircase, it was long and dark as before. The room seemed dirty and had a terrible odor. Nothing seemed to change; it was still creepy, and many questions still unsolved.

It seemed that something was rotten or dead somewhere, which had to be found in the unknown room, but not on this day. After you got past the odor and the darkness of the room, it had a misty air and mildew smell but seemed somehow airy. Your hair could stand on edge, yet there was a calmness that led me to believe that I would be OK.

I thought that a spell had been put on the room, maybe witchcraft or some unknown horror that no one should endure alone. The mist appeared in the room with a slight perfume smell, and the terrible odor went to something sweet smelling like lilacs.

I was starting to get anxious and excited. At this moment, I saw a hand reach out, a delicate small hand to touch me in the middle of the mist, which was of the color blue. The aura of the room was intense. I didn't trust my own feelings, and it seemed that the smell before was gone and the smell now was one I had smelled before, maybe as a little girl.

This was way too creepy for me. How could I know this smell, and why was I getting to be a little content with the aroma? I just couldn't wait for the answers, but for now, enough was enough. I decided to walk backward swiftly and not to question my instincts of what may be. Now I should question why this school and not others. Why did I get good grades easily in a good academy? My talent was very rewarding to me. I had to say, better than most but not brilliant. Was it all coming together why Dad was driven to this school? Was there more to be exposed that I was unaware of?

I ran swiftly back to my room, covered myself from head to toe, and made sure I had all my toes and fingers accounted for. When you want to be reassured for what you think you saw or didn't see then look for the reality for what is, what do you think? My anxiously timid body tried so hard to go to sleep on this beautiful night, but I was convinced that maybe this was what they called a miracle. I couldn't understand not having her presence, but did I have Mom's presence? This was an inner thought that I had to answer someday, but for tonight, sleep was on my agenda.

I proceeded finally to close my eyes and said my prayers and talked to my mom as I had always done for encouragement and soul-searching. It was always comforting to talk to Mom in the evening. It gave me the uplifting and soothing confidence that I needed to go full speed ahead on my next day.

CHAPTER 19

THE BELLS RANG AS USUAL in the halls for our wake-up call. The students ran to the bathrooms, and the magic that this school created was now present. Our hard work was paying off. For most of us, we were being justly rewarded. We soon knew that you would be hearing the tapping of the stick of Ms. Hornet echoing in the halls. She meant "No tardiness permitted." There it went; the tapping and the hustle and bustle of our feet soon would be heard. Getting in line promptly was a main concern since we were going to breakfast and then off to tryouts. While walking to the cafeteria, most wondered what today's specials would be on the menu. Most of us loved the cooking at the school, especially when our chef, Ms. Delight, was tossing those eggs and pancakes around. While watching her do her thing, we all cheered her on since she was always so kind and understanding. She was always open to suggestions, asking us all the time what special you preferred for tomorrow, what dessert, or for some, what vegetables. She tried to accommodate all of us with our palates' tastes.

The day was typical as we were accustomed. We attended our classes, did our chores, and had our piano lessons. As I proceeded through the day, I wondered where Rebecca was; I hadn't seen her most of the day. Usually I would see her at least once during the day, but the last two days, it seemed as if she had disappeared.

After all, she was my mentor; she was supposed to be at my disposal. My curiosity was starting to get me worried. Did she have to leave school? Was she sick or perhaps another mishap that I wasn't aware of?

I finally saw Rebecca and said, "Where have you been?"

"Even though I'm a good student and an excellent piano player, I had to do extra chores since I was caught going into the forbidden room." I couldn't believe that Rebecca went into the forbidden room in the attic. I was shocked! Rebecca said that she had heard these beautiful notes always being played and heard wonderful sounds through the hallways during the night time, while most of us were sleeping. "I've heard them since I came to school. I knew enough not to ask anyone as I too was told of the forbidden room at registration."

I couldn't wait to tell Rebecca about my experiences in the room. Now I could finally speak, thank God! I felt that we had to be brave and see the secrecy that was being projected by the mystery of the room.

I asked, "What did you see or hear in the attic?" Of course, Rebecca didn't know that I also had been there but never got caught by the witch herself, Ms. Hornet. I told her my story, knowing the same thing had happened to her. Her discovery of the room, notes, and the bad smells were the same as mine. She felt the presence of someone in the room and experienced what the room did for her spirit. As she approached the room, she also had noticed the mist of air over in the corner of the attic. The room had a horribly smelly odor, but then it turned into a beautiful aroma. As if someone opened a can of spray that was stale. Once the mist hit the air, it then became a beautiful lilac smell. Strange as my mom also loved lilac flower smells. It seemed that the smell of lilacs also meant something to Rebecca and her mom. I sat in amazement listening to her story of the unknown.

I didn't ask Rebecca about the lilacs and what the smell meant to her, but I was sure curious.

Listening to Rebecca and what she experienced was upsetting enough for me. I too was so relieved that the same occurrences happened to her exactly the same way that they happened to me. Was this all a twist of fate or reality? Time would soon tell, I would imagine. Were there deep secrets in this room? Would the faith and love of our moms make us go head-on with the spirits that were not settled?

The room was dark and creepy, and the light shined through the crack of the roof. The rain came in once in a while on the floor since it had to be fixed. The castle was so old and the money so tight, we knew it would never be resolved. I wondered about the mist, the smell, and the light that shined through. It was such a bright, wonderful light that it seemed as if the angels were playing their harps and praying in a whisper. Could this be an accident, or did our moms have a rapport with the unknown? Who knew for sure, not I!

Rebecca said, "It was kind of soothing to be upstairs. Even though it was frightening, I had a calm of relief to just be sitting there. It was getting very dark, and the light was fading into the moonlight now. *Spooky* wasn't the word. I wanted to hear the notes in my head and store them in my memory bank. Somehow neither one was scary to me. I wanted to capture the calmness and serenity that was in the air.

It's just a wonderful world—the spirits, your vision of what you think you are seeing and feeling, the connection and bond with your mom. Magnificent, splendid was my description of it all. I was trying to be so respectful about it. This was so heartening and promising to us to think that maybe in time; we would see what spirits were staying in this room. Some might think depressing, dismal, and gloomy, but it wasn't like this at all for me and Rebecca. For us it was an opportunity to have a license of freedom, and then for us to be so privileged and having the pleasure of knowing them was so surreal.

"I knew I was in the attic long enough and proceeded to go downstairs and back to my room. Walking through the hallways was scary enough. The fires in the lanterns were dim, and I was lucky to see my room. Needless to say, as I tip toed, I had to make sure the floors didn't creak. Lo and behold, I swiftly turned and ran face-to-face with Ms. Hornet.

"She was doing the bed checks for the night and asked me what I was doing in the halls. As an upperclassman and a mentor, what attitude and image was I projecting to the younger girls? I was upset with myself and didn't expect to be caught, but I was and had to accept the trials and tribulations of my actions. I was sad that I couldn't control my curiosity since I was eighteen years old. My inquisitiveness and my interest in the room led me to be nosey about the phenomenon that was a wonder of the unknown.

"Ms. Hornet was mad and grumpy about me not following the rules of the unknown room. I replied that I was quite sorry for my actions. My curiosity got the better of me. My punishment was to do the firewood for the next two nights and plenty of dishes in the kitchen. Boy, am I sorry that I was so stupid. I did acknowledge that I wouldn't falter anymore. I asked her to please let me partake in the holiday concert. I didn't want to be punished for my stupidity. As a senior, I knew I would be one to play a part." She politely bowed her head actually in a solemn way, which surprised me. It seemed that she almost had a heart.

"Ms. Hornet said, 'This is not to be spoken about, and it will not stay on the tip of your tongue to talk to anyone about. Do your punishment and we will turn the page.' I did exactly that. I was certainly not going to question her decisions. I was in enough trouble already. I was amazed at her empathy and promised my solemn oath that none of these words would ever be spoken about to anyone from me."

After listening to Rebecca, I reached out my arms to her for support. We held on to each other tightly; she was my secret big sister since she came to this school. I felt so tranquil that she had that faith and confidence in me to keep her secret. I truly was blessed with this relationship and somehow the link that we had with each other. We both were there for the same purpose. Maybe to meet and see our moms, maybe for us to mesh our families together, or maybe just for a good friendship that would follow.

Neither one of us knew what the outcome would be in our future. We did somehow know our moms were connected together in the attic. Either by spirit of their souls, or maybe they had united in the world of God and were both there to protect us at this time. We were convinced it was to watch over us and save us from harm.

"In coming here to the school, I had many doubts and concerns about leaving home and my family. I questioned myself, why would I change schools now when I'm happy? Who should I be? I am now going to be a senior and change schools? I told my dad that this makes no sense to me. Dad replied, 'Rebecca, sometimes we have to move where the currents send us. Otherwise, we drown.'

"I remember Dad approaching me and saying, 'Rebecca, you have to change schools. It has to be St. Claire's.' I questioned why again. I had a good relationship with the teachers and had good grades at my old school. No need to change I thought. Something was telling him to proceed and change my school for my final year. He was convinced I should attend this academy." I told Rebecca that my dad had the same feelings. With all the schools I looked at and could have gone to, Dad insisted upon this one. Strange that they both felt this way. When my acceptance letter was received, everyone was on cloud nine about the results. Talking about all of this now and the comparisons, it seemed that our moms' everlasting love for us and their strong inner souls gave us the path to walk on this road.

CHAPTER 20

THE DAYS AT THE SCHOOL were wearisome and sometimes disappointing since I couldn't get to achieve my excellence overall in academics. We all waited patiently to play our musical pieces with perfection, which most of us did. We also had to have a completion of our composition of music, which had already been heard. I played hard and furiously above my talent. Even I couldn't believe how well I played. Rebecca said, "I did great, and I should not judge myself so harshly." It was now time for the headmaster, Mr. Grumbling, Ms. Alice, Ms. Hornet, and the other prestigious teachers to put the best of the best together and judge us for the upcoming holiday concert. This was going to be exhilarating news. Nervous, yes, but all of us couldn't wait for the postings on the board.

This also was a very difficult task for most. Rebecca and I waited in the wings of the hallway while holding our breaths and holding on to each other's hand, waiting for the postings of the selection of girls.

Ms. Hornet came out and plugged the names on the board. We all had this enthusiastic energy that we all possessed. We ran to the board to see if our names were selected. Rebecca found hers right away. I looked endlessly on the list, I took deep breaths, my heart was beating quite hard, my finger went to each line, and finally I found my name. I was almost at the bottom of the page. This was not done in alphabetical order. I was delighted with joy that I had triumphed along with my friend Rebecca. We were known as two peas in a pod. How could one fail and the other one succeed?

We both thought that our scores had to be rated the same by all the judges. After all, we practiced, wrote, exchanged ideas, and had the same feelings on our selection of music. Once we knew both of us were selected, we became jubilant.

We jumped up and down, spun around, and hugged each other with zeal. I looked over at Alessandra and Marybeth, who also were waiting anxiously to see if their names were posted. They were feeling a little grim; thinking that they were not selected and they may not have been chosen was worrisome. Once the crowd left the board, both girls approached it cautiously. All three of us went to the board together once the crowd left. Looking very carefully at the names that were selected and the choice of girls in each grade seemed endless. Our fingers scrolled down the names that were printed. With disappointment, we did not see Marybeth's or Kaitlin's name selected for piano playing for the holiday concert. We then checked the choir and behold, there was Kaitlin's and Alessandra's name for a singing solos. I was so overjoyed to say the least and ecstatic for the selection of music both girls sang.

I then looked at Marybeth and put my arm around her for comfort since her name was not posted on the board. She bowed her head, and we proceeded to walk down the hallway slowly back to her room.

In dismay, our eyes filled up with tears, assuming that Marybeth didn't make the cut. Ms. Hornet then came over to add another listing. Ms. Hornet yelled, "Hold on, girls, we have one more selection. We made a mistake." She indicated that one more girl had been chosen, and she neglected to put her name on the list. When she posted the new sheet, again, we went over each name diligently and with such joy and cheer this time. Now there was no disappointment showing on our faces. All of us had succeeded at least for now. Marybeth's name was the forgotten one. Oh, such ecstasy that all of us had at this moment. Most of us felt as if we just went to seventh heaven and were so thrilled. Our agony was over. It was a comfort that all of us were selected for this big day. Our hard work did pay off, and we were rewarded for paying our dues. With all the excitement, we now decided to go back to our rooms. The frenzy was over!

No tears to shed, no disappointments for us this year. The alarm within our souls had now been turned off, and shock and panic were gone. We had nothing but a source of pleasure and enjoyment and a slight touch of charm.

We didn't see Kaitlin at the bulletin board; we knew she had extra chores to do and had to stop by to see Mr. Grumbling. With all of the excitement, we couldn't wait to tell her that she was selected for the concert.

Since we were only sophomores, this was an honor to be picked for any area of the concert; backstage lights would be good too! Just to be part of the concert was so exciting; being placed in any area was a good thing. How would we survive if she didn't get picked for anything and we had? We were so thankful when we found out that she made choir.

The only way that she could perform piano with us would be if something happened to one of the girls and she could substitute. At least there was an outside possibility that she could perform.

Rebecca heard about the results and knew we would be definitely upset with this outcome. She convinced us both that if we believed in miracles, not to pray on the defeat but to pray for the triumph that will come. Looking at Rebecca and hearing her strong confident words, we now knew how to approach Kaitlin. This was a good day.

Well, from this day forward, we knew it would be practice, practice, practice. We did what we were told and listened intensely at all the instructions on the performance. Before we knew it, the day would come, and we would be a representative of the school. The evenings were getting colder, and the days of the winter would nip our noses with a chill soon. The holidays were coming; so was all the excitement about playing in the concert.

I wrote Dad and my brothers a letter about my big day; the concert was going to be the week before Christmas. In my heart, I didn't think that anyone would be able to lose work and miss not getting paid, maybe even fired for missing a day on the job. I was humble with my thoughts though. Rebecca, who came from wealth, was able to have her family come anytime, Rebecca was a granddaughter from the family of the Tyrone's. This was a high society name always in the papers, usually at least once a week. They were always spoken with success stories.

Rebecca would never talk about any rumors of her family, friends, or school. She was very meek and timid in some ways. The girls and I were expected to perform well for the holiday show. The staff knew the selection was grand this year.

Invitations went out to the families of the girls, prominent families, and those of high leadership in both the states of Pennsylvania and Washington, DC. Uncle Dan always received a free ticket since he was a senator for the state of Pennsylvania. It was exciting and then a little bit earth-shattering. In my long hours of practice, I thought about my family and how I would make them so proud of my accomplishments. I didn't hear from Dad or my brothers. I knew not to question; I'm sure they felt bad for me. Then the week before the concert, Dad was able to get a message to me, telling me of his disappointment of not being able to attend. Sadly, I understood his predicament. Uncle Dan was going to try and make the performance since all his accommodations were paid for since he was a senator for the state of Pennsylvania.

I knew Aunt Suzie was making a dress for me for the distinguished and celebrated concert. She had asked me about colors, ribbons, sleeves—long or short—and other pertinent details needed to make the dress. Even though, I knew they couldn't come, I waited patiently for the arrival of my dress. My thoughts were what if it didn't fit! I knew that Ms. Hornet had a sewing thumb that I could count on.

I was reckoning that she would be my backup for alterations. I wasn't too worried about size or style. My Aunt Suzie was very significant with what she sewed for me. Time went quickly, and my delivery was here. Mr. Grumbling called me down to the office to pick up my package. The box was so large and wrapped so beautifully; I knew that it was my dress from Aunt Suzie. It was momentous and had a crucial, meaningful statement. This was her signature.

I ran to my room and called the girls in to see how beautiful it was. They waited in my room while I went to the bathroom and slid the dress on. It was beyond my expectations; Aunt Suzie always outdid herself. My friends felt this dress was going to be the hit of the parade; forget the concert. I was quite mortified and shy about these words but took it all in pride. It was gorgeous, as expected, to say the least. I had to write Aunt Suzie to thank her for her generosity and caring so much about me.

Time passed, and now the evening was here. A lot of preparations went into the holiday performance. We always presented a fabulous musical celebration of the holiday season. The invitees were arriving, and the horses were sometimes a little anxious to go into a straight line in front of the school and be still. There were so many beautiful clothes; everyone was dressed to their finest.

The playhouse was getting filled, and the music was being prepared. We had many singers and musicians and ten sophomore girls who were praised for their delightful piano performance or singing ability and were accepted to participate in the holiday concert. This was a big deal for all of us. We watched behind the curtains as the visitors started to sit down. Rebecca and I were starting to get a little nervous and anxious; it was almost time for us to perform. Rebecca managed to see her father in the playhouse already seated by her brothers.

I was a little disappointed and upset since I knew no one was coming to see me other than my friends at St. Claire's. All of us were now behind the curtains, waiting for our names to be announced on stage so we could begin. This night would be a wonderful experience of music and talent.

As the curtains were getting ready to rise, Kaitlin ran over to us and shouted with delight that she was playing tonight. "Do you believe it's happening for me tonight too? Maybe I shouldn't be so happy, but one of the girls became sick, and I have to play her musical piece." Overjoyed, we had all reached our peak of performing. Tonight all of us would perform; how miraculous was this? It was the best moment or the high point so far at St. Claire's. We were told to expect to reach for the stars during these four years of high school, and we surely were trying. It would be more than we could imagine, and so far, it had been. How great would this night be? It became an earth-shattering moment and a big, vital, important night for three girls who became friends not too long ago. Alessandra was also quite pleased with herself since she was going to be able to sing a solo tonight. She too, was so exited since she knew her family was in the audience.

Rebecca overheard the news, nodded to us, and said, "I told you all that you would perform tonight. As I said, all you have to do is believe, believe, and believe." I understood the hard times my family was enduring, but still I was disappointed that no one could attend this magnificent, fantastic show. Rebecca gave me a hug and knew about my emotions, but she had the spirit to give me the extra hug so I could endure. We were getting prepared behind the stage for the performance and so excited. The headmaster came behind the curtains and told us that everyone was seated now in the auditorium. It was now time to respect ourselves and preserve the dignity of the school. Mr. Grumbling then proudly said, "Go, my girls, and show them the talent that God has given to you so you may be the exceptional one."

We all walked out to the stage area together, and the audience stood up, clapped, and cheered for us beyond our expectations. The ushers were all in place; so handsome were the boys from St. Peter's, our copartner school. During the year, we participated together in many events. It was an opinion that St. Pete's students rightfully had the intellect and the emotions that measured up to be our best representatives at St. Claire's for the concert.

Since St. Peters was a private school for boys and St. Claire's is a private school for girls, it was just natural that we worked together throughout the school year. We always celebrated our display of talent together in unity and teamwork. It was a belief that there was a standard code between the two schools that was meaningful.

It was an exhilarating and electrifying moment to be on stage this year. Out of the corner of my eye, it became seventh heaven to me when I saw Dad and my brothers in the audience. I just couldn't believe that they had come. To see me! What a surprise; I was speechless. I turned to Kaitlin and said, "It's a good thing I play the piano and don't sing or talk during this concert. I would be no good for that display." I sat in my seat with my ladylike posture and waited to be called upon for my piano playing on my selected musical piece. It was a moment that I couldn't even bear the presence of them all. Too much for this girl to handle. Then I saw Aunt Suzie and Uncle Dan on the upper tiers. I was truly astonished and taken aback by all of this. My family really cared about seeing my performance at school. The sacrifices had to be many for all of them to come, but I was really glad they did. I didn't look for baby Claire; I knew in my heart she was way too little to be here this time.

One by one, we played or sang our musical presentations for our family and friends. We had the choir singing and the piano playing, and as each girl or group did their pieces, the audience clapped and the voices were heard cheering. I just couldn't wait to hug Dad and my brothers. When I played my piece, it was as if an angel was in my heart and sprung out into the air with joyous notes. I remembered the musical notes in the hallway that came down from the unknown room and gave so much pleasure to my heart. It put my mind in a state of a trance, and if you must dream, then think about visions of sugarplums dancing in your head. Maybe Mom was with me now to hear my precious musical piece being played. This was a piece that I had dedicated to her for this evening. When Dad and my brothers heard the piece, Dad was tearful. This was a masterpiece that Mom loved to play during the holidays. I was glad that all my family were able to hear me and see how much I had grown into quite a young lady. This was such a flawless day for me.

Rebecca played her piece beautifully, coming from her heart into the love of her dad. She too felt that the notes from the attic were also part of her day. She reflected back to the unknown room, and somehow the projection of the notes went into her fingertips. She felt that she was able to play her brilliant piece and hit so many of the piano keys correctly because of her mom.

I couldn't wait for the concert to be over. I just wanted to run and hug Dad and my brothers. The concert was over, the curtains came down, and we filed out in single order with holiday cheer. I ran around the stairs to find my family; many hugs and kisses went on. I couldn't wait for Rebecca's family and mine to meet.

It was a wonderful day. I felt in my soul that this was a time for me to rejoice and be glad to have had the privilege to be accepted into the environment of this school of distinguished teachings and their lessons of music. At the end of the performances, our dads had surprised us with beautiful bouquets of flowers. It was no surprise that they were lilacs.

Rebecca and I wondered how they got the lilac flower now in the winter when this was a spring flower. Rebecca asked her dad. He replied politely "Rebecca, I know someone who has a hothouse and was able to ship some to the school, and knowing Annie also loved them, I graciously gave a handful to Mr. Haverstein." We thought how lucky the two of us were to be presented with our best loved flowers from our dads and at our holiday concert. Oh, a special shock for all. Not so much when you had that special connection with the other side. It would become picture-perfect and absolutely complete; it's wonderful.

We all entered the dining area, had small chitchat, and enjoyed the rest of the day walking around the grounds. As both families spent their time together, our dads and brothers were so proud. Both sides got along brilliantly, sharing laugher, stories, and a few family secrets. In fact, it was incredible. Rebecca's dad was a very warm, loving person, quite personable and good-looking. Mr. Wetherbee had his own dynasty, a prestigious shipping business, many friends, family, and a lot of money to go around. He gave great advice to those who asked and seemed to be very sensitive and a caring, down-to-earth dad. Rebecca's grandfather on her mom's side was known as the Tyrone family, whom everyone knew with respect. Rebecca had wealth and status from both sides of her family.

It was such a beautiful day; we talked a lot, shared some memories, and enjoyed a hot apple cider drink between us. Rebecca's younger brothers James and Dan came along for the day. Rebecca and Randy thought James was making eyes at me. So did I sometimes. He had beautiful blue eyes, broad shoulders, and was striking for sure. When I noticed him staring, his eyes seemed to go right through me with a feeling like lightning. Through the day, I also noticed that Randy, my brother, looked like he might have a liking for Rebecca. He acted as if he was a young school boy, a little giddy and shy. I think she lit up his life.

I was thinking about the same thing to myself. James was so classy, a good catch for any girl. Everything James spoke about came from his heart. Then again, Dan was no slouch either, good for anyone's eyes to marvel at and appreciate. He was way ahead of his time. He was a journalist for his hometown newspaper had softness but powerfulness to his body. I think he had to be my favorite person in this family. He explained to me that I could be a famous concert piano player if I pursued this career. Then he went on to say, "All you have to do is try hard enough all the time and continue to do great work." James felt you couldn't make it work just because you were talented. There had to be more to a person than talent; you needed the complete package.

"You're a role model to so many other girls at the school and to me." It was sweet, the conversation that I had with James and the genuineness of how he felt. We were going to be departing soon and returning to our homes. I hoped that our memories of one another wouldn't change. I felt so privileged to have met them both. I hoped I would see more of them in the future.

Randy told me that his opinion of Rebecca was that she was really sweet, honest, and an earnest performer. He sensed that this came across through everything she did or said. She had endless enthusiasm. Rebecca had a cluster of principles and morals and a head full of romance. She gave an energetic performance at the holiday concert that was just breathtaking. Randy had to give a super positive thank-you message from him to her. He wanted desperately to have Rebecca like him, not for only today, but maybe for a lifetime. People always remembered the good guys, and he wanted her to memorize his face and retain the conversation with each other on this day. Also, in my mind, I had to be levelheaded that maybe she didn't feel the same.

It was very important to me and Rebecca for our families to like each other. We were the best of friends and had so much in common with each other. Wouldn't it be wonderful that maybe we could become one family? Was this part of destiny why Rebecca and I met and looked like we were looking in the same mirror? Was it that our moms in the spirit world met at the same time and arranged a collection series of auras at our school to watch over me and Rebecca? So many unknown questions.

Well, the day ended, and we had to say our good-byes to all with some tears and complex anxiety. We managed to let go again, knowing we would see them when school ended next week. The hugs and kisses were so refreshing with our family. With James and Randy, it was different with us; it was so invigorating and rousing, and their kisses and hugs seemed to mean much more.

Most of our classmates had apprehension and anxiety about the concert. Surprisingly though, it was very relaxing, and not too much stress and worries were attached. It went well.

The week passed by quickly, and before you knew it, everyone was packing to catch transportation to go home. All the typical good-byes and of course, tears. Girls always had to be a little dramatic, but this was part of us giving an impressive good-bye. Riding on the train this time seemed that once I closed my eyes and opened them, my brothers were there to take me home. Life should not go by us so quickly. It should be a long and winding road, taking baby steps. Otherwise, you put yourself in a spinning world out of control and you have to make sure you put the brakes on quickly to stop yourself. Try hard to be in awe of your world around you, and have a high respect for your dreaming. Take your time in your world of the unknown, and marvel at your thoughts that only you have with yourself. This is where no one else can enter unless you want them to. Dream, relax, and appreciate your moment of closing your eyes and taking that moment of being somewhere else.

The holidays were dazzling, wonderful, and incredible as always. Dad had half the town over for holiday cheer and the unwrapping of gifts. He so loved the holidays, but then who didn't? In all of the hustle and bustle, there was time for everyone to pay respects at Mom's grave site. We all held hands and prayed around Mom. The majestic moment that everyone felt in the atmosphere was grand. Delicately, a wonderful wreath was placed on her grave. It was a moment of joy but was so instant.

In a jiffy we were in and out. Sometimes I felt like I cheated her of our visit, but Dad felt that the memories that we carried with us would last forever. The time passed by quickly as usual; holidays came and went. Holiday vacation was over, and we were back in school again to finish my second year. This would be Rebecca's final year, unless she would decide to stay and teach a little.

CHAPTER 21

IT WAS NOW THE END of June. Another year went by, and once again, I had to say my farewells to my friends and sadly to Rebecca. I knew her only as a complete, humble, and warm person. Watching Rebecca, I marveled at the true intellect and childlike playfulness from her soul that would come out from within her. She was so passionate about music and her family. I could only imagine her anger at herself for leaving the school if she must and not being able to finish her role.

Her mannerisms were just like having a mousy sister but a loveable one to me. When I really got to know her, it was during the rigid school schedule for the concert. We had such fun even though this was hard work. I prayed and hoped we would stay friends over the years. She just made everything funny, and it was just such a joy being with Rebecca. I would miss her madly over the summer. You just couldn't work that close together and share thoughts, family, and the forbidden room without becoming part of each other. There was just such a hole in my heart. Suddenly, I woke up and found that I was the last one to say good-bye to her and it would be a while before I saw her again. I did hope that it wasn't for the last time. I did wish that she would get accepted again to come back as a mentor next year. I would keep my fingers crossed that she would get the position in the fall. *Mom, are you listening to me now? I sure hope you can be assertive in your world and make it happen. I want Rebecca to stay with me, maybe forever.*

Again, our tears of separation flowed down our cheeks. In a thoughtful, gentle way, Ms. Rebecca reached out to give me the reassurance that I always seemed to need from her. When the new fall would arrive this year, Rebecca and I surmised that she would not be here. Rebecca was graduating this year and wasn't sure of her plans. She put in for a request to stay as a mentor maybe a few years more. She felt she was leaving me behind and then, of course, her mom. Also, was there time for Randy in her life? This was very upsetting and a dreadful time for both of us, the unpleasant feelings we had not knowing Rebecca's path.

Rebecca and I spoke for a while in her room, and then neither one of us wanted to concede to say good-bye to the forbidden room or each other. Instead, we sought first to understand the worldview of the forbidden room and the lives of those who inhabited it. Then the emphasis came along with the study of the happenings. We felt the realism and integrity of these characters would make up a performance that would captivate and thrill us with the unknown visits of our past within our mom's souls.

We tiptoed up the attic stairs while everyone was so busy packing and saying their send-offs. Our suitcases were already packed for departure. Quietly, we crept up the stairs to the darkness of the weird room, which could be really spooky. We wanted to say our good-byes to our moms for the summer since this could be Rebecca's last visit. We both knew that we would miss the magical notes and the beautiful masterpieces of music that has been played for our ears to hear. These notes gave us the courage, wisdom, and passion to make us successful individuals. Since the beginning of last September, both of us had formed quite an exterior of growth and development that never would disappear in our hearts.

In entering the room, the sunlight was barely coming through the window. As we held each other's hands and were slightly scared of the unknown, we stood strong. We both witnessed the aroma of sweet-smelling lilacs and the mist of the thin clouds appearing over the chest of drawers. We realized that they had succeeded to gain recognition from us. They always had to make their mark when they reached their destination. The mist swept swiftly over the room as we stood there. Within a split-second of time, our heartbeats seemed fierce and our confidence seemed meek.

At an unexpected moment, the curtains blew open, notes played uncontrollably fast only for our ears to hear. The beautiful tiny satin hand appeared as it had in the past; it reached out toward me to hold. I told Rebecca to sit fast, be strong, and trust in our mom's souls. We would be fine. Rebecca always thought that someone else was also present other than us and our moms. I would tell Rebecca to shake it off and get a grip and that she was just being impulsive. The extreme odor was in the dusty, dreary part of the attic. It seemed that much junk was piled up in that corner. Rebecca felt this was why sometimes we smelled that terrible odor of death. She allowed her judgment to clog up her head with ghastly images.

This was the reason part of us existed with each other and why we were drawn to this place. It was our desire to feel them. I told Rebecca that I should sing to our mothers. They would listen to me singing, as I did in the choir. I did have a beautiful tone that was all my own. I knew how to make a song feel like a song. Today was a pure, raw, and emotional something that we were missing when we visited before in the unknown room.

It was the first day that I would sing, and I was nervous. Rebecca walked me over to the window, thinking that our moms would be present and she would be able to see more clearly. Rebecca asked me, "Are you feeling OK?" I began to tell her that I felt confidence and so much love in the room that it was OK. Rebecca was looking around making a funny face, like she smelled something again.

I didn't know how else to reach them; was this too much of a risk? She saw the look on my face and wondered, how do I react to this? She took my hand from her pocket and pulled out this toy ring that she always carried with her since her mom passed. "This is my lucky charm. Go right ahead now, and blast your lungs full blown." Rebecca made me tremble with pleasure, knowing my voice was going to be their greatest secret during this moment.

I took a deep grasp of air into my lungs and started to sing with all my heart, but softly. After all, it was time to leave school, and they would notice that we disappeared for a time. As I sung, we saw the shadows of mist and the smell of the lilacs take over the room. We both agreed that our moms had the same smell. We questioned ourselves and asked, were they sisters in another lifetime to be so much alike and arrive together? They could have been soul mates for centuries in time. The rhapsody of the music was so beautiful that we both knew this to be our moms.

The frightened, stark look became a calm, sweet smile on our faces. Holding on to each other for dear life was an enchanting time for both of us. A loss is an inevitable part of growing up, and love is a bond for that painful loss. Or, to put it another way, to infinity and beyond! Now it was time for our good-bye kisses that we blew off our hands and into the air. Did our moms catch them? You bet they did—at least this was what two young girls wanted to believe, believe, and believe.

The mist was strong and so clear, a vivid blue. When we looked hard and long, we were convinced that our moms were pleased about our good-bye performance for going home.

Now a little humble, we told our moms that the summer was short and we would back shortly. "Keep your eyes out for us running up the path when we return. It will seem as if our time not together is endless, but before you know it, the two loving daughters shall return. So anxious that our hearts will be beating fast yet furiously and you will see a little sweat on our brows. Our best world is being here with both of you." Our tears started falling, our eyes getting red and swollen; everyone would wonder why. This, of course, could not be told, so we straightened ourselves up and wiped our eyes and prepared ourselves for departing from school. Looking over our shoulders toward them, they gave us the sign of their smell in the air again. The sprits showed the image of their bodies slightly appearing to us, but most of all, their mist of departure.

As we left the attic and still heard the notes playing, at this point, Rebecca and I became almost one with more love for each other more than we had before. Our relationship was strong, and now more than ever, Rebecca didn't want to leave.

While we were making small talk, Ms. Hornet was looking for Rebecca to tell her she was awarded the mentorship for the girls. Ms. Hornet was waving paperwork frantically in the air. "Girls, girls, come here quickly. I have good news for both of you."

She explained that Rebecca was picked unanimously by all the staff for returning as a mentor. Oh, how pleased we both were. I looked for Alessandra, Marybeth and Kaitlin to tell them but to no avail. Mr. Grumbling had always looked for older girls with all attributes to stay on to help the girls, new and old, and to get them adjusted. This was going to be a good summer. I knew that Rebecca was coming back. I was looking forward to her returning in the fall. This fall would have greatness that would manifest itself in no small way, and I would have the ability to unite with new and old friends. I would look at the coming year with wide-eyed wonder. I only wished that I had time to go back to the forbidden room and tell our moms. I then had an indication of a sign. Who was I kidding? They already knew now, didn't they?

CHAPTER 22

*I*T WAS ANOTHER GREAT YEAR for me at St. Claire's Academy. But home rose to the top of the list. I made an arduous journey home from one city and then to another charming city. Some girls travelled from our school to very large cities, villages, or farms to arrive back home. This could become very tiring and exhausting to some. It wore you out before your arrival at home.

I looked forward to the summer break to take this ride home to be with my dad and family that I left behind. If I checked with my consciousness, it was a profound insight into a truth almost too big to comprehend. When a country as big as the USA gives opportunities to some of the select humans to be successful, how was I so lucky to be the chosen one? Well, Mom can you answer that?

I was now on the train and going home. I knew Dad was somewhere on the train this time. I thought that travel was always a continuing education and a never-ending adventure. I'm naturally a very curious person, and so much of what I've learned in life is from the people I've met in school or on the train rides. My commitment to myself was to see as much as possible in this world. I made a vow that my loyalty and faithfulness would be my duty to my inner soul so I would be able to reach out and be adventurous. Dad came into the cabin to make sure I was OK.

I was waiting eagerly; I jumped off the train when we arrived. Randy, Samuel, and Al, my three brothers, were waiting impatiently.

Randy, of course, more than the others, wanted to know if Rebecca said anything about him. Laughing out loud, I proceeded to get into the buggy to go home. Randy jumped in right next to me in the seat, pinched me, and even gave me a little kick, waiting for me to reply. I felt like teasing him just a little and going back to our childish ways when I left home for school. He was in an unsettling mood, so anxious for answers. There was a keen, sophisticated, understanding power play that he was trying to shape into a man's definition of love. This secret would have to wait until I was ready to discuss Rebecca feelings toward Randy. This was such a thrill, knowing that I kept a secret from Randy. Randy would have to roll over to get my comments from Rebecca. Maybe payback might be some delicious ice cream, maybe a trip to the fishing pond? I had to make sure what his payback would be for the answers he wanted.

As I lay in my bed on this beautiful summer morning, Randy pounced in on me and declared that I tell him all. "No treat or trip is greater than the remarks and your observations of Rebecca and me. Annie, tell all, please!" I laughed a little and then decided he had already paid for the explanation of my notes and remarks from Rebecca. I decided to enlighten him and let him know of the impact he had on her during the holiday concert.

Randy wrote to Rebecca through the summer. You just knew a new love was starting. This rare love was something grand yet enormous and shocking. It's the quiet moments of life that move us to put ourselves out there to get acquainted. Most of the family felt there was something in the air with the two of them, secretly perhaps? The physical thing was what Dad was most worried about.

I wanted Randy to get it right. He was keeping a cool head about himself and didn't divulge anything about his feelings. I think the breakthrough moment was here though. I expected it would be starting to happen soon. I was very grateful for these two. Randy was a pitch-perfect American that should be a likely soldier. After high school, he decided to become an English teacher but instead went on to journalism reporting for the town newspaper.

Randy enjoyed writing about things that mattered, as this could be simple and exhilarating. Yet the sleight of power was more when you watch it and think about it. After that you had the verbal fireworks to explore and open up. This, I did believe, was Randy's mission—to speak up and let the people know the truth no matter what the consequences. Which he always did.

Dad was a devoted, loving father who felt that his life may be slipping away from him little by little. Now he spent his time keeping occupied, trying to get money for another school year for me.

Dad was so busy, I hardly ever saw him during the summer months. I applied for my third year of awards from school and was granted monetary compensation the same as prior years. Dad was thrilled and knew I would do my part; now he felt he had to keep his bargain to me and keep me there. Money was getting tight, but this battle Dad would win. Dad was a little desperate and was vulnerable, an enlightened middle-aged man. Now he discovered what it really felt like getting a bit old.

He was becoming an uneasy father figure to some at home. He did the most vibrant work of his career on the train that year. He had to see whether the railroad would reward him, and they did; the compensation was great. This was a little bit of a political issue in the union, but Dad handled everything with flying colors. He did the investigations and surveys and got employees to open up and deal with the issues. A potent political statement was made, and the best kind of demonstration was displayed and was effective for all.

My dad was a hard worker, and so were my brothers. Their mission was trying to get the money for another year for me in school. My family was so diligent and full of activity. A cause was presented to them and me, and it was going to be demanding, hard, and hectic work, but in the end, it would be eventful for all of us to endure. This was enough to break your heart. Success was in the books now, and my final handoff to another school year would be put into place at St. Claire's.

This left a grown man in tears, doing what he set out to do for me and succeeding in every possible way. For any dad, this could have turned disastrous, not getting the money needed for his little girl. Things worked out splendid and great; triumph was in the air for the Haverstein family again. As hard as it was, they were always occupied with the thought of success for me and keeping the indirect promise to Mom.

CHAPTER 23

*S*UMMER WAS HERE AGAIN, AND the brooks were flowing, the sun was warm, fishing was great and swinging off the trees and rumbling around the grass was back. I so enjoyed this time of serenity with time and my family.

I enjoyed the outside and the cool times that I had with my brothers. Once in a while, Randy would take me into the barn and open up to me about his experiences in high school. Randy loved going into the barn. His well-kept secret was that he had many years of renovation work ahead of him. He enjoyed putting items together for his imaginary home. Randy would sell the items to the highest bidder.

It was such a gift for him to see someone else enjoying what he had made. He's made huge rockers, benches, and incredible swings for the backyard, which were sold at the general store.

He was very creative. Randy was always looking into writing and being a famous journalist. The railroad was not Randy's passion, as it was my other brothers. Having multiple projects going on at once made him feel as if there was a light at the end of the tunnel. Randy would rather have mishaps in front of his face to deal with head-on.

I remember when Randy built a worktable on wheels for Dad to fit between two windows, and then he stuffed baskets to make shelves to organize supplies. A band of leather was put along one side of the hutch to keep scissors and other tools handy. Once I got in there with him, it was hard for me to come out.

The barn was a nice place and had a lot of space and tranquility, and there was a lot of time for Randy to be creative at least once a week. I really didn't plan to spend all my summer there, but sometimes it was OK. Dad was busy as usual with work and getting the crops in for meals. Aunt Suzie was coming over to attend to me with my new cousin Claire during the days through the summer. She was so tiny yet cute and still quiet when needed to be—so the adults said. The days passed quickly, and as usual, letters kept coming to my romantic brother Randy. It seemed that every other day, a new letter was in the mailbox. Randy and Rebecca were now an item; this was a good thing. Love is so grand!

Summer was passing by quickly, I felt. One day of excitement and joy would turn into months of summer passing. Chat your way to happiness, I would say. People who spent a lot of their day talking to friends and loved ones were much happier than the silent types. I think that the happiest people engage in both idle chitchat and several deep conversations per day.

Vacations at home feel like a compromise. However, we soon discovered that there was a lot to like about a break that's low stress, inventive, and yet lets you sleep with your own pillow under your head with calmness. I was having the time of my life. This summer, I made plenty of time for outdoor activities—cookouts with the burning of marshmallows and family. Fishing, swimming, and eating meals in the yard were so enjoyable. Little Claire was so cute eating the hot, mushy marshmallows. It stuck to her hands and her little mouth; it was a mess. Everything we all do for the first time can be rewarding now, can't it?

I sometimes skipped the most important part of life, which was a meaningful block of time in your day for yourself. Disconnect from your everyday life and ask for the pure joy of summer to come back to your soul. When we do that, even a single day can be a refreshing break. And who couldn't use a little more of that? Summer was already knocking on the door of my house, ready to take me back to good times of swimming, fishing, and just relaxing. I could appreciate a little of that. Before the heat really got cranked up, I had a few ideas to make the scorching days ahead be at ease with myself.

I could feel the presence of Mom around me, waiting for my return to school. Aunt Suzie was busy with the baby, and at this time of day, everyone was at work. For a moment, I took a deep breath into the romance of the season's most fragrant flowers. Then I exhaled as I lay down on the blanket on the lawn with my hands clasped behind my head, looking so deeply in the heavenly skies, trying to see maybe Mom or to recollect the little moments that I had with her. So short were my years but yet so rewarding. I watched the spinning of the clouds and the rainbow colors, looking like an image of a colorful pinwheel. I decided to spend this lazy day, as Mom always did, at the lake. I wanted to remember the memories of the lilac bushes on the hills, which brought me back to Mom. Moments and feelings like these should last forever and never be forgotten in your soul.

I proceeded to go into the house, grabbed my basket, blanket, and a small sandwich in case I got hungry, and was off to go to the lake. I started the journey and the walk up the hills to the lake where Mom spent a lot of her time with herself, her thoughts, and of course, her special time with God. It took me a while to make the climb. I knew that if I didn't come home before everyone else, I would be in big trouble. No one wanted me to go there, especially by myself. The family and I had too many sad memories of Mom's death at the lakeside. Losing Mom was always in our hearts, and to put ourselves back to actually where it happened was difficult. However, today, the sky was blue, the birds were chirping, and I was in a terrific mood. It seemed that it was time for me to go to the lake and embark on an extraordinary journey with my heart and spirit. My chipper attitude was enough to encourage anyone in contact with me that this was a good day for me to remember.

It was already noontime, and I was eager to go to the lake. The hill was tiring, but seeing the beauty of the mountain, trees, and roaming animals so alive was worth the hike. My imagination was getting the better of me, and the clouds above seemed as if they were moving peacefully. As Mom would have said, "Give me the energy to proceed to the top." So, long ago, I was here for my chats with Mom, our prayers and playful times that we had together. I was so young, but it seemed like yesterday in my heart.

The fish were plentiful as they jumped out of the water quickly and moved in the same pattern. The time went fast as I relaxed. I had some great lunch and enjoyed my private time with myself. Now I knew why Mom chose this place for her contentment of the day. I knew those things you've come to know and love would vanish or die and leave you at sometime in your life. Losing your loved ones and then erratically finding a new rubber band to fling in the air and watch is exciting. Then being able to take a new ride into your life with new expectations would be a blast. I felt like I was chasing my lost youth. It was a wonderful end of a summer day.

Maybe we all had a fortune-teller who would let us know the best scenes. Perhaps the beginning was a fable of good luck with handsome people. Nevertheless, didn't you wish your luck was even better then everyone else's? I felt life was full of sound and fury, signifying much of nothing.

That was a pretty high-toned way to limit your liability for the lackluster quality of this very slight entry into heaven. Most people didn't share the fantasy world of dreams. I thought it provided a unique way to experience oneself. It was like watching a movie, deciphering a magical ring, an Easter egg hunt, and Christmas all rolled into one. Nevertheless, the best part was that your mind woke up to reality and you knew it was now time to walk back down the hill to home before everyone got home from work. If I was not present when they arrived, certainly they would worry about my whereabouts.

I knew that I was now a young woman who had paid a steep price for being the only girl in the family and having to lose my mom at such an early age. I loved to throw myself into the indulgence of thought; this gave me my strength. Hence, the patronizing lesson on the hill. Today I became typically observant and finely chiseled about lost love that marked a beautiful reunion of my soul and memories that I had with Mom. Time was ending today, and I must return home promptly.

I ran home as fast as I could. When I finally arrived, no one was there. Whew, thank goodness that I was early. Aunt Suzie was coming up the street with my wonderful little cousin. My aunt and uncle were coming to dinner tonight, and I had promised to start the chicken early for us to eat on time. I, like most teenagers, rushed the chicken in the stove. I already had the corn cleaned and in the pot; salad was done in the icebox, so most of it was complete. Aunt Suzie was just approaching the house. She asked me how things were going. She wanted to go to town to pick up some cake. Aunt Suzie felt bad that today was a busy day for her and she was unable to make the cake or pie for dinner. Since I was going back to school soon, my dad wanted this special night with family. Our neighborhood friends were invited to come over later for some fun and laughter and a good old campfire.

Everyone was finally home, and dinner was on the table and ready to be served. My brothers, dad, and uncle washed up first. Aunt Suzie put the lovely lilacs on the table as a reminder that Mom hadn't left us completely. We all held hands, said our prayers, and proceeded to have an enjoyable dinner and for me a perfect day. Our friends came over later, and of course, the laughter was hard; clapping of hands and joyous sounds from the kitchen were heard. We had such warm embraces and a good time with my family and friends

The music was quiet yet contenting to listen to. Music hit the sweet spot for me and turned my ordinary life inside out like a pocket and coated my feet with happy dust. *Your love keeps on lifting me higher and higher*, I told God quietly. This was how I felt about my music and Mom. It just never dies, true love.

For me, my love affair was playing the piano and listening to beautiful notes of music. I was a wee tot, no older than being able to sit on Mom's lap, when I was hit with the jolt of passion. Mom would sing and show me some note playing on her beautiful piano. As I got older, my love for piano playing just happened naturally. I was sheer talent, I was told. My fingers just took to those keys, and my ears were made of something special for me to understand them. This seemed perfectly natural to me, because music made me feel like I was burning up inside.

It was about being on fire and delighted to burn. And unlike so many things that banged our happy buttons when we were a kid, this feeling stayed. As I got older, I think I could remember exactly where I was every time some particular song hit me like a lightning bolt. Hearing the mysterious chords were chilling to me; you heard them the way you wanted. Sometimes the wrong lyrics could be right. Maybe better than before. Can I explain how a good song is like a good kiss? No, all I can do is refer you to a great song and say each one lifts me higher and higher. Could it be that autumnal tenderness is warming? The temperamental sunshine and the unsettling effects such sunshine can have on others. New territory for some.

Summer was going quite well, and so many joys were spent with my family. To a delightful surprise, Randy came home one day and explained that he had a wonderful surprise for me. I was so excited, thinking, *What could this possibly be, a surprise for me?* Randy continued to tell me that he had written Rebecca as always and invited her and her family out for a few days and she accepted the offer.

This was too much for my amazement, thinking that my brother had really organized this to happen. I knew it wasn't for my missing Rebecca but for his desire of missing her.

Weeks had passed, and it was time for Rebecca to come to the house. Randy and I went to the railroad station to pick them up. When her foot hit the steps, I knew it was Rebecca's. She jumped off the train and into Randy's arms, wow. I was surprised but not shocked. Not all the family came to visit, thank god. I thought, where would they sleep? Better yet, where would I sleep? I could only imagine the words that were written on those letters over the summer and how much sweat and tears went into them.

Rebecca came with her dad and two of her brothers, Charles and Tim. I wasn't surprised that they were very nice to look at. Rebecca, after all, was gorgeous and breathtaking. They were young men who ran a business of imports with their older brother Edward. I thought to myself, wow, where was James? I guess I didn't leave much of an impression on him that he hadn't returned.

Without any hesitation, I thought, which fine gentleman would like to escort me? I thought for sure Dan would have been able to come with James. When I saw them, my first response was where was Dan and James? Charles realized by my expression that I was surprised that neither one came. Charles then apologized and told us that his brothers just had too much work to perform since one of his workers got hurt on the job. I was disappointed a little, as Dan and I were good friends. I thought maybe James and I could be a new love. Well, as they said, onward and upward. I decided to set my sights on another beau.

Immediately, I was looking at these two fine silhouettes in front of me, outrageous, jaw-dropping men. I somehow forgot about the other two brothers that didn't show up. I of course had these fantasy dreams in my head, good ones though about James. I didn't forget that Rebecca was a princess on her mom's side, which was of wealth and royalty. I knew Randy was no one's fool. He would have to be tricky and yet fun and so charming to make a smash hit. His yearning and need for her was so obvious. Randy was certainly not boring or lifeless by no means. He was exciting and very interesting to know. He was a good catch for any fine woman. The town of Harrisburg and anyone in contact with Randy knew about his charms.

Currently, you would say he was on the hot list of eligible men to pursue. After all, Randy had a good job, had a respectable family, and was a charmer for sure. By no means would any girl pass him up without seeing his many attributes.

I then thought to myself, *Could this be so real, these two adorable men here in my house? Who's pulling the strings in relationships now?* It just didn't seem real that two gorgeous hulks appeared for my choice. Some may think, is this a dilemma or a strategy that may have to be taken now? Sometimes people say take the horse by its reins and pull hard but softly. I knew that tactic for sure.

We all approached the house safely, and before you knew it, we had arrived promptly and on time. Dad and the rest of my brothers met us outside with bated breath. Dad made sure everything was done above board. It was important to my family to make the Wetherbee's feel comfortable.

We showed them to their rooms. Rebecca was going to be in my room with me. Mr. Wetherbee, Rebecca's dad, had a room at the top of the house with his own privacy. Her two brothers bunked in with Randy and Al. I couldn't imagine the course of action or dealings that would be put into place in that room.

Rebecca and Randy needed to have a meaningful conversation right now. Anyone who deliberately tried to avoid the issues at hand would see that it was pointless to try and stop the chitchat of love. I will protect my brother's issues at hand and would be happy to dispense a chilly stare and a quick glimpse on the back of anyone's head who tried to stop him. On the other hand, if anyone deliberately avoided a topic that someone close had been trying to bring up for weeks, you had to change your tune in a hurry or deal with me. Everyone may have seemed to be so wildly enthusiastic that they might have wished they'd have waited, but for what? Randy had to speak his mind now; he had to speak up to tell Rebecca.

I took a broad definition of love; it could be "Oh, baby, your eyes are so beautiful," but it could also be "Hey, we've known each other for half a year, and in some ways, rejection wasn't a leap. It was a fact." Denial could be a reality that no one ever believes, but a negative response or refusal is never a good start.

I thought that if someone asked me a question today, he or she had better be ready to listen because I had a lot to say and was eager to share my opinion about them. However, I may not have been able to give a simple yes or no answer. I did have a story to tell and wouldn't be stopped until I delivered my entire response, including any explanations that you deemed necessary. Just remember that others may not have the "time for the everything" approach, so keep your message as uncomplicated as possible. When Randy was involved, I was ready to take the pitch.

This year things started slowly with Randy and Rebecca but ended OK. I told Randy not to wait until love was just right before making his move. "Start action today if you are ready."

I spoke to Randy about his feelings and told him, "Instead of getting caught up in anger over something you can't control, apply your good excess energy methodically in advance, if possible."

I told Randy, "Look at Dad for instance. As much as Dad tries to get ahead, obstacles keep appearing as if to test him. One thing, in my education process at St. Claire's, I realize you should always feel better about your place in the world and don't dismiss it. Start up your engines and go full speed ahead and don't stop until you finish your mission."

Randy looked at me as if I was crazy; I told him to talk to her today before she left for home and departed back to school. "Before you know it, the weekend will be over and she will go to school with me for another year of teaching. I'm sure her rigid schedule will keep her in overload. It's important that you speak to her father today since he must give his OK. It's the proper thing to do," I told him. After all, I did learn something at St. Claire's as to proper procedures. Randy should really open his heart and show his feelings; nothing should slip away through his fingers, not now.

"Pretend it's the magical musical notes that Mom plays when we need her in our life. This is a divine connection that not everyone will have in their lifetime. Love gives you something to care about besides having your heart scattered with nothing. Sometimes you may think of this as make-believe and so unreal, but check out your heart. It's not."

Well, Randy thought long and hard and decided to have a long talk with Rebecca before she departed. Randy managed to speak to Rebecca's dad prior. He was quite delighted with Randy and the happiness of them wanting to get married. At the end of the night, they both walked in the room.

Rebecca wanted to say her good-byes. Randy very nonchalantly made the announcement of their engagement to both of their families present. No one was in amazement about the news; everyone was thrilled.

Her brothers shook hands, gave hugs, and felt that this time was a magnificent and brilliant moment in their lifetime. They had explained to both families that they were going to keep the relationship going as they had fallen in love. Cheers were loud, and my tears were flowing. Dad was thrilled with the entire weekend, and so was the Wetherbee family. Elliott and Parker my brothers drove everyone to the train station. The Wetherbee's had many miles to go before getting to their summer home; it would be long and enduring. That weekend, the company was so worth the result.

I was so pleased with Randy. When they all departed, Dad grabbed Randy and informed him that he was so proud of him. Dad replied, "Mom would have been twice as proud of you, son." Marriage is a sweet, dying ember of romance mixed in with the pain. When time leaps, we see couples meet and sometimes come apart, and the result is far more than a showcase of love. It's a desperate piece of a puzzle of how two people could finally find each other. Yet they have the innocence of two teenagers in love.

In other words, it's really not too late to jump into love and marriage, full of thrills, strained relationships, laughs, and some acting. Randy deserved more credit for being enthusiastic and being creative in this romance of love.

CHAPTER 24

*I*COULDN'T BELIEVE THE TIME WAS here again for me to return to school. I was lifeless and limp to depart from my loved ones but so excited for my new term on learning new ideas. This year was an important year for me; after all, I was now going to be a junior. I had big concern about other events that would follow during this year besides the usual holiday concert. We had the patriotic dance, pretesting for college, homecoming dance, and of course, the always unmentionable school holidays. This year, I finally got to go to the presidential patriotic dance, which was only for third year students.

I packed my belongings and waited for a family member to drive me to the train station. Dad never drove me to the station since it tore his heart apart. It reminded him when he had to depart from my mom and the sadness he felt. He had many sad feelings when I left for school. It was a typical going-away sitcom—my friends crying, Aunt Suzie upset, and my brothers going wild. My brother Samuel took me to the train, with big hugs and kisses and the speech to take care of myself. He now mentioned to say hello to Rebecca for him. Samuel, like the rest of us, realized that Randy really fell hard and in time will be a family member to the Wetherbee's.

By the way, if I really thought long and hard, my friends and I were all very talented and our anticipation on the school's yearly show was always in our sights. Our eagerness and keen expectations of the concert made the return to school a great dream. The school had done a really good job of pushing the envelope for the school and audience. This was why it was a little easier to leave home and return to school. The difficult time of departing is always leaving my dear friends and family behind. I knew that I would miss out on some birthdays, jamborees at my hometown high school, and 4H Fairs or holidays that I would be unable to attend. Saying good-bye to my best buddies Jessica and Samantha was extremely tough since we had known one another since young children. I did reflect on what I was missing, but I also knew that at this time in my life, I belonged at St. Claire's.

Looking into our success that would follow in our footsteps of what has been achieved as young women was such an accomplishment. So with these many realities ahead of me, I packed my clothes and mirror and said good-bye to my room and couch for another year. I boarded the train, waved from the window, and was off to Philadelphia again to start a spectacular new year in school. I slept for a while and woke up at the station, seeing Ms. Hornet waiting patiently to pick up the girls. Ms. Hornet would go back and forth for those that needed the pickups during the day. She believed that it was part of her job to greet the old and new students and make them feel comfortable since we all had left our surroundings. At the end of the day, when everyone was accounted for, Ms. Hornet really looked extremely tired.

I felt that it was starting to wear her out. It was a long day for her, the running back and forth, so strenuous. I finally looked at Ms. Hornet differently, not as a cross person but as a teacher of education and perfection. She seemed to have blossomed over the summer, maybe some sun?

We finally arrived at the front doors, waiting to see our friends and meet new ones. The dormitory was just as I remembered it, still sparse and icy cold. I left at the end of the school year with new rapture in my heart, knowing that I would return. Yet I anxiously did not want to leave the unknown room. I didn't know if I could wait until the fall to hear the beautiful notes in the attic being played by Mom.

Everybody came rapidly down the halls with hugs and new conversations of summertime. Those who came to appreciate and understand the dual personalities of their friends were those that were the happiest. The storytelling, which was never too late at night, could be sometimes over the top. Then the knack to jump into new conversations and tell about your summer with others was definitely a skill and talent. This was the time when you were full of thrills and sometimes strained relationships, laughs, and nuanced acting, as if you are performing in drama class.

We had the eager beavers, the freshmen, who were united to form a warmly wacky bond with us. You could count on a grand screwball skit and, at other times, a somber, piece of conversation. Our incoming freshmen could sometimes be over the top. They just needed one day to be with us so we could set them straight on attitude, time, and being courteous. As we say, like a lady!

This year seemed it would be adventurous and exhilarating and most likely a bumpy ride. Here was hoping that this year would make more room for changes. This was the shining reason some of us had a magical allure that you couldn't wait to show up for at the start of the fall. The drama of performing on stage and this year not being a substitute was what you tried to achieve.

I was too tired to explain or even take the time to recognize the new or old students. The distance of my room seemed so far away from my baggage. I heard Ms. Hornet in the hallways, tapping and trying to get some order in the halls. She seemed to be a little impatient today, too much on her plate I would imagine. We all had to settle down now, for dinner was about to be served.

Ms. Hornet ordered everyone from the rooms into the dining hall. They shared stories, joy, and tears of missing families. I couldn't wait to see Rebecca; I had no idea where she was during this time. After dinner, we were all able to return to the classes and check out the new decor or teachers. Most of us wanted to see if our old friends returned and to meet new girls that we could have lasting relationships with now and after graduation.

Rebecca came into my room late as she had just arrived, very tired and listless. We all could see how much Rebecca loved me. She was like the big sister that I never had. The clock chimes were ringing, and it was half past nine and time for us to return to our bedrooms. It seemed as if it was an endless night for everyone; in the morning so many of us, looked so exhausted. I couldn't wait to tell Marybeth and Kaitlin about Rebecca and Randy.

It gave me such pleasure to tell everybody about the proposal, so exciting. It was a family class act with a classic portrayal of a new marriage on center stage. I told the girls that they seemed wholly suited for each other and their affection for each other reminded you that every good marriage had a code of its own; it was a secret known only to the couple.

It was always so confusing during the first week of school. Everybody settling in, new teachers, different buildings, new schedules, new and old friends, getting schoolbooks, lockers, and so on—clearly quite busy. There were those that could handle all this easily, and then there were those that got overwhelmed. That was one good reason for Rebecca.

This year she was one of the mentors for the girls at St. Claire's; any problems went to Rebecca. She did seem to heal all your wounds, though, and walked you through any dilemmas you may have had. I still realized that I was unable to find Marybeth and Kaitlin. So much time had passed and I still couldn't find them. Now, where could those girls be? I was surely wondering. I walked briskly around the halls and looked into their rooms, but to my amazement, no Marybeth or Kaitlin. I just started to shutter from fright, thinking that they weren't coming back. It was just too hard to think about.

Was I getting ahead of myself just because I didn't see them? Or was I right on the mark that there was no return for them? I had to go to Ms. Alice and asked her to check the list to see if Marybeth and Kaitlin had arrived. Ms. Alice saw my concern and reassured me not to worry and the girls would be there. They just happened to take another train arriving really late tonight. Whew, I took my hand across my brow because was I sweating now! I was glad it was not going to be a disaster this year. Without my friends, what would I do? Cry, that's what I would do, cry.

I patiently walked down to my room and decided to take a bath and take care of my fingers. We were told many times to soak our fingers daily and massage them with oil. This procedure would save a lot of pain on your hands. Night was coming on us, and one more trip to the bathroom was in order. The bathroom was cold, and no towels were stored yet in the closets. Someone wasn't doing her job for sure. In the distance, I heard some giggling going on and quite a bit of noise. Of course, I had to check it out like I always did, being Ms. Nosey.

Lo and behold, it was my dear friends acting like freshmen. I was puzzled and bewildered about their characters. After all, we were juniors this year. We hugged and laughed and couldn't wait to see if our schedules matched one another's. I was glad that the three bold, intriguing amigos were back together again. Tomorrow was another day. "Good night, ladies. See you in the hall for breakfast. Don't be late; you know how Ms. Hornet feels about tardiness."

The bells rang early in the morning for wake-up time. This meant baths, teeth brushing, combing the hair, getting dressed, and making up your bed. You had to move swiftly and make sure everything was done correctly. During the day, the headmistress checked us on cleanliness in our room. If your room was not done correctly, Ms. Alice came after you and down you walked to correct the situation. You certainly didn't want this to happen; it meant extra chores for you. The example was to do this right the first time and not have to go back. Most importantly, the corners of the bed had to be tucked under properly.

Your clothes in the closet had to be hung correctly, and the clothes in your dresser had to be folded properly, no slacking. No paperwork lying around and make sure the dust was off the floor. If you did all this, then you were OK. The big no-no was to make sure you didn't leave the lights on, ever. You may end up with a demerit on your score card.

We tried to warn the incoming freshmen girls on what was frowned on and what not to do. After all, someone at one time also had to tell us what not to do. It was all part of growing up in a fine woman's world. They were so gracious that we told them about how to handle the ups and downs of what to do. We all then laughed, smiled, and had good conversation with our newfound friends.

The next morning, we all walked calmly out of our bedrooms when wake-up call came. It seemed as if it was earlier than last year's. We knew to get into straight lines and head for the dining room for breakfast. This was not our usual breakfast room, but for the first several weeks, the school made it a treat to have our meals in this room. It somehow gave you an impressionable thought of why you were there in the first place. Looking around, there were so many new faces. Of course, we were the popular and goody two-shoes to sit with. Who would not want to join us when we sat around for mealtime? Kibitzing and showing one another no mercy at all in the name of friendship. Going through the same ordeal—introducing yourself and making new friends—was always rewarding. We knew that this year's most surprising holiday concert would be great and yet intimidating.

After all, we were all intense about perfecting our musical pieces; if achieved, this would allow us to play the piano during the holiday concert. We knew there were degrees of talent, some fakery, and egotism. It was just like the world itself. Rebecca told us that we would all reach our creative peak this year. Kaitlin, Marybeth, and I knew this was our year.

I was always worried about doing things right the first time. To be late for class was unheard of. I never wanted Ms. Hornet to be mad at me. The piano students that were upperclassmen must always show improvement from last year. We were expected to improve daily, monthly, and every semester. Piano players always had to sit erect in posture, never giving up on themselves or their piece of music. This was the law of St. Claire's.

Tears of relief and exhaustion come over us due to so much practice. Some girls caved in earlier than others because of extreme scheduling. You always had to be superb. My god, it was a miracle fighting back tears of relief and exhaustion, especially at this time, when you were supposed to be so grown-up. I tried every day to be this obedient student, friend, and daughter, but sometimes life and my dreams overtook me and I forgot my purpose at school or with myself and my family.

CHAPTER 25

I LOOKED AT REBECCA AND THANKED her for saving me, for telling me to reach into my soul and pull myself out before it was too late. Making me push hard with music and academics was not so easy sometimes, and keeping me on the safe page was a chore to conquer.

Rebecca replied, "Don't give me all the credit that you imagine. I would like you to take all the credit that you feel I should receive and give it to yourself. When we approach the forbidden room, this is where I get my inner strength to protect both of us. I didn't observe a miracle. It is the smell of the lilacs and the notes that saved us both.

"Don't you smell the lilacs in the air and hear the classical notes? I knew it was them. When it happens, all I do is become a lifeless stone statue not being able to move. It's kind of authoritative, the power of the unknown, how it enters your body and then your mind and takes control.

"God gave us both the strength to bare our feelings and just sit there with the mist around us. The marvelous notes and the wonderful aroma are a vigorous, persuasive control. I know in my heart it was my mom and yours too. This isn't just a coincidence. This is forceful magic. Some might also say a mysterious element of the unknown, the angels protecting God's children. Who really knows the answer? So many thoughts one may have at this suspense that it is intoxicating, to say the least. This time the smell was stronger. It was as if they were present and turned to rescue us in their hearts. After all, isn't this just what moms do?"

We were all so busy with our new schedules at school; the rest of our friends debated the appropriateness of classical music, using their homemade masterpiece as fuel for their startup practice. One of the appealing things about picking your own musical piece was it seemed that you wore your heart on your sleeves. The result may well be your goriest hour of self-respect. This will be rapid-fire with almost unbearable tension and never more than a brilliant social misfit, which we have tried so hard not to accomplish. If you want to see what masterful suspense looks like, then simply walk into one of these moments when someone is composing.

You sometimes can have a meltdown completely; you're appearance shows up from the dark side of yourself. This is merely an appetizer for a juicy main course, with spectacular bits of dinner. Could you pair friends and share extreme tension? We sure hoped so. If not, then departure should be part of your speech. Go home, girl, because this road is a rocky one but worthwhile in the end if you stay.

I remembered so clearly the first time Rebecca and I proceeded to check out that dreadful attic. There were a lot of anticipation and rumors. No one knew what to expect. This was attending a movie and having your own private show. Our moms made us feel instantly comfortable. In fact, they were responsible for teaching us the basic clue of playing music. All we had to do was to give 100 percent commitment to our performance, and it would be a life's lesson.

Rebecca talked a lot this evening about the forbidden room. Going there was over the top, complete torture; there wasn't much you could do to shock us. Complex, mysterious, and yet comforting was the zone of the attic.

We sat quietly on the chest and asked each other, where did they come from? What kept us wanting more? All I knew was that we didn't have to provide answering soon.

I think that when we confirmed anything about these moments, the excitement would wear off. The biggest reward for me was to see how much they were so alike. I asked Rebecca, "Do you feel they are related, if not on earth, now in heaven?" Imaginary wonder could sometimes be a burden of suspense. It was like the whispering memories of Mom that spoke gently in my ear and haunted my heart of her love.

It was a terrifying moment for us yet so wonderful. I thought that the spirit reached in and grabbed our souls and our feelings. They took over our emotions, our nerves, and our endless spirit of love. This too was part of the whispering memories that still taunted our hearts with pain and anxiety of our youth.

I started to shake a little, but I was with my friend; no harm could come to either one of us. I started to grow frantic with sin and reminded myself about my tormented soul. So confused and so much anticipation in our hearts most people would never know in a lifetime. We were quite surprised about their strong strength of aura. We didn't realize that we had to ever think about being caught by Ms. Hornet or others. This would never happen to us. No matter what the cost, we had the best people picking us up—our moms. We could never fail or falter at anything if we kept our hearts in the right place. At this point, the door slammed behind us. Now we knew it certainly was time to depart.

We both left the room quietly and proceeded to go downstairs back to our rooms. It was like a day in heaven, being with our moms' spirits. It was something you couldn't put into words—the aura, the triumphant of joy to our hearts, and the immense feelings that this would never be put to rest. At least not for a while. They were here to stay.

CHAPTER 26

*S*LOWLY, BACK TO OUR ROOMS we went, not to lose each other; it was now dark in the hallways. As we walked down the hallway back to our rooms, it became very dreary. We could hear the crackling of the wood in the fireplaces and smell, the aroma, of wood. When arriving downstairs, we hugged each other and made it back to our rooms before check-in by Ms. Alice. Whew, lucky we guess!

When we approached our bedrooms, we waved a silent good night for this special evening, which would become a special bond in our life. We were truly two girls or young ladies with their lives entwined in body and soul. This would almost be impossible for us to separate. At least not in the near future.

Knowing that we had truly believed that the musical notes were played by our moms gave us enormous comfort. It was remarkable that we managed to stay so long. It was the whispering memories that were in our souls that made it OK to stay. A pleasing visit, similar to a drama being performed in the theater but no one has witnessed.

No sooner had we closed our eyes and opened them than it was daylight shining and the birds chirping. I looked out the window to my family of ducks on the lake, swimming happily as I have left them in June. It seemed as if we had some more additions; looked like they had a busy summer, I would suppose.

It was back to the continuous, rigid schedule as prior years—practice and concentration and to excel in whatever you were doing at that moment in time. Rebecca was good with all the girls. Always a smile, a simple touch, or a praise of encouragement. "You will succeed," she repeated. "Nothing is able to stop you if you do believe in yourself.

"I feel you should always leave people with a clear impression of the key role you play. Be diplomatic for example, praise your friend's work, and mention specifics. However, take stake in your claim to what you alone want to accomplish and your accomplishments. Perhaps you don't feel entitled to do that. Build your sense of creditworthiness from the inside out.

"Review your skills and credentials you've amassed, as if you were evaluating another person. Track your achievements. In the musical life, the road takes notes of your ideas, decision making, and leadership. It will materially help your personal goals in music."

Rebecca advised me and the world at large that she sends a message that good girls cease the limelight. The behaviors we learn early can be desirable in the right context and proportion. Especially that they're so often applauded, it can be hard to see that we're using them against ourselves. Disempowering ideas about women in general become positive and sometimes even flattering terms.

Ms. Hornet heard our conversation and decided to butt in with her realistic ideas of women. She proceeded to state that the successful woman had a secret. "She's learned that she owes it to herself, her children, and to the world to make the contributions she was born to make. She's learned to ask for advice and help, to insist on getting paid what she's worth, and to set down boundaries at home, school, and work so that her needs get met, not trampled. She puts her dreams at the top of her priorities list, not at the bottom.

"She feels great about being recognized for her accomplishments, and she's totally OK with the fact that not everyone is going to like her. When she stands up against those who would put her down, she rejoices in victory. I am giving you the best step-by-step advice from your educator, your friend, and a woman not to be reckoned with.

"You have to overcome the most common acts of social sabotage and step up to the plate and hit the home run for yourself. Someday you will look back and see all the ideals, realization of the world, people, and music that this school has made you better for."

The season was upon us again, and tryouts as usual would take place in the music room. This was going to be my most intense engagement yet. I was flashing back the last two years, one at a time when I was really hustling, but I was an older hag now, I laugh. The greatest thing about the show, I felt, was how ridiculously extreme it was and how you never, ever have any idea where it was going to go. Who would play the solo piano masterpieces and who would be selected for the solo choir or who would make the choir?

It took the freshmen about four minutes and ten seconds to eavesdrop on our conversation of the concert and what to expect. Freshmen didn't really go so far in playing musical pieces in tryouts. The freshmen usually ended up being stagehands, setting up lights, rolling cameras, or being able to sit our guests properly, performing as ushers. Let's also not forget some of the important roles where help was needed—decoration committee, advertising, and food to mention a few.

It would be another glorious day, and everyone would come as dapper as always. The long hours would keep you sleep deprived and bruised. You almost ended with a split-personality disorder.

The stage crews always knew when to arrive on the set. We all tended to become these characters, and it was within our own bodies when the show settled into a reality. It was sometimes better to pretend to be someone you weren't; it was the best way to reach outside yourself, to fashion your voice into an explorer, and be an instrument of empathy. As much as I loved this event, I was really ready to shift to a slower pace. The chance to recapture the school's feeling of unplanned time was a true whirlwind.

It was a show that had been cracking out talent for decades, just done really, really well. The girls surprisingly riffed over three-part harmonies that burst open and expanded into gorgeous choruses and piano playing. It seemed that the older girls never sounded more adult than at this time. Voices changed so with maturity within our bodies and our throats. These changes could be a punch in the gut that transcended in time too; when would it end?

Monday was the start of tryouts. The first were piano recitals. This year, surprisingly, they were going to have duets in the show. The teachers were planning to put the hottest masterpieces against one another. Who (or what) would come out on top? Duets were only going to be for the seniors.

When you finally got to play your piece, you found yourself an emotional wreck, but a bit of love was attached. So you think, what are these revealing songs about? Sometimes you couldn't be surprised that some fans or teachers were unhappy with your piece selections. For some of us, we were in our third season; we watched as puzzle pieces went together and scored well. Others waited to see how it all fit together. Was our puzzle finally finished? What would we finally get from the piece? A puzzle with huge sections missing, little did we know.

The teachers were proud always of their final endings. In the end, it was all about entertainment. There was definitely no need to add more than needed to the mix. I always enjoyed watching and listening to tryouts. To see the skills and timing of my schoolmates as they played their pieces or sang their personal choices was so intense. It tended to make me walk proudly and my chest burst wide open with pride.

It seemed it was a handful of balloons flying into the air and going nowhere. When you looked above into the clouds, you saw the many different colors becoming a beautiful rainbow as the angels sat between the clouds of white mist.

Once everyone managed to get through all the singing debuts, which was the end of the day, it was over for this duration to end. Most of the girls sounded like angels singing to their God. In return, they all ended with a gold medal of hope, love, and continued trust. Tomorrow was another day; now it was for piano playing. I anxiously went to the stage front in the auditorium and sat in the first row, waiting for teachers to show up.

It was quite early, and I didn't even want to go to breakfast. This was my way of life, so at 7:00 a.m., I sat patiently waiting for roll call to play. Sitting there by myself, I had time to reflect about my piece in my head. Suddenly, the girls started showing up and then the teachers presented themselves. Ms. Hornet realized I wasn't at breakfast and asked if I was OK. I replied in a whisper tone that I was. I sat down, and Ms. Hornet asked me about my musical piece. After I performed, she was disappointed with my selection. "I won't let you do that," replied Ms. Hornet, sadly saying, "I was planning to let you do that another time, maybe the spring social? It would be a shame to not at least try to participate again with another selection of music." I understood my dilemma, and I knew that Ms. Hornet wanted the best for me. I knew now that I couldn't return without a masterpiece or miss any scheduled rehearsals that afternoon. Being in my third year at school, I was shocked that my performance was presented so poorly. I was just glad that Ms. Hornet wouldn't accept my selection.

This was the challenging platform gaming for fun and marked by exceptional pieces. This was where good and bad choices dictated your outcome. This would not be the last of my challenges in life. Now I had to bear the burden of expectations for an emotionally demanding role of musically playing a solo and then matching it with perfection.

Could you imagine all this and still hoping for an overnight recognition? Early rumors were most talked about, especially the solos. Our front-runners were Emma for piano and Alessandra for singing. There was a little bit of sparkling sunshine in my eyes though, hoping I would be the selected one for a piano solo. Who knew? I did my best, and it would depend on how they perceived me while playing. I now sat down to play another piece for Ms. Hornet, proudly I hoped.

When I sat down to decide about lyrics that I would play, it controlled all my emotions. I wrote down my process that I would go through mentally. My songwriting was a deep, personal gut thinking that made it a big part of my appeal. I certainly didn't want to disappoint anyone. All real events inspired my songs. Most of my songs were self-explanatory; who I was writing about, without me being detailed and giving names, it was known. Always the mystery in myself. I felt like I had been dealt a pretty good hand of inspiration. I just went deep into my haunted soul and listened to Mom's whispers in my ear and I suddenly got the uplift I needed to express the words to the music. My musical masterpiece was magnificent, if I do say so myself. I guess I couldn't take all the credit myself to the appealing words and sounds of the songs. After all, I had to give Mom a lot of credits for making it happen.

I also found it a shrill and an overly stylized jarring jumble of tones and moods. I thought it was a rapturous modern musical masterpiece. The opening half hour of tryouts were so frenzied that, on some level, it froze me for a second in time. After all the waiting for the moment to play, suddenly I was finished; it was all over. The anxiety, the anxiousness, being worried for myself and my friends. Ms. Hornet acknowledged me to leave; politely I stood up and proceeded to depart. I waited anxiously to hear Emma play, who was a senior and my friend. She was extraordinary, with a poignant humor worthy of a solo spot. Emma sat at the piano and gave a genuinely heartbreaking performance as a woman grappling with success. Most of us felt she was a headliner for sure this season. Emma was sure going to make it difficult since she played the piano and sang as well as she played.

Alessandra, who was a junior in my class, was trying out also for the solo lead in singing. She used her gravel-stripped voice to sing melancholy-folded hymns for the broken heart. It was mostly almost too good for her solo to have a true ending. Alessandra was magnificent in her melodious tone and sang each word with exceptional vocalization. Alessandra was also very precise in playing her musical piano piece; most of us felt she was superb. This would be a tough choice for our staff.

Yet, Emma was a senior who had most rights to the position. In her tryout, she played the hell out of the song. It would be good for the show because there were still a lot of people who watched the show and who loved the singing and playing. I arrived when everyone was talking about the choice of music. Everyone was inspiring, just as young singers of music would be. Our music teacher yelled out from the audience seating, "Make it sound like a complement-lusty vocal, and then perfectly match it with your talent." We wouldn't dream of spoiling it, but here's what I can tell you. I couldn't wait until the day when we took the spotlight off those bloody judges.

The teachers wanted to make sure that the show would be rich and have a satisfying ending. Alessandra was a terrific singer (and gorgeous), but I found it to be magnificent, the best you would ever hear, only less cool. Hopefully, she got a spot in the show.

Christmas tradition in the same room was justly rewarded. A songster turning the song's defining loneliness on its head, twining the solo's music in a soaring invocation of shared heartache of jubilance.

CHAPTER 27

*H*AVING THE GIRLS SPEND MORE time with their mentors was always a good thing. Ms. Hornet told the mentors "to pick their brains to find out what will make them huge." This would also be helpful for them in the long run. She was especially impressed by last year and how she worked on arrangements and provided accompaniments on stage. It fact, she was so thrilled by her involvement; she thought she could help end this exhaustive search locking for the best.

There was nothing so rousing as a show and about putting on a show. A great piano concert, a beautiful singing sequence, or an unbelievable solo. It would certainly kick your mood up a few notches. It became a huge hit for the school. I was a woman who wanted love and the fairytales and what we saw in movies but who also knew the harsh reality of not being selected.

I remember the first time I performed in public; it was during a church Christmas play when I was six. From there on, I joined plays, choruses, and pretty much anything in performing arts. I was only singing for fun; it was my outlet of stress since Mom was gone. It helped me process my emotions, gain confidence, and understand this new world I was in without my mom. I knew it was a way to express myself in an artistic way. If I didn't take piano lessons in elementary school or learned about harmony, I didn't know where I would be today. Certainly not at St. Claire's school trying out for the holiday concert.

It was truly that magical time of year again. As we spent, time with our families and friends and put on our magical holiday concert show. It brought special moments we would always treasure. Making memories took plenty of time of planning. Sometimes I complained a lot, and I tended to think about what I would like to say but didn't because it appears that it's rude.

CHAPTER 28

*A*GAIN, THE TIME WAS HERE and invitations were in the mail and the selections of girls were to be posted. How exciting, as it always was. Did I get chosen, was I rejected, was I to do backstage props? Oh, so many questions with no answers until the posting. We all had our normalcy of classes and anxiousness waiting for results. Classes were done, and now it was 4:00 p.m. We saw Ms. Hornet approach the board with the slips of paper of the announcements. When she left, many of us slowly ran to the board; after all, we were young proper girls.

I looked for my name and jumped with joy for the triumph that I excelled. Anxiously, now I looked on the board for my friends Alessandra, Emma, Marybeth, and Kaitlin; all did well as I expected them to do.

We watched as the younger girls, the newcomers, approached the board, checking out their success. Most were disappointed, but just one seemed to shine above all the rest. I met the girl during check-in. She was a sweetheart of a young lady and very refined. Talent she certainly had and was able to express it through her fingers. This, of course, we knew was a talent of perfection. She also had a name to match her looks and success.

She was called Margaret. Margaret had made the substitute list for anyone that was unable to make the concert on the night of the performance. Huge jubilance was beyond Margaret's expectations. I told Margaret she did grand and we were all so proud of her. My friends and I approached her and congratulated her on her great attributes. Delighted and crying, she thanked us with much sincerity. I hoped someone ended up feeling a little sick, maybe a headache, so everyone could enjoy my triumph on this evening. Rebecca looked at Maggie and, with a strong, confident voice, told her how Kaitlin was able to perform last year even though she was a substitute. "Keep the faith, Maggie, and I know for sure you will shine on that evening."

Maggie turned to me in amazement. "Annie, how can Rebecca feel so strongly about this evening? It's as if she has someone inside of her who was giving her the answers for this night."

"Little do you know, Maggie, I think Rebecca does have an inner soul talking to her. I know it's only good thoughts though, so don't worry. You will perform and have your moment of triumph. I also feel it in my guts." Humbly, she walked slowly through the halls back to her room. Tonight, she would have a calm sleep and would be able to be proud of herself when she wakes up. Good night, Margaret, for tonight. See you at practice."

Rebecca was starting to walk toward the board. She looked at us with her sly smile and her cute way about her and gave us all a thumbs-up to our success. She kept telling us to just believe and we will. She was so proud of us. Rebecca sometimes felt like we are all her kid sisters under her umbrella for the passion of music. I would think most of us were, if the truth would be told. Otherwise, why were we here at this prestigious school? Why not somewhere else? We all knew why.

"We all have notions about what we're supposed to do, yet in reality; life presents us with only a few real obligations. Some we can do and some just not meant for us to do. This means it's OK not to be in everything in school. A small voice inside you may whisper that it's OK not being a star. So put a smile on your face if you aren't a headliner. You need to take care of you. Being in the backstage or up front by the doors is just as important as the other tasks. Remember that always in your heart.

"Circulate on the night of the event and think of why you decided to participate or attend this social event in the first place. Enjoy your loved ones, old friends, and maybe some new friends. Isn't this what truly makes the holiday season so special?"

I wrote to my dad and my family of my success at the school and about my new friends. Much information was needed for Dad and the others to attend the show. This for them meant taking a holiday off work or taking a day off with no pay. We were in hard times now; not many could do this at a snap of their fingers. Dad wrote back quickly and responded to me to make sure we had enough tickets for everyone. My family was planning to attend this year. He also made a request that we all sit next to the Wetherbee's in the audience. On receiving the letter, I ran to Rebecca's room to ask her how I should respond to Dad. "Do you think it will be OK for them to all sit together, so many of them? Yours and mine!" Rebecca always was calm and said, "Not to fret, my child. I will take care of the tickets and make sure everyone reaches our destination safety, and for those that need rooms, I will take care of it." Wow, I was so glad Rebecca was part of my life at least for this moment, her loving Randy and all. A load was certainly taken off my shoulders, thanks to Rebecca.

CHAPTER 29

AYS AND WEEKS WENT BY so swiftly. I did receive my box from Aunt Suzie, as always, with a magnificent dress for me. The girls always couldn't wait to see what Aunt Suzie had designed. After all, this was done by memory, and I was growing by leaps and bounds for sure. I opened the box with urgency, and my heart was beating oh so fast. The dress was so beautiful—long sleeves, cream color, all homemade in lace. At the bottom of the hem were ribbons weaved into the lace in a color of lilac.

I knew where Aunt Suzie was coming from with this wonderful color; it was Mom's favorite. If I couldn't really have Mom in the audience, at least some of me might feel she was there with this wonderful attire. It was the best dress ever to be put in my closet and to parade. I felt so elegant and graceful when I tried the dress on, I couldn't wait for show time to be here.

Now it was finally show time, and everyone looked glamorous from head to toe, with minimal effort. I saw my family for a short moment in the audience and gave a small wave and smile to them. This year they managed to sit up closer to the stage, thanks to Rebecca pulling strings for all of us. My family was seated next to the Wetherbee family. I couldn't wait until later to enjoy the festive dinner party designed for family and friends. The great feast was to be in the royal ballroom, more elegant then last year. Mr. Grumbling liked to show off his school and the wealth it projected.

Ms. Delight was our head chef and ever so charming when she planned this occasion. Deciding what to serve could be a headache for sure. This year, it was going to be simplified by focusing on those two can't-lose crowd pleasers, chocolate and coffee. You could practically hear our guests whispering already. "'Tis the season to be jolly." Or I seem too ambitious; match it with two potential soul mates, candy and cake.

I knew that, when you felt that you needed to make a statement to your guests, you should speak up. Try adorning your dining area with vases of brown orchids, or opt for bunches of chocolate cosmos, a flower that actually smells like chocolate. Happily, there were infinite possibilities of creative coffee drinks and many deserts.

Delight your guests with an inspired dessert coffee bar. Brew coffee with espresso beans and set out a variety of after-dinner drinks, Amaretto and chocolate liqueur. Silver shakers filled with cocoa and cinnamon would create a perfect finishing touch. A fine dining experience to say the least. Truly a luxurious dining experience. Many classic dishes with a twist and sometimes an international flare for the entrées. This would dazzle our guests with great selections. Satisfying entrées using many fresh seasonal ingredients would make everyone feel satisfied upon leaving.

It gave us an excuse to meet and mingle with other parents. I tried to surprise my loved ones with a peaceful and relaxing experience that would surely warm their hearts and bellies throughout the holiday season. I just hadn't figured it out yet, but I would.

The evening went fast, and it was time for our families to return to their homes. It was hard saying good-byes again, but I knew within ten days, I would be home with my family to celebrate the holidays since school was closed then. A good time was had by all, thanks to the staff and many others who made it possible for it to be a huge success during this very busy season.

I looked for my new friend, Margaret. I was told she was on my floor at the other end of the hallway with the younger girls. Walking slowly down the hallway, I managed to see her talking to another girl.

I stopped and glanced at her quickly. Maggie (what she was called) smiled back. She excused herself from these girls and walked over to me and replied to me how happy she was to know an upperclassman. It made her think that she was entitled to be on the board with the rest of the upper classmates. I knew that there was going to be more than this moment with Maggie and myself. "Happy holidays" were said, and we gave each other a tender hug of good cheer. I was so glad that I met this new friend of mine. I thought to myself, *When I will be leaving, maybe she would need a big sister. Should I be hers? Does she want one? Maybe yes, maybe no.*

CHAPTER 30

*T*HE HOLIDAY PARTY WAS FUN, but it was a lot of work, and I was
not the kind of person who enjoyed throwing parties. While I
might have predicted that organizing the party with Ms. Delight would
make me feel resentful, it didn't. One best way to make yourself happy is
to make other people happy; one best way to make other people happy
is first to be happy yourself.

The holiday concert was finished, and we were all looking forward to
going home for a few days; those of us that could, did. The anxiousness,
the anxiety, and our expectations of the holidays were upon us. Kaitlin
and Marybeth came down to my room for our typical hugs and kisses.
As always, we would write to one another and keep in touch during the
holidays. Ms. Hornet came by for us to get our baggage downstairs in
the lobby. She advised us to promptly go outside as we had to catch our
train home. Marybeth and Kaitlin were friends before coming to school;
both of them lived in the town of Pittsburgh, Pennsylvania. I knew for
sure that they would see each other during the holiday break.

Like most people, I could vividly remember my childhood and the
excitement I always felt during the Christmas season. The air seemed
filled with energy as the holiday neared and everyone fussed for days
to help in the celebration. There was nothing like it, especially for my
brothers and me. Our home was transformed into a warm and cozy
wonderland. A freshly cut Douglas fir stood poised in the living room,
trimmed with precious generations of old ornaments; garlands outlined

on mantles; mistletoe hung over doorways; and blazing logs crackled in the fireplace. The tantalizing smell of Aunt Suzie's freshly baked cookies and holiday breads filled the air. It was a time of visits from friends and happy family gatherings. I loved it. All the sights and smells and the family and friends were all present in one room for holiday cheer. However, nothing was more exciting than the anticipation of Santa Claus's magical visit.

We all knew who the mystical fellow was and whose name was Santa Claus. He definitely suggested the spirit of the season. He was one of the holiday's most beloved symbols. He worked all year in his North Pole workshop, creating toys and gifts for good little girls and boys the world over. It was not known how he did it, but each year, children awoke wide-eyed on Christmas morning to discover the special gifts he had left for them under the tree. He traveled the world round yet had never actually been seen. You would also see how Santa evolved over time, influenced by war, politics, and Madison Avenue. Fat, thin, serious, happy, colorful, and of course, mysterious, Santa had changed, perhaps even as we had changed, depending on the world's mood and social condition.

While I was reflecting about home and the holidays, I had to find Rebecca. After all, she was going to be my sister-in-law soon, and we really had to leave. I knew Ms. Hornet was going to be looking for us soon. I had to get back to reality. At this moment, I could hear Rebecca calling me through the halls.

I ran fiercely down the hall to Rebecca's voice. Rebecca asked if I was packed and ready to leave.

"Rebecca," I replied, "yes, but you know what we have to do before going home, don't you?" She laughed so hard and grabbed my hand, and as a tear was quietly flowing down her face, she managed to have a smile for me. "Yes, I do, let's go."

We ran quickly to the attic to say our good-byes. We opened the door knowing what we would see. Maybe our moms would be waiting for us. We knew that they would be there. Being in the attic for us was humorous and delightful. It became a musical adventure that represented dancing ghosts that refused to leave the attic. Mysterious sounds of the piano were always heard as the ghosts (our moms) chased around the attic. This clever original work for these young moms would work perfectly as a novelty on our next concert!

We couldn't wait to get their opinions on our music playing for next year. We would see. We threw them a kiss good-bye, knowing in our hearts they caught them. The images that we believed we saw gave us depth at times that would give us a rich, eerie detail.

Rebecca and I both agreed that grieving occurred in linear stages and offered up a very personal portrait of pain. "I just don't miss my mother's soul. I miss her laugh, her sarcasm, and the sound of her voice calling my name," Rebecca answered. I replied to Rebecca, "When my mom put me to bed, she would tuck me in and give me a good-night kiss and told me repeatedly that she loved me to death." I knew that it was clear to me now that we could love beyond the unknown.

We proceeded to depart the forbidden room and say our good-byes. They motioned to us to sit beside them. Rebecca and I told them that we hated good-byes, but in a few minutes, we had to leave this room, and we would see each other once again, after the holidays. "Could you—would you—let us hold your hands and kiss you? Is this a possibility?" Rebecca automatically moved closer to her mom and put her hand out. The vision took my hand, pulling it up towards her and then managed to put her arms around me, and then the mist in the air became surrounding. I then closed my eyes and felt the warmth of her body and Mom's kiss that would be burned on my lips forever.

A knock was at the door, which made both of us come back to reality. Who could hear us; no one knew of our secret visits. I turned, and Mom was gone along with the mist, smell, and their images. Our hearts gave a little jump as the door slammed behind us and we knew our moms just told us to get. I opened my eyes to an empty room; both had vanished. I approached the door immediately to see if anyone was present, but no one was to be seen. I do believe it was their way of telling us to depart and not worry about them and enjoy our holiday. Rapidly we left the attic since we still had to stop on the third floor to pick up our luggage to bring outside for departure. We left our bedrooms and took our suitcases downstairs and with one more glance of remembering. I then quietly closed the door behind me.

We knew in the lobby Ms. Hornet would be looking for us. "Girls, get in the car quickly. You will be late for your train." Once we reached the station, the porter helped us on the train and then put our suitcases on the platform into the compartments. We stood there saying our good-byes to our dear friends. "Until next semester, have a good holiday!" It was sad, but then again, a wonderful reflection of love was present among my friends and me. We all waved and shouted out to one another, "Merry Christmas to all and to all a good night." Still yearning for one more look of our moms, we raised our heads toward the heavenly sky. To no surprise, little snowflakes were steadily falling to make me wonder what part our moms played at this moment. I laughed to myself, believing in my heart that our moms were saying, "Merry Christmas to you, and to all a good night."

I boarded the train and sat near a window with Rebecca, which I liked doing the most. The ticket man approached me, and I gave him my ticket to Harrisburg. Rebecca was going to her aunt's house to meet her family for the holidays. Her ticket was to Altoona, Pennsylvania, close to us but yet so far. He looked at us and replied, "Good evening, ladies, how are you today?" I knew most of the workers on the train. This time it happened to be Mr. Nicholas, a wonderful man, so gentle and always so kind. I was very happy to see him and to be able to catch up on old times. He had worked for my dad for many years. I told Mr. Nicholas that it was a fine evening yet a little cool, but I was anxious to get home for the holidays. I wished Mr. Nicholas and his family a very merry Christmas and happy New Year. He appreciated my thoughts and told me to take care and send his regards to my brothers.

It seemed that it took forever to get home this evening. I managed to get a little bit of shut-eye until I arrived home. When I finally opened my eyes and looked out of the windows, I could see so many happy faces of my brothers. The train stopped with a sudden shriek of the wheels, and before you knew it, the porters were taking the suitcases off the train for those that were departing. Randy was the first one to be at the train and was wondering about his love Rebecca. With the look on his face, I knew he had many questions to ask. He just never seemed to shut up. "Randy, you big goof, you will see her sometimes during the holidays. She will be coming."

"When, how, what day, what time?" he randomly threw the questions out at me.

"Relax, calm down, she will notify you."

"Oh, I seem to forget, I have a letter for you, oops!" Randy was unable to come to this holiday concert since work was so busy. Yet still more to come, another year, a new love still to be understood.

We seemed to arrive home quickly, and I was grateful for that as the snow was falling slightly. Once I entered the house, I took notice that everything was put into place for the holidays. Mistletoe was hanging; the tree was decorated without one mistake. Samuel grabbed me and took a kiss under the mistletoe. I laughed like a silly four-year-old girl. Samuel said, "It's about time I robbed a kiss from my girl. I missed you, Annie, and I'm glad you're home for the holidays." This moment made me aware and pay attention to the little things I didn't have anymore. I did miss these special moments with my brothers. I couldn't wait until tomorrow when the whole town came down to celebrate with us. The songs of the holidays would be heard throughout the town; piano playing and laughing would be exhilarating. New faces would arrive and be welcomed in our home; everyone would come even if we didn't know them. A glass of cheer, a friendly smile, a good laugh, and some good memories to share with one another made this a special time.

Christmas morning was here, and as we all walked quietly down the steps, we all became little tots again. The only memory that was missing was Mom. All the gifts were shaken, and we looked to see whose package was larger or smaller, heavy or light. It seemed that these years never left any of us, but now we were still missing a package—good old Dad. Suddenly we heard Dad from upstairs putting on his slippers and getting his robe from the closet. Dad came down the steps, smiling from one ear to another, expressing his love to us, and replied, "This moment couldn't be any better to have all my children by my side. This is all the present I need from anyone.

"Thank you, my children, for being by my side, laughing, crying, and sometimes worrying what would happen to us after Mom's death. The strength of our family and love gave us the fortitude to cope and manage our grief. Let's now sit down and open our presents, and Dad will then make his special pancakes and eggs." Dad then yelled to us, "Who's on first?"

Sadly, the holidays came and went, and the time was here again for me to return to school. This time it was hard to handle, knowing that at the end of this year, I would have only one more year left at St. Claires. I was looking forward to the junior dance and all the new excitement that my school brought to the table each time I returned.

CHAPTER 31

I CAME TO GRIPS WITH THE fact that I had to control and deal with my emotions again as a young lady would. Anxiously, I waited to go back to school after the holidays. I was determined to learn as much as possible this year since I was going to graduate next year. Sometimes, I thought that I was part of a not-understood world. I just couldn't believe what a great Christmas it had been. I went from despising my best friend and being upset with her then to her becoming my best friend again before I departed for school. I just wished my dad had been as cool as my Aunt Suzie and Uncle Dan with my cousin Michael. Dad did welcome my cousin Michael into our home for the holidays, but with regrets. Michael was the son of Dad's brother, Joseph, whom he obviously wasn't fond of. Joseph could have grown up being a great brother, but most of the time; he took off when he felt like it. Dad was usually picking up the pieces by helping his family and parents to survive. After all, times were hard in this era. Michael could have perhaps found out about the confusing world much earlier if his dad was around more. It all ended OK though; after all, Uncle Joseph was at fault with dad, not Michael. It was surely sad that these two brothers just couldn't see eye to eye about anything. It was just that Dad remembered when Joseph always skipped out on doing chores or taking care of the little ones. Joseph was a great carpenter and didn't want to get any more education for himself. He was truly magnificent; I guessed that may be where Randy got his talent from, Uncle Joseph.

Dad, on the other hand, made up his mind that he wanted to run one of those big old trains from city to city.

Uncle Joseph had only one son, Michael, whom we all loved very much and really couldn't be with because of family differences. When he showed up, I think he just reminded Dad about his brother. No fault to Michael; he was really a great kid.

For all their differences, Dad and Joseph were the same philosophically. They both did make a point to treat people with respect and kindness. This was not always easy; Joseph had a bad temper and a stubborn personality. They did have an understanding that if things got too heated, they would walk away from each other and settle down. After all, words cannot be taken away once you speak them, and no matter what, words do hurt.

As I sat on the train, I found myself reflecting on the long and painful journey that had brought me back to really the best times in my life. I realized that maybe one person enters your life and puts the final puzzle piece in place and now you stepped into the ownership of who you were. I don't recommend tragedy to draw loved ones closer. I looked at all of us then and realized that our love had grown stronger and had aged. It was becoming richer now and a lot mellower for all of us to be able to handle.

Before I knew it, the train came to a sudden stop, and gloriously on the platform were so many old friends and new ones, like Maggie, waiting for our pickup from Ms. Hornet. I couldn't believe that she was late—not a word in Ms. Hornet vocabulary. I proceeded to get off the train, and there were so many girls waiting for a pickup.

I never saw so many students at one time being picked up to go back to St. Claire's. We all waited patiently on the platform for Ms. Hornet or someone to come for us. Time had passed; most of us were getting a little jittery waiting.

Now, the sun was going down and the sky was getting dim. The younger girls were starting to get a little panic-stricken. I convinced them all that it was OK and that someone would come. I was getting nervous after much deliberation with them. In the back of the train station, I heard some noise and clatter of horses' hooves in the dirt. It seemed that they were prancing quite quickly. As I turned to look, we had Mr. Grumbling, Ms. Alice, and Ms. Melissa with carriages, waving us to come and board. Anxiously, we all boarded, and no one dared ask the question about Ms. Hornet's mishap. Nevertheless, little old Annie couldn't hold her tongue. "Where is Ms. Hornet?" I replied. Mr. Grumbling very softly told me that she forgot the pickups for today. She was so busy planning her schedules for the classes that would start on Monday; she just lost control of the time.

"Annie, I am quite upset with her, but after all, we all do have a moment when we forget. Since you and everyone else are safe and sound, I'm contented. I knew some of the older girls were on these trains and, as mother hens; you would protect your nests. I'm sure you were one to step up to the plate. Before you say anything, thank you.

"Let's get to the school and check everyone in. I want to make sure everyone is accounted for and the girls have their proper rooms. This was a very exhausting day, I'm just so glad that I have so many good people I can count on." The carriages pulled up, and we all swiftly got out of the carriages and ran to the desk for check-in by Ms. Hornet. Quietly, she said, "Do not run, girls. Someone will fall."

We put on our brakes and slowly got into an orderly line, checked in, and proceeded to go to our rooms. I too was so glad that this journey was finally over and now I could get down to business. Sleep was looking wonderful right now.

The morning sun came up fast, and I was so excited to see my friends Marybeth, Kaitlin, and Rebecca, who were so concerned as I knew they would be. I explained all the confusion, and at the end of the day, it was no big deal. Lining up in the hallway was such a wonderful way to start my new semester. I couldn't believe I was talking like this. If you would have asked me several years ago, I would have wanted to go home.

Breakfast was typical, and now we were juniors that everyone wanted to sit with. Who shall we allow? We ask each other. Smarter than others would be a good choice, we felt. Schedules were passed out, and the bells rang to start another semester here at St. Claire's. Here goes, off to the wilds, practice, laughing, and having a fantastic time.

At the end of the day, all the juniors had an unannounced meeting. We had to select the candidates for our senior officers. The hands were raised, and nominees were selected. The votes were tallied. Mr. Grumbling came into the auditorium and made the announcement that I had been selected for president of my class. I saw Rebecca in the hall after all was said and done. Now I knew why I was confused when I couldn't find one junior in a class or in any hallway. Excitingly, I explained we had our class elections. "Don't you want to know who had the votes for president, vice president, and treasurer? Of course you know that it was Marybeth, Kaitlin, and me. How is the class going to get any better than us running it?" Rebecca laughed and nodded to go back to class quickly and try to get serious.

As we proceeded to go to the pub in town, Rebecca asked, "Who was elected for what? Do I always have to ask the questions? Who really cares who got what position? What matters is that you are all together—working, laughing, and maybe putting in some hard time once in a while."

All day long, I was on cloud nine and so excited about the election. I just couldn't wait to return to the attic to see Mom. Boy, how I missed her immensely. I wanted to tell her everything—my feelings, my shortcomings—and question her, how do I really handle all this attention? I actually don't like the dark, but sometimes I had to go into the forbidden room, into the unknown, to get my questions and concerns answered and out of my head. It's as if the attic was a beautifully decorated bedroom painted with ballerinas and glowing sunshine stuck in the corner. In the mist of all of this were angels sounding their horns and cheering for hope and love. Once I approached it and I was in it, I was glad I'm there. I'm really afraid of it though. "Rebecca, maybe that's why I like to go to our special room. It's something you have to be a bit brave about. You have to be scared of it because it tests you not to run away from it. My first impulse is, do you want to go there again into this darkness and into the strange occurrences? Rebecca and I realized that now was not the time to wander, but surely, once we heard the notes, it would be only then that we would know our destiny.

CHAPTER 32

THE TALK OF THE SCHOOL was the upcoming Presidents' Day dance, which was only for juniors. Tickets were going on sale today and would be sold in the front lobby for those who were interested. The whole junior class of women would be attending for sure. We knew that the charming young gents from St. Pete's High School were also eligible to attend this dance. St. Pete's School was a partner school for our events when we had coed functions. It seemed that if we had an event without St. Pete's being there, it just wouldn't be right.

Mr. Grumbling was looking for girls to handle the sales up front in the lobby for the next two weeks. Someone had to balance the sale of the tickets and collect the money. Well, the trio of Marybeth, Kaitlin, and I volunteered of course; who else would be so excited with the task? The class officers did have responsibility and had to set an example now, didn't we? Since we were nominated for the officers of our senior class, we felt that it was our responsibility to put ourselves out there. Our junior class had faith in us to do the right thing for them and us too. Most likely, that was why they voted for us.

We would persuade girls not sure of attending the dance to be attending before they left the table. This was what Mr. Grumbling wanted, 100 percent participation. All the girls had no trouble talking to us; we were talented, smart, and caring individuals. We knew how to handle whom at this point. Spending the last two semesters with them gave us that privilege of going mentally deeper with each one rather than just knowing them on the surface. Most of the girls respected us, and why not? After all, we were so charming yet so damn cute.

The trio was all in the debating club, spelling bee challengers, and charm club and participated in sports on all levels. Let's not forget appeal, beauty and brains. Not to boast a little. We made up large poster signs and had other girls help us paint them. A committee was selected to post them all over the school. This was really a coming-out party for the young junior ladies to meet the fine gents in an exceptional and proper atmosphere. This was an outstanding time for sure and one that we all waited for—to be juniors. To us, that meant one more year closer to graduation. Respected young guys would be coming to this dance, and we had our pick of the litter. *It can't get much better than this*, I told myself.

We were up front in the lobby any time we were free. One of us represented the class always. Our purpose was to bury a bomb under those girls that had insecurities about going. Our aim was to sell every girl a ticket and maybe hook them up with someone from St. Pete's. It was now the week of the dance, and every junior girl had bought a ticket. So satisfied was Mr. Grumbling and Mr. Jockey from St. Pete's on the ticket sales. You definitely would have a blast even if you didn't have a beau. Today's transportation was being provided for us by Mr. Grumbling's driver. Ms. Alice had to present the money and total number of tickets sold. Headmaster Mr. Airy felt this was the best dance given by our school. Ms. Alice pulled us out of our classes, and we knew the fun was just ready to begin. We would get a head start checking out the guys. Ms. Alice knew the anticipation that we had; going over, she politely gave a pat on our laps and said, "Please cool down. Make it a memorable day. This could be a first-rate, impressible meeting face-to-face or a poor one. Your choice."

The Presidents' Day dance was coming upon us soon. Presidents' Day weekend was just around the corner. Money was in and tickets were all sold. We did a tremendous job; getting everyone in the junior class to attend was grand. I had the sudden realization that I was in danger of maybe not having a dress for this occasion. Of course, I had the concert dress that I was planning to wear, but this is the Presidents' Day dance, a big deal. I grasped two things: I wasn't as happy as I could be, and maybe my life would change at a single moment if I met the right young gent. I thought long and hard, and I knew if I would ask Aunt Suzie, she would whip something up for me.

I began with one simple strategy—sit down and write her. I told Aunt Suzie that I still felt her connection and warmth and her hugs when I wasn't with her. Her hugs were very clear that they made me feel special when I recalled my memories. Being very cool in the letter, I asked if she could whip me up a dress for the dance, maybe red, white, and blue.

Of course, in no time flat, a delivery was sent to me at the school. Aunt Suzie had already been working on the dress and was going to surprise me. It was marvelous as always. Red, white, and blue—they certainly were the appropriate colors of a Presidents' Day dance. I was so glad that my aunt used colors that matched the flag. A red and white neckline with beads and an extra skirt underneath for more flare when I danced. I was so grateful to Aunt Suzie; she was always there when I needed her. This came as no surprise to me or anyone in school that I had this beautiful dress to show off to my peers. Aunt Suzie and I had a very strong, affectionate bond with each other, and this was surely the key to happiness. In fact, it was the key to happiness. For sure it was my happiness.

This dance was so important to all of us, the moment to meet the proper gentlemen that could remain in our life. This dance had a special theme, special invitations, but always traditional tablecloths. Napkins were a must to prevent sticky fingers. Colorful cloth napkins—of course red, white, and blue—which we tied with yarn or hair bows. Not even gale-force winds could keep all the junior girls away from this fest party. "Those who brave the wild weather show up with bells, and those who are afraid of challengers end up sitting home. Your choice of what you prefer.

"You must remember that your bright, bubbly personality attracts many a friend and admirer. So does your inclination to create fun whenever you go—mixed, of course, with a bit of twinkly-in-the-eye trouble helps. Most of my friends are spontaneous solos who find joy in the little things. We think that life's possibilities are endless, and we try to seize as many of those as we can. Understanding that quick wit likely makes you the life of the party. You're determined to share generously your magical, loving spirit with others. You put true values, love, friendship, and traditional ideals over worldly gain. That's why your loved ones appreciate you, maybe more than you know. You rival the awakened spirit in your appreciation of the past seasons' joy, gathering those loved ones near at home.

"It is now Saturday night, and perhaps you will find all your dreams rolled into one basket. So when you approach the dance, go in and pick the best apple out of the bunch and walk in style, smile with poise, and remember that St. Peter's Prep is where all the young fine men come from. At this moment, you have to pick the best of the litter. Go for it!"

Party chef Mr. Ryan made it very simple, easy to enjoy items that minimized mess. Beverages were in dainty teacups for us or mugs for the male group. After all, they certainly didn't want to have punch in a tea cup, now, would they?

I was going back and forth to St. Peter's often these days. I had to drop off tickets and meet with Dex and Roger once or twice weekly. They were the responsible boys for the ticket proceeds at St. Pete's. My idea of a good catch would be these two guys. I did think that they were really cute, well "appealing," those that you would see at a college party. This Saturday night was the Presidents' Day dance, which was always held at St. Pete's. One would wonder why at their school and not ours. St. Pete's was a larger school and had a larger gym to accommodate the amount of students that would be attending. Most importantly, it was for the dancing.

Before you knew it, the carriages and cars were waiting to take us all over to St. Pete's for the big event. When we walked in the front entrance, waiting for us were Roger and Dex. They were the officers for their class, so it was appropriate that they would be at the door. We weren't surprised at all that Dex would be greeting us; after all, Dex and Alessandra were already a couple before the dance. I was sure he was eager to see her. They had met at a golf outing this past summer, which Dex's father sponsored. Most of us just couldn't wait to meet him on a one-to-one. Dex's reaction to Alessandra when we first approached was a little bit astounding. Dex seemed like he couldn't wait to disappear with Alessandra. When the dancing started, it looked as if he wanted to escape or make a run for it. Yet he never seemed that he wanted to leave her; they sure gave us that impression that they were hooked up for life.

Kaitlin, Marybeth, and I saw them in the hallway, and it appeared that this was a luscious, wonderful, and ultimate meeting of two soul mates. I got the feeling that Dex was waiting for his first kiss. Boy, was he dreaming. I didn't think this would happen so quickly with Alessandra; she knew how to be a lady. It could have been why he seemed so distant and maybe a little less agreeable with her.

What did we know, Marybeth, Kaitlin, and I? We certainly weren't experienced girls with the boys—hand holding, eye winking, and putting ourselves out there. Now we had to be reckoned with on the dance floor and make sure the boys kept their hands where they belonged. Not on our bottom for sure. My dad paid all this money for me to be a lady, and I certainly wasn't going to disappoint him with my lifestyle.

Dex was an ambitious son of a working-class Irish immigrant. His father gained entry into a world of pedigreed wealth and privilege through charm and smarts, but would he always be defined by where he came from? A gripping and sweeping rumination on the American class system of hope, wealth, and desire was Dex's dad. He was a supreme class act. It seemed no one could follow Mr. O'Brien, Dex's father.

Many energetic dance numbers were on hand. We thought that the trio couldn't be broken but we declined easily with everybody. The game of boy and girl terrified me and yet delighted me. Boys are generally simple, joyous, and goofy and yes, completely exhausting.

Dance a fox-trot, waltz, or maybe a lindy. Blast your charming talent and yet have a challenging platform of gaming fun, marked by exceptional design. This was where good and bad choices would dictate your outcome. We were mostly preoccupied with our own agenda, and we really didn't even hear one another talking. Yet not enough time at all to listen to one another for a second.

Knowing how each one of us felt about different situations, we didn't question one another. Nevertheless, we all saw the boys as heroes. Christian, one of the charmers, was a silent type with glowing blue eyes, solving intricate mechanical puzzles across surreal terrain, depicted only in a silhouette for us to find him. Were we one of his dream girls? We were not playing a jealous triangle. Just trying to make a good choice, have fun, and grow up a little more.

Lo and behold, as we approached Dex, he had several cute friends for us to meet. Dex brought with him the gentlemen that were known as the good prospects—Roger, Simon, Parker, Edward, and Christian, thank God. I was so glad that Christian was part of the mix. It surely helped us to prepare for the anxiety and idealistic steps that would happen now. I was still having trouble wrapping my mind around this stunning success of the dance and the good looks of the boys. I never imagined I'd be wearing this beautiful dress at sixteen years old and getting chased by boys, whom I hated growing up. Fooled, wasn't I, to think that way? So I was crossing my fingers that we would all have a good time.

The boys had the refreshing opportunity to give us a real performance tonight. Meeting these boys with no expectations of the outcome, they left us for a moment, and before we knew it, they were on the platform stage to perform. Performing for us, how wonderful, I hoped. They gave their hearts and souls to give us a real live performance for those in attendance in the gym. It was complete with guitar solos, piano playing, and lyrics that were astounding to all that could hear within ear's reach.

The lead singer of the band was a great guy, Keith Kenney. He had the biggest green eyes, had light brown hair, was six feet tall, and was very broad to say the least. Keith was a personable guy yet so shy in his actions. He was so tender, and his rough edge was so manly. Any girl would just fall at his feet, but his feet were falling in front of my girlfriend Marybeth. I noticed that Alessandra looked as if she was going to try and claim him first. The battle of the women—it just never ends when men are involved now, does it? It looked like Alessandra may have been done with Dex. Surprised, more importantly, I think Dex was completely baffled.

Once they were finished playing, they took their bows and the cheering was electrifying. The boys jumped off the stage, and many girls wished that they could catch them. Before you knew it, the dance music had restarted, and the floor became a masterpiece for those who loved to lindy. Keith made sure that the top fifty songs of the music world were selected first. There were boys everywhere, a whopping one hundred of them.

These boys were also in the same grade, which made it an adventure of joy and pleasure. It made it very convenient to come forth and announce any problem at hand. Any boy that went to St. Peter's Prep was from very a respectable family, either famous or highly accredited in one way or another. We gazed at them as featured guests who just made the top ten lists for the month. I was just happy to be where I was at this moment. I hoped my characteristic traits and my attributes would be my best highlights when I was introduced to one of the normal yet distinguished boys on the dance floor. I just couldn't wait to have the most excitement tonight than I ever had in my lifetime during my sixteen years.

I loved everything that Edward had done for me tonight. I felt like it was disrespectful for me not to feel anything toward Edward. You know the love thing—the moment, the kiss, and the right time. Well, I was still waiting for it to happen. I had a very high opinion of Edward, and I admired his qualities. When I arrived at the dance, he had the most beautiful flowers in his hands ready to give me. He really took the effort to find the perfect flowers to match my dress. They were beautiful and hard to imagine. Sometimes like many we have differences but I appreciate his genuineness. My mind is telling me that he was a great guy, and my biology and chemistry told me that maybe he was a loser. What I heard about him blew me away; it's that he was known as a happy party guy. Edward was totally into music writing. Now this could be the fun stuff that I was looking for but didn't see it. He had so much charisma and personality, which was usually hard to find in a sixteen-year-old boy. He wrote music for big parties that were live and for big entertainment celebrities. I think maybe this is one guy was going to go all the way with his talent, even though I had nothing to compare it to.

It was hypnotic and very catchy, his writing. The very first time I heard it, I thought it was wonderful. He was going to hit acceptability and popularity soon I was sure. He had the appeal, and I loved it. Literally, I was waiting on tables today at school since I had lunch hour chore. I was really having a crappy day. I heard his song playing in the background, and it made me feel at ease. It was one of those songs that I thought was going to be really critically acclaimed in the future. I thought this was the single recording that was going to break him out from that young high school crowd. As good as his songs were, he was just a total star. I think he had great potential and had good subject matter. God, it made me queasy when he smiled. "I'll forgive you if I outlive you." Yep, we were just two lovebirds that were meant for each other—so my friends told me. I just couldn't see it, but I was trying.

I certainly couldn't believe that my mind began wondering thinking about James and Dan; now how did they get into my thoughts? I was telling my friends that maybe I should be putting my interest in Rebecca's brothers. They surely were also good candidates to fall in love with. Kaitlin and Alessandra were gliding on the dance floor, looking for a hot date, maybe long-term or maybe just for the evening.

One boy, Christian, was surely an item to clearly think about. He was the head of the class in academics. Now we all knew this was a good trait. Would he be the select one or a good possibility for one of us? I caught Roger checking out both my friends; it looked as if he fell for both of them, but that was not possible. Christian, on the other hand, was about 6⊠3⊠ tall and had the broadest shoulders and deepest blue eyes that you would like to look into. He was so polished, sweet, and gentle. I didn't think Christian had an angry bone in his body. I noticed that he asked Kaitlin to dance several times tonight; maybe he was a little sweet on her. My friends and I noticed that she didn't seem to push him away so much while they were dancing. He held her really tight to his body when they were dancing slowly. He was physically a powerful, strapping man for sure. I thought, could I like a guy like this? Standing on the sidelines, we watched as she was delirious while dancing. My guess was that we would see shortly after this event. Sometime soon, I was sure.

Marybeth was stuck on Keith, and I was truly trying to give some of my thought to good old Edward to love. Well, it wasn't easy for most of us to get hooked up on this evening of dreaming and hoping that our vision would be a reality and not a pipe dream or a castle in the sky. I told my friends, "You just can't fall in love with every boy and dreamy yarn spinner. It packs heart, humor, and more tragedy but more hope if you do. We know that we will see them again at the spring formal or the school's picnic. We're certainly not going to make it like we'll never see them again. It will happen, maybe the next co share school event?"

Looking back in my memory bank and remembering the hopeless romantic girl that I once was, I remembered the innocent girl who once had a crush on a wonderful guy and how careless I was with his heart, which I should never have been. I suddenly had a realization I was in danger of wasting my life being with only one man. Breaking up with Sean Cassidy around Christmas last year was a difficult time, which may or may not have been a coincidence. I just sat back and tried to remember my emotions, my first love, first kiss, and heartbreak and didn't know if I was ready for that again. Sean would always be part of my heart, today and forever.

He was a sweet boy from a small town outside the city of Harrisburg. I met him at the farmer's market one day while Dad and I were shopping. After that day, I made a point of always going with Dad to the market, hoping to see him again, which I did. Time went by, and Sean and I became good friends. He was so adorable that I just couldn't resist his muscular, well-built body. His family owned one of the farms on the other side of my town. It became a date every time I saw him. Dad knew I wanted to go with him only to see Sean Cassidy. I melted when he held my hand and gave me my first kiss. No girl forgets this at all. I would say my good-byes and leave him to go home regretfully.

This was very difficult for us, to depart from each other time in and time out. When I reached home, I wrote about everything in my daily journal. I never wanted to forget any details of our time together. He was gentle as a dove, and with him I felt like I was always flying over the beautiful clouds in the air. Romantic, yes it was. We always enjoyed each other's company, and our market dating went on for years. Sometimes I would wonder what his family was like, his home and surroundings. I never had that chance to do so. I would regret that sometimes.

I explained about Dad wanting me to go to a private school, and most likely, it was going to happen once I took the exams for several girls' academies. I knew it would only be a matter of time before Dad selected a school for me in the upcoming fall. I was going away to school, and who knew when I would ever see him again? Summers would be with my family and friends for sure. I told Sean that I most likely would never be able to get back to the farmers' market again. It was tough and hard to admit this, but it had to be done. A very effective way for me to change my emotions was to act the way I wish I felt. "Fake it till you feel it." Really does work. We walked our last walk, and he gave me a gentle kiss of good-bye. I walked away with my heart broken, and I'm sure he felt the same. It just had to be done. We both knew this was going to be our history and hoped in time, if destiny was for sure, we would meet again.

It was an emotional roller coaster being in love. I told the girls to just be aware that love was grand, but the hurt that may be attached was horrifying. The first minute that I got that halfhearted response from him, I knew I was in the wrong place. We sometimes look for a deep dive into a fascinating family that feels very real and fully grounded in our time. Prestige, power, and respectability were so grand to wear on our sleeve. Think about the issues that may be a conflict if you're not on the same page. Separations and breaking up is hard, but the results will be good. It is what it is.

The dance was over, the balloons fell from the ceiling, and the last song was played. All in all, it was a very demanding evening for most. The guy you met, the dance you had, and his gentle touch on your body would never be forgotten. Most of us used our precious time for academics or practicing our piano not for romance so this evening would become very emotional. Ms. Hornet and Ms. Alice were two of the chaperones for the dance. As we boarded the bus, we giggled and laughed how the two of them were on guard duty, making sure the hands stayed in place. They went into a sweat at one time; counting heads, checking the punch, and making sure no one disappeared on the courts too long. It seemed for a short time, though, that some of the girls drifted outside without them realizing.

Saying our good-byes to the boys after the dance was difficult, but we knew we would see them again since Alessandra and Dex were an item. Some of us were trying to make arrangements on Sunday that some of the boys would come over to our school and hang out by the lake. I thought to myself, would I see Roger, Simon, Christian, Edward, or Parker again? Maybe we could meet by the lake in the future? Or meet in church? Who was to say? Life is what it is. I did know that maybe Marybeth and Alessandra were in a fantasy world when they departed. The trance that they both were in was a hallucination I would believe. I told the two girls to open their eyes wide. "Don't look now, but we are on our way back to school. It's time to put your feet back on the ground and get your thoughts back to this world with us, OK?"

Overall it was an impressive and majestic time, and I hoped if some would match up, they would have the opportunity to see them again. Just another day of enjoying life and being a teenager and having the social event go well. Here's to our presidents, hip, hip, hooray!

Ms. Alice clapped her hands as usual for our attention and then said, "As we celebrate our independence and express our gratitude for our freedom that we enjoy, thanks to all the military and public servants that keep our country strong and are always ready for a fight to win." She reminded us the reason for the dance and what and who we should be celebrating—our country, presidents, and our grand old flag. Ms. Alice was one to keep us grounded in our ideals.

CHAPTER 33

ARRIVING LATE AND HAVING CHURCH early the next day, we all quickly went to our rooms. I think, in a flash, when our blanket came over us, it took seconds for most to be sleeping. Rebecca stopped at my room to see if it was as wonderful as she had remembered. "It sure is," I replied. I started to tell her about the young gentleman that I met who was quite charming. She looked at me so seriously and said, "What about Dan, my brother?"

"Oh yeah, I forgot about him." I started to laugh, and she realized that I was just teasing her. Wondering about our moms, I asked if they were up to their shenanigans. "Not for tonight since they had a dance to go to, remember?" Rebecca gave me a sweet kiss on my forehead and made sure that I was tucked in for the night. Here I thought I was so much of a hotshot tonight, going to this dance and meeting a great guy. At this moment, I felt as if I was four years old again when Rebecca gave me a tender kiss on my forehead. It was a humble gesture from Rebecca to me. I respected her; she was not any ordinary person. If I had to label her to anyone that asked my portrait of her, it would be wonderful, distinguished, striking, impressive, and let's not forget beautiful and kind.

Morning came so quickly, and those of us who were ready for church were in the lobby to go to mass at 8:00 a.m. Sunday was your own personal time. Rebecca and I always started with the Lord. Rebecca and my friends went to mass early since this day would be fresh air and physical activity. Riding bicycles was going to be a big part of our new physical activity by the lake. Many of the girls at school received them for Christmas this year. It was a new way to get exercise and to have fun. A few of my friends brought them back to school for all of us to enjoy. It was fantastic for us to try them out, difficult and challenging for most. Stretching out on a blanket on the damp grass and feeling the balmy breezes on your face also was breathtaking.

It was mid afternoon, and the day was picture-perfect. The sun was warm, and the food in our basket was cooked just a little bit delicately. In the opening of the trees, who appeared but a few of the chaps from St. Peter's? The boys had arrived to play some ball. Dex, Roger, Parker, Christian, Keith, Simon, and good old Edward came running over to be part of our game. Alessandra, Kaitlin, Marybeth, and I were having a great time throwing a ball around on the grass. I told Maggie to come over with some of her friends, which she did. Once Maggie walked over, the heads sure turned wondering who this beauty was. I introduced her and her friends to the guys. Needless to say, the charm and the politeness were seen and were evident from the boys. They definitely wanted to impress Margaret and her friends.

Maggie was so glad to have the offer to come. The boys ended up joining in, and of course, boys will be boys, and they just had to show off their masculine ways. The shirts came off and the pants rolled up, and before you knew it, some of us were being tackled by those big old brutes. Hmm, maybe not so bad after all. Rebecca and a few others decided to take a walk around the lake. After all, Rebecca was way too old for this nonsense. As the sun went down and dinner was almost about ready to be served, it was time for all of us to go.

How exciting was this day? Fun and laughter all rolled into one, plus we were able to see the guys. Rebecca gave us the look to depart. We gathered our items and proceeded to go to the dining room. We said our good-byes politely to the guys and hoped to see them again. "Let's not forget to wash first," yelled Rebecca. She sometimes could be a mother that's not around. Amusing sometimes, but also could be a pain.

We proceeded to go to our rooms, drop off our items, wash quickly, and meet one another in the cafeteria. I suddenly felt a tap on my shoulder. I turned quickly to see that no one was present. My imagination was questioned. Was it Mom, making sure I was OK tonight? I nodded to Rebecca that I had concern, and she knew it by looking at me. I left the cafeteria in a panic. Somehow I had to go to the attic now. Quickly, I ran to the attic, and Rebecca followed me. I had to see, like Rebecca, if the room was secured. After all, it was mine and Rebecca's entire universe. Were they concerned about the social? Were they thinking of what happened to boys and men when they realized that the world wasn't the sparkly planet they had been hoping for? Did they just leave you, feeling no hope and feeling hungry for life, and drop you on the dance floor, questioning what you did? Or did they wish more was at stake this evening, a kiss and a touch? Believe me; they weren't just looking for the doughnuts.

I went reluctantly into the attic to see the usual mist, aroma, and shadow of someone in the distance of the room. We looked at each other. We somehow knew this was not our moms. The truth was, I think neither one of us thought that this was very promising, though I was nervous. "I understand that you may want to speak to me since I received the tap on the shoulder during meals?" The shadow nodded. I was baffled and more and more; all I could do was see a change in the mist. It was sure frustration. There was a stare too. It was a look that I had never seen but never could tell if it was joy or disappointment. Who was this unknown soul looking for someone to notice him or be aware of his presence? Maybe wanting someone to just take an interest or awareness that he did exist.

I knew that there was a reason for all this to happen now. I asked Rebecca, "Why were we told during registration that the attic was the forbidden room that no one shall ever try to enter? Why would Mr. Grumbling be so concerned about anyone knowing this? Right from our first meeting with Mr. Grumbling, it was mentioned. There is a mystery to this room. Forget our moms; no one understood their existence, only you and I. Mr. Grumbling certainly wouldn't be telling new students about them. It had to be another issue, something that no one ever spoke about. Well, it is my duty," I told Rebecca, "to find out the truth about the old attic room."

Without anyone realizing, I started to question the older workers on campus, the head chef, and the gardeners and started to read about the school in depth. It was known that during the history of the school, a young guard, who was posted at the front gate, got involved deeply with a girl at the school. They would meet in the attic to spend time with each other. He was much older than she, and they fell deeply in love. Once the parents found out about their romance, they made many waves and wanted many questions to be answered. How were they able to see each other? Where were the teachers, the headmistress, or headmaster during all this involvement? It caused a rumpus on the campus, and the school had to stop the gossip immediately.

After all, who would want their daughter to go to a school so renowned and respected if this went on? Time passed, and they managed to break up the two. The girl's parents removed her from school, and Mr. Grimes was able to stay on until the semester ended. The couple was so heartbroken to think that they would never be able to see each other again. It weighed very heavily with both of them.

The last day of school, no one was able to find Mr. Grimes. He couldn't be found in his post, which was at the front gates. It seemed that Mr. Grimes had vanished into thin air. Knowing that he couldn't see Beth ever again was ghastly and gruesome to him. The day passed, and Mr. Grimes became missing, not showing up for his job, and not calling in sick. It seemed as if he had just disappeared. A campus—and town-wide search was done for several weeks, trying to find him, but to no avail. The town police, the campus security, friends, and family were questioned about his whereabouts. Time had passed, and on this one dismal day, when the sun wasn't shining and the birds weren't chirping, the maintenance men were asked to go to the attic to get some desks down to replace the old ones for the upcoming classes in September.

To their dismay, as the workers advanced toward the attic, there was a terrible stench. They had to cover their mouths with handkerchiefs; it was so wicked. Opening the door very carefully, they approached the room to see where the horrifying smell was coming from since no one knew where or why. It was a shock, what they saw. Mr. Grimes wrote a suicide note to his lover, Ms. Beth. As they slowly got to the door, they lifted the lamp once more to make sure that their shock was correct. The light shined fully in the mirror of the old bureau where it was left last year tightly against the wall. The worker in charge saw a cloud of white vapor and a mist surrounding a head and shoulders of a man. A rope was knotted tightly about his neck, his eyes were bulging in their sockets, and his tongue slightly protruded from the side of his mouth. He looked straight at the men as if he could see right through them. Mr. Grimes just couldn't live without her. Of course, a story like this had to be stopped and not gossiped about. Who would attend St. Claire's if the cat got out of the bag? I didn't think my dad would have let me come here, knowing this. Rebecca couldn't believe what she was hearing from me. Very softly Rebecca asked, "Annie, is this all true?"

"What do you think? Am I the type to tell old wives' tales over the truth? Come on, Rebecca, you know it's the truth. But it is so sad though, isn't it? True love and yet lost so early.

"Maybe, this is why our moms are so protective of us. His soul still lives on in the attic. Now I know when we go upstairs, how reluctant our moms could be with us being present. I do believe he's a good old soul and wouldn't hurt a fly. I sure hope, he doesn't decide to present himself to us on any occasion. I'm sure Mr. Grimes, this poor old soul, just has to reveal himself to anyone so his spirit may have some outcome of destiny."

Reluctantly, I proceeded to get up and back down the stairs; I couldn't say a word in this small room. I felt trapped but knew there was nothing I could do about it. I told Rebecca the feeling was one of protection and for me to be aware, that there was a presence still in the room. Not gone forever, just for this time to be brought back with the exquisiteness of music. Mr. Grimes was to be pitied; imagine being taken away from your loved one then separated forever. How could one deal with this agony? I did hope that someday, he would be at peace and return to the wonderful white clouds of heaven and be happy. Maybe our moms could help him on the other side. Rebecca reminded me not to whisper this to anyone. Mr. Grumbling could take action against the two of us since we didn't obey the sacred St. Claire's rules.

I was sorry that I couldn't stay any longer for tonight. "It's OK, just go to bed and relax, and maybe our mothers will put us to sleep tonight with the sounds of their magical notes. I'm sure of it, Annie. Good night for now."

The time flew by, spring was here, and the end of June was in our midst. We had so many events this year The spring was so exciting; it introduced the new blooming lilacs. It's a bloomer range in May, this powerful lilac flower. It soon would be covered in heavy clusters of sweetly scented blooms. The bush continued to bloom until the frost. I, like Rebecca, loved the blooming of the lilac, and it took us to memories of our moms. It seemed as if they came back to life every spring and then spent time with us till the flowers withered away in the fall. I was glad they were home now for a while.

CHAPTER 34

PRING WAS IN THE AIR, and our spring concert was prepared to be a typical triumph as always. The underclassmen would give their best performances for their families and friends. It gave them the opportunity to play superb and stand up and be counted. The eleventh graders usually performed the solos, and if a ninth or tenth grader got fortunate, they also would have the opportunity to show their special qualities. The instruments got tuned to perfection, and voices were blessed. You knew the moment was timely when you heard the fingers play flawlessly and the voices sing to what the doctor had just ordered. The performance is a picture-perfect textbook. The bows are taken, and you know at this time it is a splendid concert to acknowledge. This is to be admired and put in the books as one of the high-flying, outstanding concerts. Our younger girls were so gifted with much talent and poise, thanks to all the educators in their life.

The girls clear the stage and go promptly to their loved ones. They now became striking, respectable young ladies not to be reckoned with. Now the cheers were loud and everyone celebrated these well-liked young ladies who were not yet famous and were just ordinary people.

Everyone gave their thanks to the staff and nuns who oversaw their girls during these special years at St. Claire's. It did prove to be well worth the effort, money, and time.

Again, the hugs and kisses and a few tears for some when departure was accepted. Summertime approached, and I went back to my hometown to visit family and friends from childhood. It was a great way to clear my head and get away from it all. I thought about fireworks and homemade popsicles and farmers working so hard to make sure their harvest came in for the summer. You captured and enjoyed the very best of the sun. Because it's the first month of summer vacation, June is the perfect time to just play, relax, dream, and enjoy every moment.

In school, sometimes everything becomes overpowering. I knew when I got home, it was now time to relax, enjoy family, and have great fun. In the end, it could diminish your frustration, anxiety, and a lot of unknown questions. Learning just to let go to enjoy playing outside was so wonderful. Not to worry about exams and practice and sometimes also reminding yourself that you didn't have to be so perfect.

To have relaxing fun took no effort; you didn't have to work on skills or make plans on how to do this. I looked forward to this summer maybe more than others. I knew that next summer; I would have to pursue other ideals such as college, maybe marriage, who knew what path my life would end on? I did wish that I would always have the energy, though, because without energy, I wouldn't be able to do the activities that made me the happiest now.

When I would go home, I would take my cousin Claire out for a nice walk and sometimes pick up a treat on the way back. Ice cream always put us in a great mood. I found reading a good book and sharing my thoughts by writing them down were easier to handle when bored. Spending time with each of my brothers and Dad was an important part of my summer days. We ate dinner as a family, and for those forty-five minutes at the table, it was as if time has just stopped. Summer allowed me to pause temporarily and chat with family and friends and stroll to the lake whenever the mood arose. There was nothing wrong with listening to my own needs once in a while when life felt swept away.

My special thought of one day was when I remembered my time with Dad up at the lake. Dad found it difficult to go back to the lake; after all, this was where Mom passed away. It was a wonderful day, and of course, I was swimming. I turned around briskly, and there was good old Dad deciding to take a time-out for a nap. I thought it was the perfect time for a water fight. I surprised him with a bucket of water, and at that time, our battle had just begun. Dad jumped up quickly and managed to get one empty bowl to fill and repeat the same routine to me. We chased each other around the lake until he gave in and said that I was the queen of the water splash. No way could my brothers outdo me on this battle. We laughed for a while; in fact, I had to sit down on the blanket because of the pain in my stomach from laughing.

However, laughter turned into more splashes. I proceeded toward the water then lost my balance and grabbed Dad and dumped us both in the water. We were laughing so hard, we could barely get back in the boat. When we paddled back to the dock, the canoe had to be hoisted on our shoulders. We all knew that the best part of today was that tomorrow we could do this all over again. The day was absolutely watertight, maybe even picture-perfect.

Day was starting to turn to evening, and Dad and I knew it was time to head on home. We knew that the family should be back from work now. I was sure my brother Randy did a good job of cooking. His special dinners were fabulous and superb. He wanted to cook something special tonight before I went back to school. So much time it seemed before my return to school, but ironically, it would go at a speedy pace. Randy and I had that special bond between us. Most of the time, I felt like bopping him over the head, but usually, I loved him tremendously. He really was a cool guy, my brother Randy.

This year was one of those record-breaking hot summers. I enjoyed this season so much, not because I went home to see my family but because of the brightly colored flowers that produced nectar throughout the season. The best was that you can cater to butterflies right now by planting late-season flowers. Butterflies actually preferred untidy gardens, giving you permission to sit back and enjoy the show. One thing I knew was that summer flew past us so quickly.

We didn't have to plan fancy dinners just to be able to hang out with our loved ones. Figuring things out together was all part of keeping your attachment to one another strong. I knew that when I would leave home, one of the most important things was to stay connected. Just not too connected. I found that family, friends, work, and play worked as one. They all came together in a house built for get-togethers for all seasons.

Summer's big hurrah was as casual as a holiday—food on the open fires, going barefoot, and splashing in the lake on a delightful day. I couldn't wait until the Fourth of July; it was all about having old-fashioned fun with family and friends. To look out my window and find my best friends Jessica and Samantha sitting on my big old porch swing and waiting for me to come outside is superb. Usually we stayed on the swing for most of the day. During the day, you could count on Aunt Suzie to bring out some of her special cookies. Down the road a bit was a pond that some of us would go to on really hot days. We swung from the tires over the pond and just let ourselves see who could go higher and higher, you or me. Eventually we dropped in and cooled off. "Watch out for the water snakes!" I would yell in the background. Remember, snakes and I had a bad memory together. A spin in the air of fire sparks and a gathering by the fire, cooking marshmallows, made every day a celebration. I was so looking forward to this summer, my last one to enjoy before college or maybe marriage. Who knows where my life would lead to? My imagination sometimes went into flight, wondering what my later years in life would be like. I wished I could talk to Mom; I was sure she had an inside knowledge of what would be.

Sometimes, when I mentioned the word *mom*, the wind would get strong and the air would get cooler. When this happened, I sometimes believed that it was my mom giving me a strong sense of her awareness. Wasn't this what all children wanted to believe in their hearts? Just to try and believe and trust their inner feelings that maybe their parent didn't really die because her spirit returned when she was needed. I knew this for a fact because my mom had many mysteries of her unknown soul.

CHAPTER 35

Dad had planned a few weeks for our family to have a memorable summer vacation. "Vacation in style," he replied. "We're going to Philadelphia and will spend some of my vacation days there to enjoy each other's company. For me, just being away with each other will be exciting. What a city, Philadelphia, a great place for us to be together and enjoy the atmosphere and the ambiance. It will be memorable for all of us to be in one surrounding rather than us being here, there, and everywhere."

Philadelphia is a grand old city, which made us aware of the best pasta and seafood, relaxing moments of shopping, looking for ice cream desserts, and maybe that special restaurant that set the scene of what America was all about. Shopping downtown, antiques, paintings, and seeing some of the incredible head sculptures on display of our presidents was what I expected. The museums had so much history and extraordinary displays of sculptures. The grounds were as green or greener then an unripe apple. The fountains had many spouts, and yet if you sit close enough, it was refreshing.

Dad took special pride in preparing this special week. When the time was here for all of us to depart, we all received our train tickets. Dad politely told us to bring necessities but pack lightly. It was my day for me to depart and travel with my brothers and Dad, what joy. If only Mom could be here to see this sight. So many years had gone by between us. Now all our lives had taken on different roles but pleasant ones. We knew that our road trip must continue with one another and having these special connections with family was a must. Dad always wanted us never to forget our roots and what Mom started out to do. We arrived quickly; maybe we were all so eager to have a wonderful time and a great vacation in Philadelphia. The train trip didn't seem endless, but it was so pleasant and with such joy and love in my eyes and my family.

Checking into the hotel was a trip in itself, unpacking our clothes and then onto sightseeing in this beautiful city. I loved the food, history, building structures, and all the summer fun. Dad took us to one park in town; we stretched out our blanket on the grass and relaxed for a while. Our picnic basket was filled with great food that Dad had picked up earlier. With all of us being there, so much food had to be packed. It was now time for us to eat our lunch and feel the breeze on our bodies and the sun beating down with extreme force. Seeing children of all ages playing with their shovels and pails made your memories of fond summer days. It was wonderful for us to share special times, love, and a summer vacation together. How grand was it to have this marked on your soul and hearts forever? This was a first for us but I was sure not an ending. Dad surprised us at the end of the day with tickets to a baseball game. Wow, what a surprise. We were so elated and breathless, and yet it was triumphant in a majestic way.

Dad told us that he wanted to do something very special while in the city. He knew the baseball game would be a highlight for our vacation. It sure was. We got to the game early enough to see some of the teams practicing and in the dugout. It was very impressive to see Philadelphia playing the good old New York Yankees team from New York City, New York. You couldn't ask for two better teams to see; it was an amazing game. My brothers just couldn't believe that Dad managed to put aside money for the trip and nevertheless money for the tickets. Dad was a superb, wonderful, and outstanding father. He was so grand; some of my friends at St. Claire wanted me to loan him out for a few days. My brothers and I knew how hard it was for Dad to come to this chapter of his life with us and to lose his one love, my mom. He was so remarkable and fantastic—some would say groovy—but his journey had not been spent alone. With the love of our family and friends, we climbed the mountain together, and with beliefs and good values, we never felt alone.

Before we knew it, our five days in Philadelphia were over; our sense of direction of who we were was now clear with each one of us if we forgot. None of us wanted to leave the fine qualities of this famous city. The enjoyment we had with one another, fooling around, pillow fighting, and making fun of good old Dad was all so marvelous. I didn't know if Dad sometimes agreed with me and my brothers on our selections of touring the city and the stops. It was now time to depart; Dad wanted us to meet in the lobby within the next few minutes. We were getting picked up to return back home. What a bummer, to give up these good old days of great vacation time with one another.

I decided when I got home to spend my last few weeks by the water, eat fresh foods, and maybe waste an entire afternoon at a baseball game with my friends Jessica and Samantha. I did enjoy watching any baseball game, no matter who was playing and where. I asked the girls if they wanted to go to a game. Of course was their reply. I asked Uncle Dan if he could please get us some tickets before I returned to school. Uncle Dan was a great guy, and within seconds of conversation, he was already making my plans to attend.

I truly wanted to see if one of my brothers would take me to the farmers' market during my stay at home this summer. It was a meek memory that I had with Mom and my first love with Sean Cassidy. Memories between Mom and I were very meek since my time with her was short. I had limited time left before returning to school, so I didn't want to restrict my degree of fun. I wanted the rest of my summer with my friends and family to be boundless and complete.

My celebration before I left would be parties with my hometown friends and getting a few party-planning tips from Aunt Suzie. Maybe even a great-tasting recipe that I could share at school could be ingenious. After all, this year would be quite busy, and I would have many after-school meetings. I knew we are able to use the school's kitchen if we wished to make special dishes for our friends at the meetings. But of course, this had to be done with the chefs overseeing our dish to see if it was complex or just plain easy for us to do.

I was hoping that Aunt Suzie would give me a dish that was easy for me to do. I could surprise the girls with my delicious recipes at one of our meetings this year. I was excited about everything this year—returning to school, my new and old friends, holiday concert, college testing, and entrance exams to schools. The king and queen of the senior prom would be a highlight, but the prom would be the main feature for me to focus on. Maybe some stress, but life is not easy to endure sometimes. This you might say is not important, and yet I felt would have some anxiety and tension. Overall, it would be a superb and glorious year. Come on, senior year, hit me head-on. I'm waiting!

August came quickly, and I knew it was time to start my weekly planner as I always had. This did become a lifelong organizational skill. I knew that when school started, it was check-in time for homework and exams, and you didn't hover. If you didn't learn to organize yourself, it could lead to failure of not being prepared. There were always bumps in the roads to make into mountains. High school brings on a slew of new challenges each year, especially at St. Claire's.

Academics became a piece of the pie, along with your music and talents of charm. After all, school sports and activities became more competitive, and you may not make any of the cuts. Confidence could take a beating, and so could school performances. It's during downtime that the brain processes has new learning.

Before departing from family and friends, our town has an end-of-summer tradition. It was the effective, clever Haverstein apple party. Dad had many trees growing in the backyard, which came in full bloom before going back to school. He invited all to attend; it gave us time to celebrate a beautiful season and say my good-byes. It was nothing fancy, just very old-fashioned and very relaxing. The get-together included games, a tractor ride by farmer Phillip down through his orchard, and jumping into the pond off the tire wheel for those who wished. Dad always had some great games planned; I think he was going back to being a child.

His favorite game was to have the kids make up teams, and the team who picked the most apples and had the most baskets would win a grand prize. Of course, the kids didn't realize that Dad was having them do his apple picking before they fell off the trees and rotted. As I had said, many times Dad was no old fool. As the kids get set for "On your mark, get set, go," the excitement was splendid. Everyone grabbed their baskets, got the color of their team ribbon, and off they went. We all watched in anticipation, passion, and much excitement. The kids cheered, the adults cried, and I just watched in amazement, wondering who would finish first, second, or third.

Dinner was always quite delicious; Aunt Suzie headed the ship featuring many pie dishes. My aunt's favorite dish was peach cobbler. She tried to keep things simple but so mouthwateringly scrumptious. It was easy to over think things when entertaining, but the reality was whenever you gather great people together with good food, they were going to have a blast for sure.

Dad made a great fire pit for the roasted pig; the corn got hot, and we made sure to burn it a little. Farmer Phillip got the fire going for the little ones to roast their marshmallows. Dad's friends made the roasted chicken and great vegetables for all. Food was so plentiful, sweet, and mouthwateringly pleasant. Moments like these were hard to get away from, but the return was so yummy. Some departed to home sooner than others; some stayed and did cleanup and helped Dad. The younger children were usually the ones to go home earlier, but overall it was quite an enchanting and delightful day and night. The adults that remained stayed around the campfire, relaxing, laughing, and singing. There were many good campfire stories to tell, some comical but mostly mysterious. We let our imagination wander into the stars and heavens and maybe look for God. You could call it a private retreat for me; I always hoped that mom would give me a sign to know that her presence was with me always. I looked hard and long and watched the stars move swiftly by and hoped that Mom was hanging on to one of them. Very carefully, I hoped.

CHAPTER 36

*L*ABOR DAY WAS APPROACHING US, which was the first sign for us to return to start another school year. There were signs everywhere of summer's end, new lunch boxes, and special good-byes to mention. This was an exciting time of year for kids, parents, and teachers. This was a time of hopes and dreams for a happy and successful school year for many.

The month had now arrived, and September was here again and classes would begin. Seeing friends, old and new, was always special. Our teachers would enter our lives for our solo trip that would end this year since we were now seniors. This year the school added some additional enrollment for students and teachers to increase the total on campus. We now were ready to graduate in June next year. I knew the year would pass quickly, and I was going to dread the departure. While I sat at the train station, waiting for Ms. Hornet to pick us up as usual, I reflected on my wonderful years I have spent at St. Claire's. I had many wonderful memories, some good and some bad, to reflect on.

The schooling experience was highly structured, and how these structures were continuously reconstructed by the actions of staff and students was amazing. Among students, those with the most control over the conditions of their education and musical talent of piano playing would be the students who would succeed first.

I remembered my friends, the ones we chose. The ones we wanted to invite to our parties and share our private thoughts to. Of course, it's always about love, family, or the unknown. But did you know those handpicked companions are also scientifically proven to help us lead longer, healthier lives? Most of us usually choose friends with similar values and belief systems. They're often better equipped than family to provide comfort and motivation. Having buddies is so good for us, researchers say; the opposite, social isolation, is a risk factor.

In fact, we can master new skills and be creative about our lives. Now are we genetically hardwired with artistic gifts or a lack of them? Factors and willpower are just as important. Genes affect our lives, but our lives affect our genes. The brain changes shape according to the experiences it has. The implications of this are so profound. Most of us don't understand that our true inner potential is extraordinary, not just in our twenties, but well into our senior years. The main reasons people stand still is that they limit themselves through their mind-set or habits. Or they simply have their sights too low.

Recently, my mentor sister, Rebecca, paid me a compliment that led to another insight. "You have a gift for helping people see themselves in a new and powerful way," she said. I realized that this was a good description of the parts of my work I had most enjoyed. I knew that whatever path and future I would take, helping people see themselves differently would have to be a part of it.

"Sometimes the things that give us the most pleasure, meaning, and purpose in our lives are obvious to everyone but us. So if you're wondering where you go from here, the little reintroduction may help you see that you're hidden self was in plain sight all along.

"Time and experience allow you to distill those feelings and your skills so you waste less effort. It's the difference between a sauce you make in five minutes and one for which you reduce the heat and cook for thirty minutes and then the flavor gets more intense and deeper in taste.

"You're left with a smaller amount, but the flavor is amazing. Each has its own unique charms and pleasures, and all are safe and welcoming, plus, you'll find more appealing and affordable items in your life. I'm talking about seeing yourself the way others see you. I've learned we don't always know as much about ourselves as we think we do. Many experts on reinvention agree that before you reinvent yourself, you need to be reintroduced to yourself. I know that I have.

"Accept yourself. However, demand the best of yourself. To dance and play the piano demands the best of me. To dance with your mom in your spirit, you've got to be fully committed. I was pleasantly surprised to hear the musical piece from someone who has used her attributes to entertain and awaken the music in all of us. You have to have faith, and you have to give yourself over to something greater than you are. All those things are enormously helpful for the rest of your life.

"Almost all my life, I hadn't considered myself a 'real' musician for some reason. I had never been able to read music, though I'd tried often to learn. When I learned to play the piano, I couldn't read notes, so my mom taught me to play by ear. My talents and my flaws were in my genes, passed down to me through my generations, my mom's. Finally, I knew where I belonged.

"Americans finding deep fulfillment through the arts and immersing themselves in new pursuits learn later in life. Some do it just for fun. Others have won public acclaim and do it for the inner feelings that you receive in your soul."

Rebecca found my talk to be significant and astonishing and told me that she was impressed with my character and my noteworthy reasoning in life, me, and the world around me.

CHAPTER 37

*T*HIS WAS THE TIME FOR me to have my heart touched by my friends and relatives. An indication came to me that this was my great moment in time. To think, this would be my last concert at St. Claire's; after all I was now a senior. Many of my teachers watched over us when we performed for the moment called tryouts. It took many rehearsals and our experience that we strengthened every time we played; it became that holiday moment. The understanding of my music was the impact on me while I played my musical selection.

I told my friends Maggie and Alessandra to believe in their voice. "You both were born to sing. Whether you win or lose, walk away with pride and be remembered for your voice, which is out of this world. Stop thinking about the school expectations, and start listening to your voice. Focus on singing the right words. It's like me making sure I hit the right keys. You have to be extraordinary and be a little imaginative for success."

Tryouts for our concert are a good experience. They have to be done the proper way. Practice and practice assure a successful job when presented. It develops leaders and ensures quality. No one wants to put all this effort into the time and then have a bad review on the night of performing. When we have the solos, the teachers want to make sure that those girls are up for the task in these important roles. So every year, do the same girls step up? Sometimes, but remember, every year we do have someone else that shines, as Maggie did this year. She is a role model for the younger girls and an encourager for our incoming freshmen. A talented girl cannot stay in the shadows. She may be quiet but so talented and so unreal.

"You think to yourself, how much longer can I do this? How many more hours of practice? It's the same thing over and over each week until you try out. It becomes the same story each week, but the setting is a little bit different. You become more and more incredible and say to yourself, can I top my performance from last year? Certainly, you can. Your moment is just for you to grab, and stand firm. I know both of you are well worth the applause on the night of the holiday concert." I walked away giving them both the encouragement that they needed. They nodded to me, and both gave me a little smile. I knew it was a sign of a thank-you.

Everyone was second guessing herself, because everyone wanted to be so perfect. Senior tryouts for the holiday concert were coming on us shortly. They would be there before you knew it—the tryouts that no one would ever forget in our high school years at St. Claire's.

At this point, I knew life was full of surprises and serendipity. Always being open-minded and putting your feelings in tact was an important part of success. If you walk every step in life and don't stumble, what are your challenges? Enjoy your moment and think about what could come next. I told my friends it was just another day.

My qualities, along with my irresistible appeal, made me the number one pick. Love it or hate it, I say. I didn't let tomorrow get to me because I was going to hit the keys in perfection, and I was going to do it regardless of anyone else's performance or attitude.

I still recalled the fun and friendships that I made during these four years. The girls that helped me do better, the girls that whispered, and those that were behind me all the way throughout my years.

St. Claire's had been a wonderful rewarding experience for my soul. Who knew that I also would have met Mom and Rebecca here? I know the stress gets the better of me during rehearsal tryouts. I had to remember that every performance was unique. It was a commitment, and you had to show your music teacher that you were not to be reckoned with. I witnessed many tryouts, and they went so differently every year. It was like a candy treat that melted in your mouth when you performed well. This was certainly a confidence booster to exhibit and parade proudly. This year we decided to name the concert the Holiday Great Expectations rather than the holiday concert.

The girls wanted a stage name instead of the same old name. It was time for a change declared the student counsel. It seemed that the holiday concert sometimes singled out some of the girls that didn't perform that evening.

The choice of name was to make a statement that the show was equal for everyone, stagehands or ushers, whoever participated in the show. Everyone had to reveal their assertiveness and prove their great expectations for the show.

Well, now it was time to shine. You listened intensely to the voice of Ms. Hornet saying, "Hit it, girls, and make sure every one of those keys are hit perfectly in tune, and bring tears to some and hope to others."

"Play, Annie, play hard," Rebecca yelled out. Rebecca was present while I played my piece. It sure was wonderful to see her there. She was always in my corner and was not a fantasy that I made up. Today was the day these masterpieces would be offered.

The pieces selected would be part of the fabulous musical celebration of the holiday season. Mr. Wolfe, our assistant chef, would present a fabulous dinner, and then we would have our annual tree-lighting ceremony in the lobby.

CHAPTER 38

As we waited for the postings, now we had apprehension and fear as the climax built up. This was the hard task for most, not knowing. Did you impress them or not? Did you really play your best? I hoped everyone had a high point of playing their wonderful piece. Whether it was concert piano playing or singing like an angel, we had to manage to beat all odds and succeed. Since I was not able to read notes, I counted on my keen ear for listening to notes being played. I felt this sometimes gave me an advantage, and it felt awesome that I was able to do that.

Well, tomorrow would tell all. I did hope every senior would be able to perform in the concert this year. The teachers decided to go with a larger chorus, more solos in singing, and piano playing. The talents were becoming more and more spectacular.

This year fifty girls could participate. We had one of the larger classes in the last four years and so much talent. We had the highest expectations of ourselves and were so eagerly devoted. We all wished to be picked for the solos or groups this year. Nevertheless, each senior would have a part for sure in the holiday concert. Some of us would have tiny parts, and some of us would have massive parts to play out for this evening. Either way, it was a rejoice full evening of sharing your talent of music with your loved ones during this magical moment during the best holiday that God could provide—Christmas.

This was our moment of truth, our days are now completed. Now we counted down to the end of the year, and you know it, prom time and graduation was here. No need to think about it; it only brings tears to my eyes.

All of us waited until our friends were finished, and then we continued to dinner and a good night's sleep. "See you in the morning," replied Kaitlin and Marybeth. Sure, keep our fingers crossed and then our dreams would be hopes, promises, and perfection. During the evening, some of us were able to get together before going to bed to talk about some of our anxieties. I just had to tell the story that Sister Harris told me about fear. "Fear is only what you make of it," I told my friends. "So, now I go to bed saying good night to you because tomorrow everything will be so magnificent now, won't it?"

I told my friends that when I played on stage during a concert, I would decide to get emotional and sensitive. "The new piano songs feel pretty raw and yet moving. Its fun when people enjoy it and sometimes obvious if you're feeling it. To be successful, my vision will have to be different from yours, but it's pretty exhausting. I feel it's about understanding the world and becoming as immersed in the show as possible."

It was now time for us to try to get a good night's sleep. "OK, my dear friends, much stress will be on us for the results of the school's selections." We now wondered who would play on the special evening of the grand old show, the Holiday Great Expectations Concert; time will only tell. We all decided to pray together this evening for some of us were worried about the outcome of this year's selection. As seniors, we already thought that we made the top of the list.

Morning seemed to come around quickly, and the notices were to be posted at 4:00 p.m. after class today. The day was nerve—racking, not knowing the outcome. Morning classes came and went, and we all proceeded to the cafeteria after day's end. Patience would be put into place, and our eagerness had to be put on a back burner. We were aware the teachers are very critical about their choices.

Ms. Hornet posted the results for the seniors on a separate board. It was an exciting and disturbing time in our lives to find out who would be the final choices. What if I and my friends didn't make the list? It would be our last chance to shine. What a shame not to have recognition and go out being a legend.

I looked for my friends as I had always done, but I didn't see them in the hallways, bathrooms, their bedrooms, or down at the library. I just couldn't find anyone. I was so surprised and shocked. *Where did those guys go now?* I wondered. I walked over and checked the lists and saw Kaitlin's and Alessandra's names first, then Marybeth's, and with no impartiality, also Margaret's. Where was I? I wondered. I had to walk away and give myself a far-fetched talk that this was so bizarre. If I didn't make this performance in my senior year, then what could I hope for in my future? It just couldn't be happening to me not to be selected, not now. This had to be my worst nightmare to imagine.

Rebecca saw me in the hallway and looked at me doubtfully, as if she saw our moms or a ghost when she approached me. She asked me, "What's wrong, Annie? The results are up, correct? Why do you look so perplexed and confused?"

"Rebecca, I looked on the board at the list of names and saw Kaitlin's, Marybeth's, and Margaret's names on the sheets. Then I proceeded to look for Alessandra for at least making a singing or piano solo and found her also, but I didn't see me. Rebecca, you know I'm the best, and I should have been the number one pick. I've been selected since I was a freshman. This doesn't make any sense."

"Calm down, Annie. I'll check the list. You are so clearheaded sometimes and mixed up. Wait here!" Rebecca went to the sheets very calmly because she too wasn't sure about me if I was selected. I had always been the top choice, but maybe something happened with the Bernadine sisters' choices or other teachers'. Rebecca knew though that she would make it open for discussion to the staff if I wasn't chosen.

Slowly, Rebecca went from name to name, checking out solos for piano and singing and even choir selection. She too was at a loss for me. She was really saddened and frustrated with the outcome. Ms. Alice was in the hallway, and Rebecca approached her. "Rebecca, what's wrong? You seem quite upset," said Ms. Alice.

"*Upset*, that's not the word. I am really frustrated since Annie wasn't selected."

She then smiled and laughed a little. "My child, do not fret. The sheets aren't all posted."

"Yes they are," she replied.

"No, they aren't. Don't dispute me. We posted them differently this year. The staff had determined that one girl made so many contributions to the school, in academics, charm class, music and toward her classmates that they decided to handle things a different way this year.

"Annie will be performing a solo opening, and she will also be closing the show with a performance. Never ever has the school bestowed such an honor on one student. Rebecca, listen to me, it's Annie."

Rebecca just couldn't hold her composure on the thrill of it all. "Ms. Alice, Annie doesn't even think she was picked at all. She's quite upset at this time."

"Give me a few seconds and I will post the last sheet and tell the school our new procedure for the holiday concert. Go find Annie, please, and bring her to the board in about fifteen minutes.

"Please tell Kaitlin and Marybeth to fetch the underclassmen and the seniors. The staff knows to come to the board shortly. Find Annie for me and tell her that I must see her in fifteen minutes." Rebecca went up and down the staircases and hallways to look for Annie, but she just couldn't find her. She knew that Annie had to be mortified, humiliated, and embarrassed of what she believed to be the worst outcome of her last year. How could anyone survive not being able to play the last year of high school? Rebecca knew in her heart to find Annie quickly as she would be quite uncomfortable to see her friends. After all, she would have to explain her shortcomings.

She thought long and hard. *Where would Annie go with this dilemma? I know she feels it's a predicament and a tight spot to be in. Where, where, where would she go? Of course, how stupid of me not to know where she is.*

She would go to the attic where she will not be judged and get the confidence that she needs to proceed through this disappointment. Rebecca ran as fast as she could up the attic staircase, stumbling and scared, saying to herself, *What if Annie is not here? I feel in my mind that she has to be with her whispering memories that haunt her soul. I'm sure she would go there for tranquility and silence. The spirits of our moms were clear to me and Annie since we saw nothing but serenity, harmony, and love in our special hideaway. I know for sure Annie would be in her secret, hush-hush, undisclosed room.*

Rebecca opened the door slowly to see her dear, sweet little Annie shouting to her mom, "Show your face, Mom. I need you to appear right now." She went over to me and placed her hand on my shoulder to give me comfort. "Annie, it's OK."

"No, Rebecca, it's not OK, and I failed myself and everyone I know. How can I go on and walk out of here feeling good? Maybe I'm not cut out to be the famous concert pianist or the fine young woman that my family wants for me."

"Annie, you will be the prominent, legendary, famous musician that everyone has their sights set on. Now get up and calm down. Grab my hand as if you will never let go, and let your heart release your pain. Your mom will catch it and replace it with good emotions and affection. No concern for you my dear little one. Change your mood and consider a different point of view other than what you saw on the bulletin board."

I wasn't sold on Rebecca's speech but decided to go with her. As we started to go down the stairs of the attic, she yelled to me to slow down. "Ms. Alice wants to see you now. You must go down to the board with me, but just believe in me that I will not let you be hurt, and remember that our caring moms will prevail. Annie, give me your hand and wipe your tears because your destiny is to go way beyond your years."

"What are you saying? Are you going a little nuts or maybe just crazy? It's posted. Once it's done, it's done."

"Just say good-bye to Mom for now and come with me, swiftly please. Your opinion and concern will be over soon if you trust in me. Continue walking downstairs. We need to hurry."

I very reluctantly came with Rebecca down to the second floor where the postings were done. As I proceeded to the floor and around the winding staircase, I saw so many faces and teachers and the Bernadine sisters, it seemed as if the whole school had arrived. *For what?* I asked myself. *To feel sorry for me, give me a strong shoulder to cry on, or just enjoy my misery?*

Ms. Alice came over to me and took my hand as we went in front of my classmates and teachers. "Annie," she said, "the school of St. Claire's has bestowed an honor upon you and has decided this year the concert will change for the best. We have one girl who has surpassed her expectations in every way, whether it's academics, leadership, or playing. The staff has selected you to be the first girl to be able to open the concert with a solo and close the concert with a solo of her choice.

"Annie, congratulations on your honor." I was so thrilled, overjoyed, and tickled pink to be the exceptional one to have this first-time honor bestowed upon me. Me, could you imagine the little girl from the farms creating all this fuss? I turned to Rebecca and my friends and said, "First I was disappointed and now I am elated." Life sure was strange now, wasn't it? Rebecca gave me a great, big bear hug, and my friends jumped up and down with joy. My mood certainly did change from a tense roaring lion to a calm wave going out to sea.

My friends knew of my sensitivity and how I would be so concerned about what I thought happened. When the good news was reported, they sure cheered and we cried together. All of us made a big circle of love and jumped up and down a few times, and they held on to me tightly for reassurance. I looked around the room to see if I maybe could get a glimpse of Mom around somewhere. I was sure she was there, but right then, only my heart was feeling it.

"Rebecca, I wanted you to know that I was OK in our special room. Before you came in, I spoke to my mom, and she gave me the reassurance that all would be excellent. She replied that everything will be just great for me and it's OK to return to the hallway. Boy, was she dead on. I guess this might be a pun on words."

CHAPTER 39

*O*NCE MS. ALICE TOLD ME the results, I thanked my educators, my friends, and gave a special thank-you to my mentor Ms. Rebecca. "I want you all to know, I will be happy when my day comes, when the audience never second-guesses my performance. I know that we owe the audience fresh new music, something of character, and something that makes us driven. Yet, I want to have fun and enjoy every second of my piece selections that I will play to a captive audience, and why not. In a tryout, not everyone makes the team. Not all of us land a part to sing or do a solo. It seems that the adults rarely play in our game, but the stars can skip through the devastation of failure.

"We learn to handle most situations. Talent is so more important than the hard work. To most of us, it comes naturally. Success is years in the making. Life is always filled with talent. If not so, then is there no future. Sometimes I think these musicals could be performed without single tryouts. I learned to believe in myself and that failure isn't a final tragedy. We will have applause and standing ovations as usual and record our moments in our souls. No one wants to do all this work and end with a poor production. Celebrate our accomplishments for everyone that is involved and create a sense of unity and teamwork. Remember that a musical can't be successful with only one or two people or even several. I now realize that rehearsal and performance ensure that everyone's roles are important to the concert." After my short speech to all, I walked away elated and yet so thankful.

CHAPTER 40

THE DAY WOULD INCLUDE MASTERPIECES, and our concert would highlight a guest this year. The girls' choice of concert pieces would be breathtaking and amazing as always. Students would sing and play, and performances would be as good as many books that have been written. So many of my classmates would participate and be able to have the thrill of my roller coaster. There were numerous bumps but you may fly high; it would include the elements of disappointment sometimes, but when you held on tight, you introduced your attributes. Watch out, girl. It's a tremendous ride. So you can be your best, remember you must have the speed and fury daily.

We would present a fabulous musical celebration of the holiday season. Tickets would read, "Please come to the Sean Center for Performing Arts. Starting time will be 4:00 p.m. followed by an annual tree-lighting ceremony, which will be held in the middle of the campus grounds. Our guests are welcome to help us decorate the lobby tree in the morning if they wish."

One more brilliant night to enjoy our families and show off our expected talents. Many would be present in the hall, behind stage, up front, and in the audience. Everyone would have a job to do and would do it superbly.

The program should have everybody's names printed, maybe in red (for the holidays), and what their participation would be in the concert. Everyone participating in the show had to be recognized; you certainly couldn't select just a few. These acknowledgements showed the hard work and dedication that everyone had put into their task. Every task was a responsibility, and every role was crucial. Equal recognition was given to all from the staff during the practices. The night of the performance, our headmaster, Mr. Grumbling, and our headmistress, Ms. Alice Snap, came on the stage to give credit and thanks to everyone that had anything to do with the performance or the setup of the event.

They proceeded to identify the seniors that were performing and said they would always remember this class as one of the finest. "We give our gratitude to the teachers, sisters of our school, and parents for being behind these children. Recalling them as entering freshmen, you can say they came a long way to this moment. Their moment is now, and I would like all the seniors to please stand and take their special bows." We all stood up and took our bows very humbly. As I came up from bowing, I did see my dad and family looking so proud as if to say, "That's my daughter and her friends." Oh well, you couldn't blame them now, could you?

However, of course, St. Claire's was a class act, and it always showed. They acknowledged the underclassmen and asked them also to take their bows. "Please stand up," said Ms. Snap. Mr. Grumbling also thanked the winning performance of its star this season. Mr. Grumbling was modest and wanted everyone to give me a special applause for the two private solos I performed with an outstanding and brilliant choice of music.

Alessandra and Margaret were also some of the crowd-pleasing sensations of the show. Maybe some of their selections were not meant for everyone, but for most it was a great production with a slam dunk. So far, the show's excellence belonged to my friends Alessandra, Kaitlin, Marybeth, and Margaret. Margaret had a beautiful sound that comes out of her cute little mouth. Her looks didn't seem like she would project such a strong voice. Margaret had jet-black hair, dark eyes, and the whitest skin that you could imagine. She was very petite and had a twinkle in her eyes and a smile that was wide. Her beautiful teeth that were as white as the beautiful clouds of heaven were her best attribute.

She sang as if God gave her a special voice to sing and play the piano to his angels with such perfection. There's a saying that one song can put you in the mood and a good song can bring you back to your memories. This was what Margaret did when she performed.

No one was more surprised than Margaret and her family. She was the only tenth grader who was performing a solo. Sometimes it was luck and timing, and of course, the voice helped too. I thought she was new and refreshing; most of us had been here in the concert for four years now. Could it have been boring for some to see us over and over again highlight the program?

Not for us, though. Every year it was an excitement, and you got this special feeling deep inside you that made you want to explode. Maybe same old things tended to be boring. She was the fresh new face along with some of the other tenth graders that so far had succeeded. I think people are just bored with familiarity. I hoped that wasn't the case since we all worked so hard to make it a perfect evening.

Alessandra, my newfound friend, was next to perform. She was not part of the original threesome, or should I say the three amigos. She managed to slide right into our graces with her sincerity and charm, and there was no slouch about her wits either, which was amazing. She had talent so magnificent that she could succeed in both roles—one as a young pianist or one as the splendid singer. She always wanted to please everyone other than herself. I told Alessandra that she would be happier and more interesting if she had her own life too. "And then you'll have more to offer your family, if that is what you desire to do."

Alessandra always constantly felt pressured to get somewhere in her roles. She was a powerful woman to be reckoned with. She was a really fun bullet from a gun pointed right at you and was a straight talker and took no prisoners. Alessandra was a rare beauty with hazel eyes and light blond hair with a beautiful, sincere smile from one side of her mouth to the other. She walked onto the stage tonight and lost her confidence immediately. But despite that one big weakness, she glanced over at me, and with a thumbs-up, she became alive and vibrant. She had a talent for atmosphere, pulling you into her vivid performance. She became powerful and universal once she started singing her solo. She knew how to get her audience's attention. Great job, Alessandra, well done. The applause she received related to her that everyone felt celebrated about her performance.

Kaitlin and Marybeth played their musical pieces with power and strength and had charm like no other artist on stage. Rebecca played a duet for the first time; it seemed there were a lot of first times that went on this year. Well, you always need change now, don't you? When they played their music, it seemed so real and could be romantic in a weird way. At the same time, it just went right through you, and the chills were abundant. They certainly did win over the audience. It was as if my friends all became starlets on stage this day. They were just so glorious and grand. I was so proud of my group of friends, who all became brilliant with their performance.

Well, if I have to speak on my behalf now, I do believe I was a hit, but I was expected to be. I stopped the show with everyone standing, yelling my name out, and many tears from the right corner from my family and friends. I was so excited to land such a vibrant role in concert piano playing this year. I tended to be a feisty one, not your typical little girl. I did astound and amaze myself. I thought, *Wait, is this right, what I am doing? It seems that my mother inspired me. Perhaps.*

I ended the show with an outstanding piece, and then decided, since it was the holidays, to ask everyone to sing along with some holiday selections. It was as if a magician came into my soul and I was waving a magic wand. I was speechless and taken by surprise always with my unassuming talent and the privileged knowledge of music.

It was a wonderful, terrific, and dazzling first-rate show. The event was flawless and exceptional, but it always was. I bowed humbly and showed my eternal love to all and no one in particular. It was exactly the kind of risk that some never would attempt to do, but not good old Annie.

It was important for some of us to get behind the stage since we were presenting flowers to some of our teachers and to others that always helped to make this a special day during our years at St. Claire's. As their names were called out by me, the senior class president, I presented the staff and others flowers that had been selected for each recipient. We had decided to thank Ms. Delight and Mr. Wolfe also for the fine food each year.

Well, before you knew it, the curtains came down and the show was over and it was now time for our dinner. It was such a gratifying and pleasing night to say the least. I hated to get off the stage since I knew my feet would never walk up those steps again and I would never sit on the stage to play. The tears came to my eyes briefly to this disappointing yet rewarding time in my life. For one moment, I asked myself that maybe I too would be a mentor next year like Rebecca.

CHAPTER 41

I KNEW THESE HOLIDAYS WOULD BE different; Randy and Rebecca will be getting engaged. I was so proud of my brother. Somehow, I turned around and saw Randy—my brother, a wonderful, fine man—now in love with Rebecca, my mentor and friend at St. Claire's. You just never knew what road your destiny would take you on. Hold on, I say. It may be a bumpy road or it could be a relaxing bath; either way, you're going to have to accept your challengers that God would present to you.

Despite their attraction for one another, I wondered if they were a match. Randy was fretting that Rebecca might find him too rough-edged. She was wondering if he was going to be that successful in life. Maybe she was way too quiet for him. Rebecca grew up in England, with nannies, maids, and gardeners and singing in the Church of Christ. Randy grew up caring for his baby sister and with routine chores. Mom and Dad both worked hard and long hours to make a living for their family.

My mom and dad were a visible twosome, this town's most romantic, true power couple. Mom and Dad always remembered the long journey that brought them to what they called the best time of their lives. Somehow, we all thought that family, friends, work, and play all came together in a house built for gathering. This was our home for sure.

Rebecca's ideas were to be a good mother and an outstanding concert pianist. She wanted to succeed in the role of family and career. She knew that her family would not take a backseat to her profession. She was getting older now; this was the ideal time in her life to launch the next phase.

CHAPTER 42

$\mathcal{A}$s I left for home this holiday, I knew the excitement that would be rejoiced in our home. The Wetherbee's were coming to spend a few days with us, all of them. What a hoot this would be, all the brothers, dads, me, and Rebecca all in one covering. I thought to myself, *What do I wear when I am walking around the house, getting an extra cookie or apple before bedtime? Who will take a bath first? I sure hope that we don't all want to use the bathroom at the same time. It will be amusing. You will have to keep your wits about you. Mentally, psyche yourself out and don't take offense if someone disapproves on any of your ideas. There are so many of us if a decision has to be made on those few days. Most of all, the saga will be about Randy and Rebecca.* Aunt Suzie was making some of her special dishes for the holidays, as always.

The Wetherbee's arrived on time; Samuel, Al, and Adam picked up the bunch. When they arrived at home, Samuel made a joke saying he had to do a head count before leaving the train station. He probably did, I thought. We had a loft in the barn, and some of the older boys were planning to stay there. They felt it surely would be adventurous. After all, the Wetherbee boys, I was sure, had never slept in a barn. I couldn't wait until they heard the cows mooing, the chickens hackling, the pigs snorting, and the horses prancing at 5:00 a.m.

The mornings come mighty fast on a farm. We told the boys that they may get cold in the loft. They should think twice about staying in that darn old place. Dad said, "Most can sleep in the screened-in porch that we have. If not, double up on the floors by the fireplaces." After all, it wasn't for a century, only for a few days of love. We were all keyed up for the nighttime sleep. It was going to be the Wetherbee boys versus the Haverstein boys. The boys were so jubilated and energized; I knew we certainly weren't going to be bored.

They were looking forward to just getting to know one another to share stories, adventures, families, and how each one of them got to this point in their life. I couldn't wait to hear the yelling, pillow fights, and who was on what team. In the morning, I was sure many laughs would be at the table, but the most important point was that we all shared love, faith, and the belief that God had given us this path.

It was easy for me and Rebecca since she was sleeping in my room, nice and quiet. Thank God. I told Rebecca, "I was sure we would have guests on that evening that only you and I will know."

"Somehow, they will let us know with their smell, mist, or the wind chills going through the dining room on the event of the announcement. Watch and see," Rebecca told me. "It will be a climax for us."

"Rebecca, what if they don't come? Does this mean it's not right, you and Randy?"

"Don't get your mind jumbled up, my child. Randy and I are perfect for each other. We will have no mishaps on that evening. All is good. I will pinch you when I know that they are present, deal?"

"Are you kidding? Of course, a deal."

After dinner, Rebecca and Randy proceeded to go into the dining room. I watched with caution and felt this was it, the moment in time. Could my brother handle all this? Did he have what it took to be a dad and husband? In my heart, I knew he did. I trusted him about all his instincts. Randy believed in God and trusted in him. He would have no doubts about Rebecca in his heart. He would sometimes speak to Mom, as we all did when we had those times when we wondered, is this right or wrong? No doubts for this couple. They proceeded to leave the room.

"It's OK to be nervous," Randy replied. "But it's not OK to be paralyzed because of it. Life is unpredictable, and sometimes you move along with no road map. Just use your gut and feel your toes and just rely on each other. You may fall, but that's OK to do so. Your partner will pick you up, and together the groundwork and foundation holds firmly."

Randy proceeded to tell Rebecca how their love would age and grow with leaps and bounds. "I get this feeling when I look at my family and yours and see the challenges in store for us. We are richer now and mellower. It's like an aged bottle of vintage wine. I know in my heart that I love you with everything in my soul. I know I want you to be my best friend, my lover, mother to my children, and my wife to cherish for all the rest of my lifetime. Are you able to accept these conditions of my expectations, Rebecca?"

Rebecca stood there looking at Randy with his big blue eyes, like Mom's. Her eyes were filling up with good tears, some rolling down her face at this point. He reached out to Rebecca, got down on his knees, and promised her everything that a woman would want to hear from her lover. In his hand was this little box of velvet. Randy pulled out a miraculous ring, delicate, yet with a diamond so brilliantly placed on the band. As her heart was racing and beating with fury of her love for him, oh so meek and yet forceful, Randy asked for her hand in marriage. Of course, what could her response be other than, "I love you, Randy, and I will be yours forever in this lifetime, and we will see beyond our expectations and our love that we both have for each other."

She knew it was time for him to get up off the floor now. As he managed to stand on his feet, he grabbed her by her waist and put her over his head and then brought her gently down to his body. He held her tightly up against his body as if they were one person. The heat and feelings were as intense as we kissed. Rebecca thought, *So this is what love is all about. What have I been missing, and why did I wait so long? Who knew? All I did know was now it was the right time for me and Randy. There will be many wonderful moments to anticipate. This was my choice, the man I shall marry, the children we will have together and love. The blanks have now been filled and no surprises are left over whom I shall love forever.*

Our life is good, and we just can't wait to tell everybody about the engagement and show everyone my gorgeous ring. Oh, so proud my dad, brothers, and I will be. Let's not forget Mr. Haverstein and my new to-be brothers-in-law. This is a wonderful holiday and not one that we shall soon forget. With a glance to the heavens and white clouds that were passing, Rebecca raised her hands up to God and asked for him to make sure her mom and Randy's see this wonderful blessing through his eyes. She then thanked God for loving us and reminding us to always be giving and loving. She knew that when she went back to school, she would run up to the attic where her mom was and tell her about the exciting news. How it happened, where, and when. She knew in her heart that she had already known.

As they both had time to reflect out the window and gaze at the stars, the windows blew open dramatically, and the lilacs fell over on the table due to a tremendous gust of wind. Randy asked her, "Rebecca, what is happening? Could a bad storm be brewing soon?"

"Relax, Randy, I know it's the culprits. Our moms are coming through. Hold on to my hands and wait for the blue mist to appear slightly around us. This will be the time when we will receive good wishes of love from our moms." Randy stood with me as straight as an arrow. He never moved and held tightly on to my hands. I think Randy was afraid that if he let me go, I too would vanish into the blue mist.

It was amusing to see this hunk of a man so nervous about a smell, wind, and a few flowers being knocked over that made him shake. "How do you know this, Rebecca, that it's our moms?"

"It's a long story, Randy. Sometime I will tell you a bedtime story of love."

They went out to the room where everyone was celebrating. Songs were being played, laughs were heard loudly, and of course, the piano was being played by Annie. Excitingly, all our family circled us with cheers to "He's a jolly good fellow" and "Hip, hip, hooray, and three cheers to all." I showed my ring to my new family to-be. Her dad asked Randy, "My goodness, are you now broke? Are you not able to marry

Rebecca now?" And then her dad laughed so hard. Randy, at first, was taken back then realized her dad was joking. "Heaven's sakes, she's yours now, no going back." At this moment, Dad opened his best red wine and the wine glasses came out of the china cabinet. Before you knew it, half the town was in the house, enjoying the moment of joy with us and celebrating the gift of Christmas and meeting our new family, the Wetherbee's. The church bells were ringing fiercely and the walk was long, but all of us put on our jackets in order not to miss midnight mass. What a day to remember.

The Wetherbee's stayed for a few days, and the moments with them were supreme. I just couldn't imagine this wedding, the splendor, excitement, and decor it would have. Not to mention the important attendance that it would attract. Well, the next morning, with no further ado, the Wetherbee's were packing up and saying their good-byes to us. Many great hugs and a few tears from me and Rebecca, but overall a good send-off from each other. Adam and Randy were taking everybody to the train to make their schedule on time.

Rebecca and her family had another home close to ours, where they were planning to spend some of the holidays. They were good times, and I just couldn't wait for what was going to follow. All I knew for sure was that I would be back to school soon and I would have so many preparations to do for the senior prom and graduation.

As Rebecca reached the doorway, she turned to me and gave me one good pinch. I yelled to her, "What are you doing? Are you crazy or something?"

"Darling, Annie, don't you remember my promise to you? If our moms showed up during the proposal from Randy, I would let you know. Well, they certainly did. They scared the heck out of poor old Randy. I told him not to be scared and just hang on to me, that it was OK. It was just our moms agreeing to this marriage. Randy thought that I was really losing my mind. He told me to settle down and relax. He replied to me, that he knew the night was overwhelming for me but he didn't know that I was a little crazy. He then said, 'Rebecca, your mom and mine? Isn't this going a little too far with your fascination on spirits or the unknown world?' 'No, dear Randy, have faith in the unknown because they are definitely with us tonight. Sleep well, my dear man!

"You had to see it, Annie. The winds came in, the curtains were blowing, and the dust off the floor was plentiful. They had a good time with us though. They even made some of the pictures spin. What characters these two are together now, aren't they?" I looked at Rebecca and thanked her for reminding me of her promise. It was just great! "Does Randy know all?"

"In time, my darling, in time. Have a great holiday and enjoy. See you back at school."

As they all departed with my brothers, I quickly nodded to Dad that I was going to bed. It had been a long weekend, and I was surely ready to go into slumber world. I was dead to the world and now needed more than a siesta.

CHAPTER 43

HERE IT WAS AGAIN; HOLIDAYS had passed, and so had the wonderful Christmas morning. I was truly not shocked with my brother's intentions with Rebecca. I was sure this was no surprise to any of us. It was a wonderful, dynamic, and zealous holiday spent by all.

Now I had to board the train and question my panic and confusion as to what I had to do head-on when I arrived at school. I have many obligations to my senior class and much puzzlement to make sure everything the rest of the year is in order and done correctly.

I couldn't wait to get back to school with my old high school pals to join in our usual end-of-the-holiday gossip center to chitchat about our time back home. Some would have stories that would be of comedy, and some would have heroes for the big event. It was kind of funny what everyone pulled out of their bag of magic: some of it made you cringe. A few would tell of disappointments that weighed on them and the hard times that they had to endure. The gawky, blank-faced freshmen would try and be an overachieving squad with no problems whatsoever. Then as we proceeded with our stories, something would happen to the underclassmen as they listened to our fables. They would decide to lay it all on the table; they would lose confidence, botching up even the smallest tales of their holiday adventures.

Then as the stories projected to more elevation, we saw from the corner of our eye a new girl in school who stood in the corner, watching. She seemed as if she would make someone an inspiring friend. We questioned who is she and where she came from, what grade she is in and whose buddy she would be. Without any hesitation, as we sit around our circle, she approached us and introduced herself as Isabella. She explained that she was an incoming sophomore and had transferred midsession to our school. She indicated to us that she was there for the same purpose as everyone else was—to achieve and be successful. As we all sat there inspired by this sparkling young girl, down the hall, Margaret came. All of a sudden, Margaret saw Isabella and told her how she had been waiting for her to arrive. Margaret replied, "Your room is right next door to mine."

"How exciting," she says. Margaret has a talent for atmosphere, pulling you into a vivid portrait of campus gibberish.

I told the girls about all the excitement that we had in our house with Rebecca and Randy and their announcement. Ms. Alice approached us to remind all of us that tomorrow would be a busy, hectic schedule. "Remember that you all should make sure before dark that you have unpacked your bags in your rooms. Trouble will brew with the nuns and good old Ms. Hornet if things aren't properly put away." She reminded us that we would have plenty of time to talk about our fame, family, frank discussions, and boys, new and old.

She then laughed at us and walked away. Time passed by, and most of the girls were departing for their rooms to spend some extra quality time with their closer friends. Margaret came by my room to ask if she could just have a moment of my time before I went to bed. Margaret, of course, was one of my favorite girls here at school. She and I had made a strong friendship that seemed very binding. I hoped that I would be able to have her meet some of my brothers and let her select just one as her suitor. This would be so magnificent for us and Rebecca.

Even though it seemed wonderful, I could see something was weighing on her shoulders. "Sit down, Margaret. You do seem troubled now. Are you?"

"Well, Annie, I was talking to Isabella, and she informs me that she has a twin and her sister's name is Irene. She then goes on to tell me that her sister is the naughty one, seems never sober, and has witnessed a murder from their small town of Blaire, Pennsylvania. It seemed that someone hit one of the townspeople by a car, trying to pass the railroad lights before the rail came down. He didn't see it coming. Her window of her home faces the railroad tracks, and she watched the accident in progress. She really didn't see the person that was hit, but her sister is quite bothered by all of this. Most of the time, she thinks she's drinking. I guess Isabella felt she had to tell me."

"Sometimes, you just have to get things off your shoulders. Feel great about yourself, Margaret, as she obviously felt she could unload her thoughts to you personally."

"Isabella comes off as being the rich, spoiled, and small-town girl with all the answers. I would like to be her friend. I surely won't get involved with a classic horror story."

"Margaret, whoa, pull back on your reins. Her story of her sister may be a little strange and out there, but her story isn't your story to carry. You have dominated many challenges, but you also learn from other mistakes. If there is anything we can do together to make this road easier for you, let me know. We will work out a strategy and then consider her arrogance as a plus rather than a negative. It's OK to be concerned, but please don't blame or be fearful of little old Isabella now. Do you really think that St. Claire's would take in a girl that would give the school any issues as they had years ago with the murder in the forbidden room?"

"What are you talking about, Annie?" replied Margaret.

"Never mind, someday I can explain what I know or heard. When you embrace the insane and mindless, you then can make your wish and walk through the demented doors by yourself, but it's really no fun. Lighten up, Margaret. Classes start tomorrow, and just think school is almost coming to an end. Good night, my dear friend."

I proceeded to go back to my room, and my heart was in an intense, strong mood. Just thinking about what Isabella told Margaret was so serious and grave. Was this new girl just looking for attention? She convinced Margaret that her sister was not such a fine young woman. Why would she even, on the first night, want this to be told to anyone?

Was she a good person, or had she definitely made a deal with the devil? Eerie, now wasn't it? I wondered who the town thought her sister saw at the hit-and-run. Puzzlement if you didn't see the face. Her town felt, because of the sister's reputation, that she most likely saw who hit the man but just can't remember. Shame how life had all these unknown decisions set upon us. You know, my curiosity would make me get to the bottom of this mess. I wondered if she was a churchgoing girl. We would soon find out if she would join us on Sunday in church. God would help her heal her wounds with her sister and put a smile on her face. All she needed was a little time of prayer, I was sure.

She seemed sappy but sweet, and you had to love seeing her among the girls. You had better believe that I would get to the offstage shenanigans. I realized time was passing, and I had to hold many meetings this week for the prom social. Oh, what a day today was. I told myself to go to sleep and rest, for tomorrow would be a long day of exhaustion.

I could hear the bells ringing and Ms. Hornet tapping away going up and down the hallways to her own dance. It was good to be back home to the old noises, my teachers and friends. As we were getting lined up, I wanted to make sure I had my pencil and pad with me to take notes.

Briskly, I walked into Mr. Grumbling's office to tell him today was a day that we were planning to have some committee meetings about the prom and graduation and any other issues the seniors would like to discuss. "Surely, you are heads-up, Annie. I will tell Ms. Alice of your plans."

During classes, each teacher told our senior girls to meet the officers in the gym after school for a meeting of what would be going on the rest of the school year and who would handle what. "Do not delay, girls, since supper is done and you still have your chores to do, and for some others, there will be practice."

The school day ended, and before you knew it, the senior girls showed up in the gym, very eager to learn about the rest of their school year at good old St. Claire's. My officers were present—Marybeth, Kaitlin, and myself. I started out saying to the girls, "Well, are you ready to party? You know me, I just wanna have fun, which is the kind of girl I am." I introduced myself and my officers for those that didn't really know us. I simply couldn't understand how though.

"Well, ladies, let's talk about the prom. What would you like to see or hear at the prom? Open for any suggestions now." Emily raised her hand first and felt maybe we should first decide if we wanted a jazz band or solo singer. "After all this is our first adult social event for teenagers, the first time taking a family car out after dark. There is the famous Mark's jazz band that plays in New York City. I think this has to be our main concern right now—what kind of music and players do we want?"

"Good idea, Emily. Any suggestions from the floor? Let's have a raise of hands for a band, solo singer, and blues or jazz band. Raise your hands, ladies, as we announce them." We tallied each group, and the jazz band won out over the others. Emily suggested that she would like to handle this part of locating a good group. I agreed, and so did the rest of the class. This was not an easy task.

"We need food, art, tickets, a chaperone list, and maybe some performance from the boys. The prom will be great fun but will be a lot of hard work. For those of you that don't really want to put your heart and soul to work, do me and everyone else a favor and just practice. You might say that I did predict that organizing a party would make me feel resentful. It doesn't. I will swallow my impulses to nag, to criticize, to point out your mistakes though, so be on your toes, ladies.

I was always looking for ways to make my friends feel important and yet not worked too hard. I asked for hands to be raised for the committees that they would like to work on and with whom. Alessandra raised her hand first, then Nina, Sara. Whoops, there went Caroline and Sophia too. I knew these girls were leaders. The best thing was that they decided on all the committees needed in the allotted time. Of course, I knew things would come up and favors would be asked, but overall, I knew my class was one of the best. I really searched in my conscience to have them help me without giving them a lecture at the same time. I knew this was very difficult to do but so important. I asked myself,

Am I a cheerleader agreeing to get things lined up in a row, or am I going to keep rescheduling meeting times for no reason? No way, I certainly don't want the latter of the two.

I had great working groups, and I was sure that they would all be very cooperative and help in a blink of a second if needed. Well, all was set and done. I reported back to Mr. Grumbling and told Ms. Alice that things were on a roll and not to worry. Everything would be placed accordingly to need and money.

"Ms. Annie, I don't worry about your intense and strong personality that you have. If you have to use it, do so. I know the steps will be put into place in order of importance and burden. Full speed ahead, Annie. Go for it and show us and your classmates that the officers in charge were the right choice for their vote. If any help is needed in any decisions, please yell out any name on the staff, and we will guide you if so desired. Don't forget to fall back on your mentors—for example, Rebecca and Gladys."

Prom time was for the girls that were wallflowers and didn't sparkle or shine, or was it for the gorgeous ladies that were already popular class acts? Let's never forget that tonight no one would ever miss out on the fun. But you might say the meek, reserved girls seemed to always miss out. This night was for both of them to enjoy, overcome their shortcomings, and enjoy the slow waltz or enjoy the boogie and party. But on this one special night, we all could become angels. We become dazzling, stunning, and certainly not ugly for any one second in time. It was for the romantic dreams, maneuvers, and plans you have toward the ultimate date night.

On this night, the senior king and queen selection would be cheered, and they would have a special dance all their own. It was the moment of sparkle, glamour, smiles, and engagements for some. Prom gave you charisma and royalty you wanted to have on this one evening in time.

In a systematic manner, so many arrangements had to be handled. Procedures to be put into place, chaperones to ask, decorations to arrange, and the guy that you would ask. Prom was the evening that you would never forget, even when you were old and gray. Prom time was finally here, and this week was going to be a crazy. Of course, prom week usually was. The boys were always nervous about doing the right thing. What color flower would they have to buy? What time should he pick me up? Would her parents be present or a family member?

They had many questions to decide on and to be answered. I really didn't know where to start. The boys, above all, had to be obedient and well behaved and do their families proud of being disciplined. No complaints would be handed out tonight unless they became disorderly with the girls dancing on the gym floor.

I was busy with the prom decorations and tickets during prom week. The committee had decided that our linens for the tables and flowers would be the school colors of red and white. Appropriate, yes? We had banners to put up over the stage and some balloons to be blown up, but we weren't doing this until Friday night before prom. We needed girls to collect the tickets and either parents, nuns, or teachers as chaperones. Marybeth was putting together a list of chaperones, which seemed always easy to do. For some reason, parents and teachers alike all wanted this job.

Who knew why? I believed that it was probably to listen to beautiful music, to taste the delicious food, or just to reflect in time back to their youth. Either way, it didn't make a difference; our duty was to get an appropriate amount of chaperones, which was done. Once prom was announced, her list was soaring; some had to be refused. Her job was done in a speedy fashion.

An arch was going to be made by the art group for the entrance into the gym. A beautiful rainbow of butterflies and birds were going to be handmade and hung all over the gym. Then of course, don't forget our school's name, St. Claire's, being very bold and in big letters, that would be hung over the stage.

We knew we were the best radio in town for the notes; some of our talented girls were going to sing, dance, or play an instrument. Most of the girls had dates from boys at St. Pete's school, and some of them were going to participate entertaining this evening.

Our committee was going to meet on Thursday right after school at 4:00 p.m. to set up tables, chairs, and do last-minute practice. We had decided on a jitterbug contest, and our king and queen had to be announced. I needed someone to make sure about the choice of flowers since I didn't want to buy my own flowers. I didn't say I won yet, but maybe.

I knew I had the nomination for the queen. I really didn't know why, but then again, I guess maybe I was a little cute. Don't forget, I was a great kid too! Some of my friends thought I had it in the bag. Maybe I did. I had the hot date for the prom, the football quarterback, and the dress. Let's not forget to mention that he was quite handsome and was part of an established family of wealth. How cool was this? Outside the gym doors, we had a courtyard where you were allowed to go if you got a little too hot. It should be a majestic evening for me and my class.

I hoped the stars would be out and shining boldly. Of course, you may go outside for that little kiss or hand holding. You never knew during the night if you were going to end up being kissed by your special beau.

Only one thing that would get in the way and those were the chaperones, especially the nuns. They could be brutal. Sometimes they sent you back to your room for misbehavior. Certainly no one wanted this, but I knew it had happened. It just kept you on your toes and out of trouble. As seniors, you got a little smarter the older you get.

We had a lookout outside the gym doors just in case someone may have that moment of romance. The seniors were very clever now, weren't they?

CHAPTER 44

THE JOURNEY OF LIFE IS a long and an arduous one, and unfortunately for us, it was just as long to be at the prom. If you weren't having fun, it certainly could be a bore. I was going with Franklin DeHaven, who was also a senior at St Pete's. His family owned one of the concert hall theaters where talent was recognized in Philadelphia. In fact, my mom played a performance there.

I met Franklin when I was on the junior dance committee. Roger introduced me to him one day when I dropped by to hand in money for the dance tickets. I noticed him giving me meaningful glances and long, full pauses. He made me feel so totally alive. He was handsome, honest, smart, successful, and a real likable, good guy. I found him so fascinating. He romanced my heart to skip a beat and, in the kindhearted department, manipulated me and his dad very easily.

I had been in his company several times since then. Playing ball on campus or sometimes coming over with the guys to chat on our blanket on Sundays. He won his sweetness points and harmonized with me when he offered to take me down to the pub in downtown Philadelphia to buy me something to eat. Franklin wanted to go to O'Hanley's, one of the best pubs in town. He achieved what he wanted with me, to impress me, and he did.

I did believe that this evening, you could have a carefree, ready romance to build on, but for me, my greatest struggle was to break through all that aggressive pleasantness. Luckily, I was more than a smile. I was smart and talented, and I could be a hair-toss-over-my-shoulder-type girl if needed. This was bittersweet sometimes and could be a whimsical experience for me and him.

We knew at the junior dance that prom time came the following year, and this date was ours to be asked. I was sure glad I didn't have to think about it long and hard. Rebecca had reminded me that Dan or James would surely go with me if asked. "Rebecca, he's instantly a likable guy and nearly too good for himself. But when you mix his silly, stupid quirks into his corny attitude, that's when he becomes golden."

"I do like them both, but Franklin and I had an arrangement, and since I am so ladylike, I'm not going to break our promise to each other."

"I understand, Annie. It's OK. People have to do what they feel is the best at the time they are doing it, and this is what's right for you at this moment."

Prom had always been the stuff of which teenagers dreams were made. The excitement surrounding the occasion was nothing new. It was amped up like never before. You had so much preparation leading up to the prom, trying to find the perfect dress, hairstyle, or date. You must, for this evening, be delightful, charming, gorgeous, and let's not forget, adorable in a lovable way.

The emotional buildup was an inherent part of prom. It was about teens moving from childhood to adulthood. This was the night that we felt like adults. We dressed up, rode in maybe an awesome car, and if we were lucky, we went to the ice cream parlor for music and ice cream afterward. We counted down the hours to prom, but it was a bittersweet occasion for our parents, friends, and teachers. Everyone shared our joy, but they also realized it wouldn't be long before some of us wouldn't be leading our own lives.

Tensions rose because kids were trying to assert their independence while parents still wanted rules and restrictions. There was always someone that would try and spike the punch during the evening for sure.

The one different thing for most of us at St. Claire's was that we lived in the dorms and our dates would greet us at the gym or pick us up at the lobby. There were very few parents present, mostly teachers and some of Mr. Grumbling's friends. They came aboard as extra chaperones to help keep the dance controlled along with faculty staff from St. Pete's and St. Claire's.

Overall, the prom would be a memorable night for pictures, dancing, and your imagination going wild. Yes, think about the stars, the lightning bolts that may hit you, and just the simplicity of enjoying your friends and having a great time, maybe your last time with these coeds. What an evening of expectations.

CHAPTER 45

Prom was all that I thought it would be. Yes, I was the queen for the evening. Kaitlin, Marybeth, and Alessandra couldn't have been happier for me being selected. Of course, they had to tell me that they voted for me. I looked at them in amazement and said, "Oh my, I voted for you all." My handsome king was a boy from St. Pete's, a senior who was very gracious and polite. His parents taught him well; just as Dad wanted me to be a fine woman, he was quite a handsome gentleman. I was told his name was Mr. Connor Brandt Harrison from England. I'm sure his folks wanted him to succeed and most likely go to law school. I'm sure their intentions were not for him to fall in love or go into the service. They had great dreams for this boy of theirs, and why not? Don't all parents expect the best from their children?

After Connor and I were announced as king and queen, I felt a little gun-shy yet so excited. They put the crowns on our heads, and we were expected to do a special dance on the floor. The cheers came, the lights were dim, and most importantly, he placed his hand in mine. He helped me off the stage onto the floor with such tenderness and gentlemanly politeness. Franklin was not enjoying this time at all, watching us close together and smiling at each other. I have to admit, Mr. Harrison was a great dancer and very smooth on the floor. He kept me close to him and laid his cheek next to mine. I looked up at him quickly during the dance, and he gave me a sly little smile. My heart melted, but then I woke up from this dream to see his girl on the sidelines. He was dating

Emily Hatmellow from Chicago, Illinois. Her father worked for the Chicago News as the editor of the newspaper.

Emily and I were friends since we were freshmen. She was in a different class from me growing up, but now I became her equal in every area, which she wasn't too crazy about. All I thought to myself was, *Emily, it's time to grow up, every man for himself.*

He twirled me and dazzled me off my feet. Connor Brandt Harrison was a fine catch. He asked me later for a few more dances through the night, which was wonderful. I did feel a little bad for my date and his during the evening. Franklin DeHaven was a great guy too, but I wasn't committed to him. For the first time, I had a bit of self-worth as a woman and didn't have to go to anyone and wonder what I should do. I was kind of telling myself that I knew what I wanted and you were not it, Franklin.

Franklin was quite baffled to see me with other guys, dancing. Was I considered to be an easy girl? After all, Franklin was not my steady. During the Presidents' Day dance last year, Franklin and I decided to go with each other to the prom since we were friends. It just became easier that way for me so I wouldn't have to think about it anymore. All the boys from St. Pete's that were seniors were able to come to the Prom as long as they brought a ticket. My assumption now about the boys was powerful and unexpected. I knew I wasn't going to give too much of myself to any one boy. This was how I felt about Connor Brandt and Franklin. I was confident that I handled it the right way with the two boys. I had my own reaction of self-respect, and then realized I would end the evening without any reservations. It made me feel good that I now knew this. It was shocking, but that was life when you turn seventeen years old.

I looked over at him several times and noticed he wasn't having any problem with the girls. I did say he was hot, correct? It was prom night, and I was going to take every second in. Connor Brandt, near the end of the night, asked me to meet him outside the gym doors. I went and told Marybeth and Kaitlin what was happening. They too were having a blast. Their dates were also great guys, and my two friends were sultry, needless to say. Both of them had beautiful jewelry on and gorgeous dresses and anyone would want to be with either one of them. They stood out among most of the girls on the dance floor as the best choice to be with. You know, the smart ones, talented, and let's not forget, very good-looking. Kaitlin ended up going with Keith Kenny, and Marybeth was with Roger Pittman when they started the dance music. What charming couples, I do say. They all moved across the dance floor with grace and style. Lastly, let's not forget Alessandra and Dex, who seemed to be hitting it off better by the end of the night. We all knew that they were perfect for each other, but they didn't know it yet. You do realize, girls are so smart now, aren't we?

Connor met me outside for a quick moment. He danced with me, looking at the stars, and in a swift jiffy grabbed a kiss from me. It was tender, delightful, and I felt so out of breath, a little star struck. He really caught me off guard, so romantic; maybe I should see him again. I told Connor I had to get back to Franklin; after all, he was my date. I replied to Connor, "You know where to find me, and maybe I will see you at graduation." It was as if I was a well-known celebrity and he was the leading man.

"We'll see," he replied. I laughed a little and then very meekly told Connor, if he had no prom date, I knew a girl he could ask. Somehow, I just didn't think that was part of charm school, but I knew it was part of me, good old Annie.

I knew that sometimes responses like this would go nowhere. It was just the time when the little girl now turned into a fine young woman on a special evening. So grand it all was. I told Connor to let me go back and find Franklin for the last dance. I did have to go back even though I wanted more to be with him then good old Franklin. Was I being mean or nasty? Not really, I knew my heart was taken over by some incredible force, and I couldn't control myself for wanting him. It was only fair that I ended up on a good note. Connor looked at me with a wise smile and proceeded to find his girl, Emily, who he came with. The last dances were wonderful, and sometimes a tap on the shoulder from someone gave you the opportunity to dance with someone new.

CHAPTER 46

THE STARS WERE OUT AND the music was starting to play, and Franklin and I were dancing to the last dance of the prom. After several steps and spins, a tap was on Franklin's shoulders, and our dates passed us on to each other. As I glanced up to see my new partner, I could feel his arms around me and the intense feeling in my heart. I knew it was Connor; he held me so tight next to him, I thought I almost couldn't breathe. His touch, his magic, and his knowing how I felt when he held me was enticing. I didn't have to open my eyes to know who I was with at this time. Before the final note, Franklin regained me back to his arms for his time with me to the last musical notes of the evening. We turned; swayed and dear Franklin tried to pull me into his body tightly. Instantly, I bent over and fixed my shoe, and when I came up for air, I was fully at an arm's length. He surely received my message.

I didn't think I was ready for that part of a relationship. I still thought about Rebecca's brother and how I had this special feeling when I was with him. Maybe love? Who knew? It was confusing the feelings, the special kiss I received from Connor; after all, he was my very first romance. I did remember Sean, my young love at the farmers' market. I was very impressionable then and just a kid. How could I compare all of this to the other guys when they never even had an opportunity to do the same? I felt that James and Dan, Rebecca's brothers, were wonderful, good-looking guys and great, but they were going to be family soon. Not a good mix, I thought. Could I possibly date either one of them and fall in love. Sure, but was this what I would want? I guess I would have to ponder over these things and try and be selective when choosing my loved one. Right, Mom? Wouldn't you say so? I guess, for her to respond, I had to visit our room. Maybe I would have my questions tonight. At this time, the wind blew through like a rapid hurricane and items fell, and a strong scent was left in the room. You got it, lilacs. OK, OK, I got the picture. I would think wisely, Mom.

Our dates brought us back to school, and some girls stayed overnight with their parents. This was a costly affair for my family to come for one evening. I would have enjoyed Dad and my brothers seeing this special night, but I knew they just couldn't. Franklin was to be dropped off after me. As I arrived in front of the school, he leaned into me and stole a little kiss on my cheek. Do you believe he even did that? Holy cow, what was he thinking? He must have been caught up in the thrill of it all.

Graciously, I said good night, gave a slight wave to Franklin, and proceeded to go to my room with the rest of the girls. We all rushed up the stairs to go to bed. Exhaustion had now set in, and we promised one another that tomorrow would bring much conversation, good talks, and some good laughs.

The next day, everyone was talking and was so excited to tell their adventure with their dates. We ran down to Ms. Hornet and Ms. Alice to tell them of our wonderful experiences. So pleased they were for all of us. They knew of the good times that were in store on this evening, good old prom night. This was the night that everyone felt like a princess. Ms. Alice grabbed my hand and told me that she knew, once she heard the nominees for king and queen, I was a shoo-in. I knew Ms. Alice had me on her list as one of her favorites. She never could say, but her looks, her reactions to things I said and did were always caring.

Never did she want me to do badly in any thing I did. If we had any problems or just couldn't figure things out correctly, she was always there for me but also for all of us. I sure wished sometimes I could have told her about Mom and my visits. Maybe she could have met her too.

The conversation about the attic with Ms. Alice never happened. It could have resulted in her losing a job if she went with us and was found out. This was the reason I never told Ms. Alice about me and Rebecca and our involvement with the forbidden room. But, I knew she had a special spot in her heart for me. When I had problems with piano pieces, she would help me get into a room not scheduled for anyone for practice. She would do my bed if I was late for lineup for breakfast and made sure my room was always tidy. No one knew she was helping me out, but I did. She was a special woman to me, almost like a mom should be, I guess. Ms. Alice always gave a positive impression toward everyone.

She taught and reminded us to always be respectful and courteous and to always keep our grades up at all times. Music was an important part of our role in life, but with no education, we could only succeed so far.

CHAPTER 47

BEFORE YOU KNEW IT, PROM was over, and for those of you that haven't put it together yet, yes, Connor did ask me to go to his prom. We had a marvelous time, and all of my friends also got to go. He made sure his friends asked Kaitlin, Marybeth, Margaret, and Alessandra. He made sure that I was going to be comfortable and not feel out of place, not knowing anyone. Connor, being as smart as he was, I certainly couldn't refuse if my friends were going now, could I? Rebecca wasn't so thrilled with me since she really wanted me to try and get to know her brothers Dan or James better.

Connor was just an individual with character and soul that you couldn't deny. His nature had so many varieties of being a genius. Passionate I always was with Connor. I found his soul to be so genuine.

Together Connor and I knew much had to be discussed with our lives and our futures. He was planning to attend college and go to law school. Myself, I had so much uncertainty. Time would let us see each other in many places with extreme eagerness. It was a journey for me to watch and another wonderful time to explore.

Graduation was coming; I contacted Dad on the invitees. Dad knew that tickets had to be ordered, and since it was outside, everyone in the family was able to come. Mr. Grumbling said, "No holding back on this occasion. You girls worked hard and endured the socials and academics that St. Claire's played on your life. Certainly your time is here, and I ask the world to come, if you wish to do so." There were 120 seniors to graduate this year, and about half the class was going on to other schools. Some were staying behind to be a mentor at St. Claire's.

Marybeth and Kaitlin were leaving for sure, and good old Alessandra was staying to mentor girls. Rebecca and I were also departing, but sadly. Plans had to be put into place for Rebecca's wedding. Ms. Snap told me that anytime we changed our minds, we shouldn't hesitate to return to them again.

I do believe I was going to contact Franklin and see if I could perform some evenings at the concert hall in Philadelphia as Mom has done in the past. It was a wishful thing that I had in my dreams, maybe as if I were walking in Mom's shoes. I didn't know if I would see him before graduation. A short note would have been a little awkward, but acting like a lady and handing him a note is the way to go. I had plenty of time to plan and arrange my life to come at a later time.

Concentration was now on graduating this year in June and maybe furthering my education by attending college in the fall. Whoever could believe that the years would go by so quickly and my life would soon be going on to a new adventure? For me to go on to another school would be a strain for sure on my family. I did feel that these last four years were exhausting for my dad and brothers. I felt now that I was on my own; would there be a possibility of me getting my own monetary grants since I would be eighteen years old in August? Who knew at this point? Could my love show up and I and Rebecca have a double wedding?

As I was thinking about my scenario, a whirlwind came by me so fast, blowing the brush around on the lawn. I looked up because as I knew the mystery of the unknown, I knew that they could show up at anytime. "Mom, I feel your presence. I smell your aroma of the lilacs. So glad you could take the time and listen to me with my speeches and accept some academic awards. I do need a sign of help making some lifetime decisions. I guess, the marriage one wasn't a good one, right, correct? Got it! Thanks!"

The graduation would provide so much talent of instrument and piano playing. We would have great speeches to listen to and some awards to be presented to several seniors. Of course, the valedictorian and the president of our class would do speeches along with some diplomats from other countries.

Good sportsmanship, English, Math, and Science awards—to mention a few—would be handed out. Also a most talented music award was going to be given out this year. This had never been done before. Mr. Grumbling felt he had to add something else to his program and felt that someone should be recognized.

Flowers had to be ordered; seats had to be assigned according to your status. Teachers were always applauded, and the mentors, such as Rebecca, were recognized. Our music teacher had to get the music in order, if and who was going to play and practice for the marching precession, what songs would be very important, and our caps and gowns had to be ordered. Since we paid so much for going to the school, the ordering for the girls' caps and gowns required no cost.

We had to check on the graduates to see who was sitting where, what height you were; would you have heels on this evening? All of us had to wear a white dress with a red ribbon around the waist, and if desired, you may have a ribbon in your hair of matching color. The dress had to be right below your knees, and no off-the-shoulder scene.

God forbid no skin on this day. What would Ms. Alice say about what we learned in charm class on becoming a fine woman? I do mean a fine woman.

We had to make sure that the underclassmen would stay to help out. Some of the boys from St. Pete's on the student council were selected to help that day. Tickets had to be disbursed. Each senior was getting four to six tickets per family. The campus was large, and there was plenty of room to go around. Some townspeople attended this ceremony, and other invited guests as well, our mayor and governor to say the least. The surprise of the day during ceremonies was that we had the vice president of the United States, Mr. Thomas Marshall, under the presidency of Mr. Woodrow Wilson, would be making a speech to our class. This was going to be a surprise to our class and our audience. Mr. Grumbling and our Governor pulled some strings to have this important, respectable figure on this day. How much more would you be proud that you were an American and a graduate from St. Claire's Academy?

CHAPTER 48

R
EBECCA DECIDED TO GET SOME tickets for her family to come. She was just so proud of me, especially since I was going to be her new sister-in-law and the president of the senior class. I just missed the valedictorian by half a point; it went to Ms. Kaitlin McGuiness, my dear friend. Marybeth was going to play a piece of music of her choice on the piano. Margaret, even though she wasn't a senior, was going to sing a duet with Emily. I was playing a duet with Alessandra on a special piece that I dedicated to my mom. Alessandra was thrilled she was doing this with me. She felt that I was special to her, maybe a little better friend than the others. Not really, but she wanted to think that. I certainly wasn't going to burst her bubble.

When you hear Emily and Margaret sing together, it just takes your feelings to another place. The words were sung with such impact and perfect notes, high and low, and with such beautiful harmony. It was just something no one would want to miss. I was so proud of my circle of friends at the school; each one of us did very well and was outstanding in different ways. I felt bad leaving Ms. Margaret, but I told her I would keep in touch and help her in any category.

She was so gracious and told me maybe she would come and visit me sometime. Sure, summer was long, and we had plenty of room at the house. "I am sure one of my brothers would be thrilled to have you stay over. Keep your door locked when you come over, though," I said laughing out loud to Maggie. We had time to give each other a big hug, and the tears came flowing down our faces.

"Margaret, remember that you are a fine young adult lady. Now we shouldn't show how we feel in public. Let's close my bedroom door, and then we can cry hard." Maggie, grabbing my hands, did just that with me. Maggie and I became very close friends during this year. I felt as if she was my little sister. I hated to think that this was all coming to a finish with her and I in school together. We spoke about our different stages and our good times and bad. I told her that she must come over this summer for a visit.

I wanted so badly to tell Margaret about Mom. I knew Mom would take care of Margaret, and she could share anything with her. I knew it was now time to wrap things up and go and participate in the graduation.

Our families had just arrived and checked into the hotels where they were staying. Dad came over to see how I was doing. I had to meet him in the lobby since no one was allowed in the bedrooms or other areas of the school unless escorted by a staff member. I told Dad saying my good-byes to friends was weighing on me. Saying good-bye to some of my teachers was also going to be a concern and an issue for me to deal with. I had some selfishness in departing and giving up my room that I had for the last four years to a new girl in the fall. I had my mark on the windowsill and my family of ducks I had to leave. Would they have additions to their family in the fall? I told Dad my heart was breaking as I reflected on my high school years.

Margaret was special to me. I remember myself when I was that age and starting school. I had many questions, as Margaret did. A lot of soul—searching, and sometimes I was confused why I was really there. I too had to leave family and close friends, a wonderful neighborhood, and a great school. I knew I had to tell Margaret about Mom though. I had to share Mom so Maggie also had somewhere to go when the days became overbearing. All of us needed that special friend in our life to share ups and downs, sorrows, and happiness and to look forward to sharing their thoughts and feelings. I knew it had to be Mom. I just had to figure out a way for Mom to meet her. Mom would love Maggie for sure, as I did. I realized it was a significant issue for me to leave.

Dad looked at me with kindness and sympathy and understood what was going on in his little girl's heart and mind. On the other hand, Dad realized now that I had turned into a wonderful young woman, as his wife and my mother Brenda wanted. There are things that happen when you're going to be eighteen years old. You know that most of your important choices in your life are done, and you start to look back to see what you did with your dreams and relationships. For me, that was not so scary because I lived my dreams all the time.

CHAPTER 49

I**T WAS GETTING CLOSER TO** graduation, and before I knew it, my friends were at my door. The day was finally here. The campus grounds were filling up rapidly. I got to see my brothers before I walked down and gave them a big hug and kiss for good luck. "Where is good old Dad?" I asked. "Where do you think? He's arranging everything with Mr. Wetherbee for later. They are thinking about going downtown to one of the pubs after this is all over. OK with you, sis?"

Of course, this should be a great evening with us celebrating my graduation with my family and our new family, the Wetherbee's. I just had to tell Dad that I wanted to invite my wonderful friend Margaret along if it was OK with Dad. "You must all meet her. She's delightful and gracious and just one of my best friends here at school. She just must come along for the fun tonight. Hey, guys, let me see which one of you would think this was a wise choice I made today by inviting her along. You will all thank me in the morning."

It was now time for us to gather our thoughts, line up, and put on our best poised look and smile, smile, smile. We had our caps and gowns on. We were ready for our walk more than ever. Our family and friends departed to their seats on the lawn. They were escorted to the seats by the juniors, which was a big deal for them. Next year they would be the seniors just like us and would be able to experience this moment in their life.

We were all so excited and overjoyed with so much love of our school and what happened to all of us in these last four years. We had now all grown up and became fine young women. Since we had now learned about ourselves and our lives, it was time now to start a beginning of a new one.

Our marvelous educators were there, and the complete staffs of nuns were seated also in the audience. Most of the time, not all of nuns were able to participate in our activities. It was great having them all present at graduation. Since we had a really special speaker at this graduation, it was most likely why they were permitted to attend. Mr. Grumbling welcomed everyone and was glad that many attended this special day for the graduating seniors. The music was played, and the march proceeded with all of us to go to our proper seats. Once we were in our rows, Ms. Alice clapped her hands as always for us to sit or stand.

Sister Harris said her farewells to us with a tear rolling down her face. In the background, you could see our teachers, Ms. Alice Snap, Ms. Beth Hornet, Ms. Melissa Atkins, and others smiling from ear to ear. Ms. Alice proceeded to get up in front of all of us and thanked us for giving her the pleasure of being able to be with us for the last four years. To her, we were the best group of girls she had taught in her last ten years at St. Claire's. She wished us much success in our future.

Speeches went on and on, and awards became so many. I was one of the lucky girls that did get scholarships for my talents. The speeches were said, and it was time for each graduate to get their diplomas.

Dad, Rebecca, and my family were all so proud of me. Names were called out, and each one of us went up on the stage and then walked humbly back to our seats. We looked for one another and cheered loudly for all, and rewards were given out in abundance. Then of course, they asked the valedictorian to come up and say a few good-bye words to the class. No one knew other than me what girl was going to receive this prestigious award.

It was to be Kaitlin's, but I knew, of course, a mistake was made and it was me instead. I felt bad for Kaitlin since she was one of my best friends. At first the staff felt that I was behind Kaitlin with a one-point difference. I challenged it with Ms. Hornet and Mr. Grumbling. I received all A's the four years and couldn't imagine that someone also had that honor of doing this. Some of my friends were close but never straight A's; after all, girls do talk to one another. I did remember one year that Kaitlin received a B in history, which would make the point discrepancy. I was sorry to oppose it since the school's choice was my friend Kaitlin, but it is what it is. I also worked hard and deserved it.

I had to keep my lips tight and never repeat it to anyone once I was told. It was so hard not to tell anyone about the delighted reward. I did work hard, but so did a lot of other girls. I knew to have this honor bestowed upon you all through school; your grades had to be straight A's. I had to do this anyway, or Dad would have lost my financial packages for me. Once I was in school. I knew what had to be done. I never wanted to leave here or my friends after a few months. I knew where my life was heading and I never wanted any change for me.

Friends cheered and hats were tossed in the air. This moment was one that had to be stored in your soul, if this was possible. I knew that I would see them forever in my dreams and thoughts. I will laugh and sometimes cry when I think of St. Clare's and my dear teachers, my friends, and dreary hallways and remember my good old Mom in the attic.

Thinking to myself, *Now where to? College, yes. Marriage, who knows?* I just didn't know where Mom would go after this triumph. I know she would be on the campus grounds to be proud of me and what I had accomplished here at school. I knew that Dad, as we were praying, looked up to the heavens and nodded with a smile. Just who do you think he was thinking about?

Before we were ready to depart the grounds, Mr. Grumbling went onto the stage and thanked everyone for coming. He proceeded to say that he also was so proud of this class and their accomplishments. If you are not aware, many would receive other academic honors in colleges, and some would stay as mentors for our underclassmen. Others would be accomplished concert piano players abroad or in the States, but wherever these girls would go, they would all triumph in this world.

He ended his speech again with a soft-spoken thank-you and reminded everyone that plans had been made for breakfast in the ballroom at 7:00 a.m. for those that would like to attend. "I want to remind you that there will be no cost to anyone. Ms. Delight, our head chef, has planned a wonderful breakfast in our ballroom. For most, this will be the last time we will be together. So please join us for good conversation, good food, and great memories that we will talk about for years to come."

People stood up, cheered, and applauded, some more than others. Our music started to play for us to depart. As we passed one another, the tears fell from our eyes; smiles and rejoicing came over all our faces. We knew our lives would now change for the better. We had been handed off the tools to do the right thing for ourselves and to accomplish our goals. As we say, onward and upward.

CHAPTER 50

*O*NCE WE WERE ALL OUTSIDE, I reminded my family and friends not to forget breakfast. It was still early enough to take a stroll around campus, which we all decided to do. Mr. Wetherbee had booked a pub for around 6:00 p.m. after the graduation performance. As we started down one of the paths, everyone was hugging and giving out last words of love to one another.

Out of the corner of the lake, I saw someone starting to approach me and my family and the Wetherbee's. It was good old Connor Brandt Harrison and his family. They too came up for the festivities. Connor was going to graduate in the afternoon tomorrow. The two schools always tried to keep the graduations on different days but the same weekend. Some families had daughters at St. Claire's and boys at St. Pete's and wanted to attend both ceremonies. Traveling was an all-time high expense for most families and also could be an inconvenience. Knowing that they could see their children, family members, or friends over a weekend was a pleasure. Both schools had a marvelous display of talent on stage; the boys usually had a small band performing for their guests.

I was surprised to see Connor. It was a bit uncomfortable since Rebecca's family was still with us. Connor politely, as always, introduced himself to my family and to the Wetherbee's. I could see that my brothers and dad were impressed with him.

You just couldn't help liking him; he was wonderful in so many ways. I glanced over at Dan, Tim, James, and Mr. Wetherbee and the other Wetherbee boys, who weren't really thrilled that he came. So much displeasure was on their faces that it showed. I was so glad that suddenly I saw Margaret approaching us and was so glad she could come to meet everyone. Her family was not here since she was not a senior but had to stay since she was performing during the graduation services. She was just in time to take the looks off me and Connor showing up. Perfect timing you sure could say. Thank God for little favors. Great timing, God.

Mr. Harrison invited us all to attend a pub in Philadelphia with him and his family. He also said, "Since Annie is the graduate today, I would like to give her a gift by treating everyone to a few cocktails, if you accept." Graciously, Dad accepted, and so did Mr. Wetherbee. Mr. Wetherbee had already made reservations at a famous pub and invited the Harrisons to come along. He felt this was a great idea to meet new friends, have a few drinks of cheer, and let the kids socialize. The families had no idea what went on during prom time. Rebecca, Connor, and I were the only ones, of course, that knew what went on that evening. It was a grand evening at the pub. We then all departed for either school or a stayed at a hotel. Connor asked my dad if he could have a few minutes with me by myself.

Dad, being such a nice guy, said, "Sure, go right ahead, but she has to be back in school shortly. Annie, we will see you in the lobby at 6:45 a.m. for breakfast. We are all planning to go."

"Great, Dad, see you tomorrow."

I turned to Mr. Wetherbee and reminded him about the breakfast that everyone was invited to attend in the morning. Mr. Wetherbee and everyone else were excited to have breakfast and get to familiarize themselves with one another. All of the family could attend; wasn't it wonderful that we could have more time together before we all departed in different directions.

I spent a few extra minutes with Connor, walking around the campus a little. Plenty of lights and plenty of people were present. The night was just beautiful, and a warm breeze was blowing by once in a while. Wondering about the gentle breeze, I did think maybe that was Mom. She showed up at unexpected times. He expressed his feeling that he hoped to see me during the summer break. Gently he grabbed my hand and gave me this wonderful kiss and then a second one. My heart beat triple time whenever I was with him. The kisses also helped out. His lips were so gentle, and he pulled my body so close to his in such manly ways. Was this love?

Who knew? I told Connor that I would keep in touch and wished him and his family good luck tomorrow since I was going home with Dad. I gave him my address to write to me if he cared to do so. A wonderful good-bye was put into place by both of us.

CHAPTER 51

*I*T WAS MORNING ALREADY, AND Ms. Delight made a wonderful breakfast for all of us to enjoy. At this time, Sister Harris asked us to hold hands and repeat with her a special prayer. "For those that know the prayer, please join in." One of the lessons that St. Claire's did teach us was that religion and happiness were linked together.

Church attendance was just not enough. It was attending church and seeing you and your close friends together visiting God. Church regulars without pals were like pews that nobody sat on. Therefore, continue your faith and participate in church services with your family and friends. We should never ever forget our memories that each one of us would keep buried in our souls about St. Claire's days. As we prayed out loud, some squeezing one another's hands tightly, the tears came down our faces. It was surely an uplifting moment of God and faith. I hated to let go of my friends' hands; they were my shoulders to cry on, my confidence when needed, my backbone for my challenges. Over the last four years at school, I now held on tightly to my friend's hands that I had known to love and respect. They would be my dear fiends forever in my heart and stenciled in my brain.

I talked to Rebecca how these four years had been so special to me, having her here, our moms, and our special times. We sat on our beds and had many talks about being visited by close dead relatives who pointed us toward our destiny. It was an awesomely promising time that we had with both of them. It was an atmosphere of unmemorable pleasantness but, to some extent, kind of fun, moderately enjoyable, and reassuringly great.

Finally our words had been turned into an audience-participation chant for recognition for us that someone was listening and cared. "Sometimes it seems that our moms have goofball charm, and they begin to dabble again just as we hear about a bunch of mysterious happenings that start plaguing our campus town. Annie, you and I knew who this was! How does the supernaturally high, unpredictable twist and conclusion come when you say good-bye? This was a wild ride and you say to yourself, what am I doing here? You see that they believe in what they are doing and what you will do in the end. They were clearly pretty genuine. It's truly about what happens at the end. Do you wait for the mist, aroma, or maybe a gentle touch to your sprit? They have listened to us, directed you and me, and gave us courage to be together. The rhapsody of their magnificent music playing in the forbidden room of no hope was truly ours. Melodies of great concert music for us to hear during the wee hours of the night made our souls delighted and peaceful. This was true for you and me, Annie. Annie, this was the best place on every occasion where we could be with them in spirit and mind.

"Now you will have memories for a lifetime! You'll go home after four years at St. Claire's and yearn for the option to stay. But you will take with you developed leadership skills and the confidence you need for success. Your character has been tested, and you apply courage and curiosity in your life. Some have opened doors with developing songwriting skills, learned new techniques, how to rehearse and practice to perfection. We learned about the importance of female leaders in history and the opportunity of meeting current women leaders in congress.

"The thrill of public speaking with experienced women presenters are only a few of your skills that you have learned. I will have many memories of my four years of high school. The school focuses on grades nine to twelve, and studies reveal that to develop confidence, you do this through discovery, rigorous academics, and performing arts. St.

Claire's is a network of college preparatory schooling dedicated to the development of character and leadership of their students.

"We will leave with preparation to navigate the tough choices that we will all face in our everyday life of today, tomorrow, and our future. Kaitlin, Marybeth, Alessandra, and Margaret, now picture that this is all coming to an end, how dreadful."

CHAPTER 52

*K*AITLIN AND MARYBETH WERE OFF to college in the coming fall. As we started to depart, Kaitlin repeated that college was all about parents and children learning to loosen the ties—a process that could be hard for both. We should remember that every college has its support systems in place. Now we sat down with advisers to choose classes that suited our needs. Students who lived on campus had residential advisers to guide them through roommate squabbles. For academic assistance, most colleges offered tutorial centers, and there were counselors and medical professionals on campus. But I knew it would never be the same as our dear St. Claire's.

Productive homework routine, including minutes a day on math, just one minute would make your facts automatic and would reduce fatigue and frustration when you needed to complete more difficult problems.

What parents need to remember is that school is a preparation for real life. The more you coach your child toward independence at every level in school, the better your child's preparation will be for the future. Thank God for St. Claire's training and guidance in faith and relationship. Students at St. Claire's never experienced a bad apple in the bunch when they departed.

I now sat in my room, packed my bags, reflected on my education and friends for a lifetime. I had experienced charm and other qualities that now made me, Annie, a woman. It was a journey rich with courage and loyalty and some evil. What was the purpose of never being able to mention the unspeakable attic? Rebecca and I had unexpected great years with our moms plus all the creative forces behind us. Approaching the attic with unexpected anxiety, we had special talks, visions, doubts of fear, and apprehension of the sights in the attic with our moms. The shrieking hallways, howling sounds, and the beautiful music playing were beyond our expectations.

I asked myself, *What will be the hot topic for the day? Now who will I ask?* When I would leave, so would my friends, my beloved teachers, and some special people that I have met in my life. Who would I ask now about my feelings, my grades, or just girl worries? I had family members, but they were all men; this just didn't work somehow. I sure hoped my mom was able to leave here and start on a new journey with me. I would never know until it happened. When this would happen, then my expectations and my questions would be answered. I also thought that I shouldn't be selfish as to not let her stay with Margaret. I did know that some of my friends this year were staying as mentors; this sure eased the pain of me leaving her behind. I would have to talk to Margaret before I departed and tell her all about our moms.

She too—as Rebecca and I had that someone special during our crisis in school with music, friends, and charm—needed someone to count on. I did believe that our moms would be that special adventure that Margaret needed in her life too. They would comfort her and soothe her with any fears and doubts that she may have over the next years. Maybe even help her pick out her beau for the prom. The spirits of the unknown and the wind that rides through the air, and the whistle noises it makes will chill your spine and make you feel much love and comfort. Mom, what do you think? I know you're listening.

CHAPTER 53

Now it was the end of my senior year with Rebecca and my friends. I looked for Rebecca since we were going to leave at the same time today. I found her in the hallway with some of the underclassmen, crying and hugging. I yelled, "Rebecca, come on, let's get ready. It's time to go." As we walked down to our rooms, I told Rebecca, "This was the best time of my life, and I didn't even realize it until I was in it. The way things appear is not always the way they are. Sometimes when we withhold our strengths and our imagination, it's for the best."

After all was said and done, I looked at Rebecca and reminded her that we had to say our good-byes to our special connections—the women in our life, our dear moms. Rebecca, with so much concern on her face, realized the issue at hand. We had to leave now and say our good-byes. We ran as fast as we could and managed to get lost in the crowd. Waving to Dad and others, we explained we would be right back. The apprehension with the two of us was a little bit like being panic-stricken. How would this end? Approaching the room with tension and increased worry, we took the steps to the attic room.

"Don't be scared, I'll be with you every step of the way. I feel already safe yet somewhat sad. The life forces are here in the room. Sometimes they twist and whiz by us, fast in a rage. We then know its all wrong and we should depart. We just need now to let them through. They need a clearing. They need to know that it's OK to leave us." We held on tightly to each other, closed our eyes, and waited for the life forces of the presence of our moms to appear. They were in flight, but we knew they we would catch up to us shortly. Right now it was not important to know when they would return but where. Was it the spirit world that they were off to now? When would they come back into our lives again? Rebecca and I had the wrath of passion to wait for them.

We remembered, as we sat there in our special room, where we had our fantasies and our play-acting stories. To us it was all a game in the beginning, just fun and being silly and immature. I suddenly felt a tap on my shoulder. "Mom, is that you?" There was nothing unusual about these two women, on the small side perhaps, but there was every indication that they weren't gone. A few freckles on someone's face passed me by, and a shadow appeared in front of me. It was very promising that I could see her now. I did feel as if she was in the real world with both of us.

We managed to convey the haunted complexity that we showed on our faces. There were tears in our eyes, but we knew we had to be connected with them one more time. We succeeded to say our good-byes, and now it was time for us to go and do great things. Tears were flowing down our faces, and our hearts were thumping so hard. A smile was exchanged with all of us, and at this time, it was destined for us to depart. Hands were held tightly; as we sat down on the chest, the mist was back in the room. The lilac aroma was there again, not to disappear but to leave the smell on our clothes.

The alarm of distress and fear set into our bodies as we sat waiting. Our arms and legs went limp, our fingers tingled, and our hearts started beating double time. The pounding in my chest seemed as if I couldn't breathe through this, too much anxiety, too much pain to let them go.

Rebecca and I realized now at this time that we had to open our arms and swiftly release them into their world of the unknown. To some extent a bit overpowering and crushing, but they must leave us.

Oh, so breathtaking and grand to watch them in flight. The air became thick with the smell of them; the shadows of their bodies were shown to us. The wind went into a tailspin, spinning all over the attic as their visions appeared to us. Shutting our eyes and holding on to each other became comfortable to us and peaceful.

As we watched in amazement the thrill and excitement of it all, we stretched out our arms for them to touch our hands and hoped that they would give us a sign of their love. As always, our moms did not disappoint us. They were an enjoyable twosome to watch. We were so grateful to them for nourishing us these last four years.

Of course, our moms did not discourage us, knowing what we expected from their love. Gently, a warm breeze came over the two of us. As we sat on the trunk, oh so still, the mist of blue clouds and the smell of lilacs engulfed our bodies with so much power. A small touch on our cheeks and a wrath of wind encircled us while we sat on the chest. The wind lifted all the dust on the floor and made it rise and proceeded to sprinkle a bit of dust on our clothes. Reaching out to touch us was the best thing anyone could ask from the spirit world.

To show themselves to a human being was not in their rule book. Primarily, this was a no-no. Knowing our moms, they threw the rule book out and did what they wanted, which was us seeing their silhouettes, maybe for the last time. It was so fulfilling and gave us enough nourishment to sustain us until we saw them again.

We had an emotional impact of tears, which we told ourselves we would never forget. I reminded Rebecca of how they both died so tragically. I said to Rebecca, "Now look at them, seemingly as if they have so much life." Never understanding the reason why they died so young in our eyes or how much love we had for them until they died. I was thrilled with the opportunities our special room provided for me and Rebecca. I was now excited with new adventures and unknown expectations that life would bestow on us. The key was that I didn't believe anymore that this was all make-believe; it was reality, my mom's spirit and Rebecca's.

I have received everything, and I knew this experience would bring me much harmony in my life for years to come. The light coming through the attic window was getting very dim now to see the forces. It was now time for us to leave until another day shall come. Soon Rebecca and I were dazed in unison.

We closed our eyes, and both of us felt the tiny pecks of a kiss on our foreheads. Did we want this for our last good-bye, the feelings, the kiss, and their smiles? Only they would know what the new world of marriage, children, and maybe war would bring to all of us.

As we slowly got up to depart, the window blew open, and the mist and smells left the room. As we looked out of the window, the beautiful clouds turned into a soft color of blue. It seemed as if they were riding the clouds to their place of somewhere.

Rebecca and I looked at each other intensely because we both knew no one would leave us until they were ready to do so. Well, Mom, in time I'm sure I will catch up to you in our house with Dad or maybe at one of my brother's homes.

As we now knew, it was time to depart from this wonderful forbidden room. It had always kept an aura over us; a special trance of love and weakness known only to us was irresistible. Looking for them and trying to see which way they went was impossible; our kiss was sent off from our hands for them to catch in the air. Hopefully they did. Backing up slowly toward the steps, we tried to keep their likeness in our minds. The amazing strength that they possessed was fulfilling. We held on to them as their intensity, power, and life forces became splendor in the grass.

Going down the steps slowly, we knew this would be our last time to have them near us. The power of forces became present again only to us. Music of delight, joy, and ecstasy was playing. Their beautiful notes that were seventh heaven or like riding on cloud nine. Shutting the door behind us was the hardest thing we ever had to do. Holding on to each other and shaking and trembling was treacherous. We knew as we looked at each other, time was now over for us and them. This was not an easy task for Rebecca and me to do, but it was now done.

Knowing that we would be able to come back to this school every year would give us excitement and enthusiasm and an anticipation of hope to look forward to. When I would return to see the girls on graduation day, it would be rewarding. It would be a gift of love for me and my soul in different categories. Maybe I could still get a quick glimpse of Mom in our room, or maybe just one more time hearing the notes being played when I returned. Where would they go? Here or there or stay? Only time and visits would allow us to find the answers.

Four years—that was a long time to be in the same world and the same page with the unknown spirits that embraced your heart. I remembered that we spent a lot of time in the beginning trying to make things seem real when we knew that we invented and pretended to imagine our moms. Or did we? There really wasn't another world similar, we would say. But now four years later, we realized that the spirits and shadows and mist were truly them. The dust was no longer an effect; it was real. Rebecca dreamed of another world where our moms lived and were happy. They became to us protecting angels soaring through pink cotton candy clouds and vying to be mysterious women. Who else other than me and Rebecca would know this?

Rebecca and I understood and recognized that you had to make yourself familiar with the angels. Hold them tightly against your heart, and celebrate them frequently in spirit for without them being seen, they will only be in your imaginary world. Reach out and present yourself to them so you can grasp the anguish and resentment of them leaving you, whatever age it may have happened.

Open your hearts and feel their embrace upon your chest, then you will be able to have a moment of whispering memories that haunt your soul. Release your feelings to them and feel free to show yourselves, circle them with much love, and hold on tightly before they leave you again. They will descend from the heavens to heal your heart. You can count on it.

Be safe, you wonderful women, and whether you live in a place where it rains all the time or where the snow is three-feet deep, just relaxing with a loved one is much more appreciated than being by yourself. In time, Mom, in time, you will start a new phase of your spirit world, but for now, just stretch out for a period of time until you decide to show up for that one special occasion for a new generation of life to love you. Love and kisses, Mom!

THE END

ABOUT THE AUTHOR

I AM FORTUNATE THAT I HAVE a very vivid imagination and a thirst to create. In this instance, it moved from a thought process to an inspiring novel about a girl's childhood and her journey to womanhood.

I have been told by many that I do have quite unique attributes. I use my innate abilities and character as guidelines when I am writing my books. Some of my formidable traits are as follows: imagination, adventurous, humorous, joyful, and ambitious. My days are of dreams and my nights are of reality, telling me to put them on paper. To make someone believe your dreams is phenomenal and then to have someone come into your soul and heart is pure joy.

My mother was a writer with a vivid imagination, and she instilled her love of words into my heart. I was born in Harrisburg, Pennsylvania, and was raised in West New York, New Jersey. I married and moved to Paramus, New Jersey. I've been married for forty-eight years and have two girls and two boys and sixteen grandchildren. I also worked for thirty years in a corporate environment. Along the way, I am now able to have many stories that have yet to be told. Some real, some fiction, and you can cry or laugh with me along the way. Why not have the world read about sentimental, imaginative, and joyous stories! I now will put the pen to paper and allow my readers to come with me on a journey of a lifetime.